To Lynn Hagan,
In appreciation for
your vision for ed
and your passion
that vision as a To
Ed
1-23-1

IN PURSUIT
OF
SOMETHING BETTER

A NOVEL

Ed Varnum

IN PURSUIT
OF
SOMETHING BETTER

Ed Varnum

Cover Design by Chris Varnum
http://www.asleepstanding.com/

Edited by Cara Lockwood
http://www.edit-my-novel.com/

To Jan
Your constant encouragement keeps me going.
Your unconditional love keeps me grounded.
I never need to pursue something better.
I have found it.

PROLOGUE

Jean Mayes rose from the sofa and walked across her living room in Casa Nueva, a suburb some twenty miles north of downtown Phoenix. She drew a deep breath, sighed, and smiled as she turned off the television. It was June 11, 1963, an amazing day for news.

The Chet Huntley Report summed it up well. Governor George Wallace stood defiantly at the door of the University of Alabama, but the Alabama National Guard told him to step aside so two young Negro students could enroll. President Kennedy had federalized the Alabama National Guard, and he ordered them to insure the students' admission to the school. Federal marshals escorted the students to the university door, with the Deputy Attorney General leading the way. The world watched as Governor Wallace finally stepped aside, and the University of Alabama was officially integrated.

At first, Jean didn't know quite what to think. It was a stunning step toward racial justice, with all the power of the presidency behind it. But it would also be an incredibly unpopular step to so many. There would be backlash and mounting resistance to change. Jean's hopefulness was tentative at best.

Then, that evening, she watched the television, poised on the edge of the sofa, as the president, *her* president, addressed the nation, speaking of the University of Alabama incident, telling every American citizen not to feel superior or smug as they watched Wallace stand in the way of liberty. He told them all, he told us all, she thought:

racism is everywhere, in every section, state, and city of this great nation.

President Kennedy spoke beautifully, eloquently, of the need for us to live up to our constitutional heritage of freedom for all. And then (this was the best part, she thought), he called all American citizens to do their part to make it happen, to work for all Americans to enjoy "the kind of equality of treatment that we would want for ourselves."

She would remember those words forever. She wished Andy were here to share the moment with her. Where was he? Often, too often, her husband had to work late, to take advantage of every bit of sunlight and stay ahead of construction deadlines. Sometimes, it was dark by the time he drove the twenty miles home from Phoenix, a city growing at such an incredible rate that construction could barely keep up. But it was good. He was working, and the family was on solid financial ground for the first time. If he worked late, Andy always said, that meant more hours and a bigger paycheck.

But she hated how long and hard he had to work. She could tell it was starting to take its toll, and she hated never being sure when he'd get home. Besides, he'd never been this late. Something must have happened. Something bad. It's not just dark, it's after ten!

Jean shook her head. *Stop it! Cut out all that negative thinking! So much to be thankful for!*

She thought again about Kennedy's incredible speech. Yes, Andy would have loved it. He was the one who opened her eyes to the evils of racism. Her family wasn't rich, but they were certainly on the upper end economically in her hometown. She was sheltered. She had no idea about the ways the poor and minorities struggled until Andy opened her eyes to what was already around her. And he introduced her to his very best friend who lived in the same town, but they were kept apart by the barrier of segregation.

Now, that barrier was being struck head on by nothing less than the President of the United States! She was so proud of her president. And she was so glad that her two teenage sons, Michael and Marty, had watched with her. They had a chance to talk together afterward before she sent them on to bed, and she felt sure they grasped at least some of the significance of it all. The news held potential not only for their nation at large but for their father's best friend, whose own son could have ever-increasing hope for his future.

But the boys were in their rooms, the TV was off, and Jean Marie Mayes suddenly felt swallowed by the silence. Did Andy have a chance to hear any of today's happenings? If so, he would certainly have been even more intrigued by the news than Jean, especially since all of this broke in Alabama, the state of his birth.

Andrew Mayes was only ten when he moved with his parents from the tiny farming community of Dearing, Alabama to Donelsburg, Illinois. He did remember some things about his life before that move: all those fields of cotton, his school, a couple teachers, and some friends. He remembered their tiny shack and its crowded living space with his grandparents, parents, aunt, and uncle. He carried fond memories his wonderful grandmother. But the time young Andy loved the most was joining his father as he made his handyman rounds: building fences or furniture, repairing just about anything that was broken.

Jean's husband's opinion of his birth state was shaped not so much by his own memory as the attitude of his mother and father. Andy's parents both hated everything about Alabama; above all, the poverty and prejudice they were trying to escape.

Jimmy and Barbara Mayes moved with their son, Andrew, from Dearing to Donelsburg. Then, years later, that son would move his family from a town he'd learned to hate; from Donelsburg, Illinois, to the middle of the hot, Arizona desert. Andy even convinced his lifelong friend, Bill, to join them in the move.

Bill Davis went to a different school than Andy or Jean, a big part of Andy's hatred of Donelsburg. He lived in a different neighborhood and, outside that neighborhood, had to be careful of where he went and what he said. That was the overt, unapologetic racism of the mining town of Donelsburg, Illinois, and why Andy was so passionate about escaping.

Jean quietly sighed and glanced over at the clock. *Good Lord! It was after ten-thirty! Where was he?* The sound of ringing jolted her from her thoughts. Filled with a sense of dread, she walked slowly to the phone. This just could not be good.

"Hello?"

It was Bill. He wanted Jean to know that he was bringing Andy home.

"Don't worry, Jean. He's really okay. Really. I'll explain it all when we get there. I'll see you in just a few. I promise. I'll see you in just a few."

And he hung up with no further explanation. Jean watched her hand tremble as she lowered the telephone receiver slowly into its cradle. *Bill is bringing Andy home? What could that mean?* Her mind raced with question after question. And none had an answer she liked.

***

Marty took a deep breath, exhaling quietly as he stretched back onto his pillow. He had been sitting up in bed, listening intently ever since he heard the telephone ring. All he could hear was his mother's low voice, intense and concerned. He figured it was Dad. It had to be Dad. Of course, Mom had said nothing about being worried, but they all knew he was late. *If it's buggin' me,* he thought, *she's gotta be upset.*

Marty stared at the ceiling, wondering if he should get up, but then thought better of it. Even though he was fourteen and it was summer, Mom had made it clear he should be in bed.

Tomorrow was Wednesday, and it was Michael's early day for work. "He's seventeen, going to be a senior in high school," she said. "And he's gone to bed with no problem. Don't give me any talk about you being too old."

With a grumble, Marty had made his way to his room. He'd never admit it, but he was tired. Something else he would never admit: part of his hesitancy was a slight dread of his new bedroom. As far back as he could remember, his family lived in a small, two-bedroom house on the other side of Casa Nueva. But his parents said it was time to move to a bigger house in a "better neighborhood."

Marty wasn't so sure about that last part. He'd lived his whole life in the same neighborhood and it seemed perfectly fine to him. All his friends were there, kids he knew from first through eighth grade. Yeah, he'd see them in high school, but it was summer, and they were no longer next door or just around the block. He missed the neighborhood and, to be honest, he kind of missed bunking above his brother in their shared room. That was part of his wanting to put off bedtime that night, that and the creepy shadows he kept seeing on his bedroom wall.

Nothing in this summer move seemed to be working out nearly as perfect as his parents promised.

Marty sat up in bed when he heard the doorbell. He ran to the bedroom door, opening it just a crack when he heard his mother call, "I'm coming, Bill! I'll be right there!" Then, he stiffened in shock when he heard his father's voice as Mom opened the door. It was indeed Dad's voice, but he couldn't make out any words.

He opened the door just a bit more so he could hear better, and he realized there were no words, just sounds, slurred and guttural. His father sounded sad, like an apology, but spoken in a language Marty didn't know. But, no, it was his father, and it was English, just slurred beyond recognition.

Slurred. Slurred like someone who had too much to drink. Was that it? Had Dad been out drinking all this time? With Bill? It made no sense.

Then, Marty recognized Bill's voice, soft and apologetic. "I'm so sorry, Jean. This is my fault. I told Andy I shouldn't stop with him. I just knew it was going to go bad."

Then, Marty heard his mother, in her kindest, most patient voice, as she said, "It's okay Bill. I want to hear all about it. But right now, let's get Andy into bed."

Marty looked across the hall and saw Michael staring back from his own bedroom door. Michael shook his head, and Marty felt his eyes well up. He was startled by his mother's voice, closer now.

"Boys! I see you there. Get out here and help us get your father to bed."

Sheepishly, Michael and Marty stepped into the hall and saw their mother and Bill struggling to walk their father toward their parents' bedroom. Actually, they were dragging him, each grasping an arm under his shoulders, as Andy Mayes had apparently passed out on the way down the hall. He was a mess. His dark brown hair, usually neatly parted at the side, was disheveled and parts stood straight up. His left eye was swollen and dark. His lips were also puffed up, crusted with dried blood.

"Dad's been in a fight," Michael whispered to Marty. "And I think he got the worst of it."

"Boys!"

Marty and Michael looked into their mother's stern face and moved quickly toward the trio. Marty wasn't sure how to help. By this time, his father was completely stretched out, face down, with his feet being dragged behind him.

Michael stepped forward and grabbed his father's left arm, nodding for his mother to step back. Michael was three years older than Marty, tall and muscular, an athlete, everything Marty was not. No way could the younger boy take over for Bill. Marty looked at Bill who, like his father, was slight of build but powerfully strong. It was then that he noticed that Bill, too, had swelling around his mouth with a trickle of dried blood. Bill also had been struck in the fight.

Marty shook his head. He needed to at least have some appearance of helping. So he just awkwardly put a hand under each of his father's arms and walked backwards, knowing full well he was being no help at all.

Andy was not a big man by any standard. He was thin and wiry, 5 feet 7 inches tall, the exact same height as his wife and shorter than either of his two sons. But that was deceptive. Andy was all muscle and bone, powerful for his size from a lifetime of hard labor. Moving him was an effort, but the three worked together to bring their father and friend to the bedroom and drag his upper body onto the bed. Jean followed behind, finally lifting his feet and shifting him awkwardly, still face down, to the center.

As they all stepped back to gaze sadly at their shared achievement, the unconscious frame suddenly jerked, coughed, wretched, and heaved the entire contents of his stomach onto Jean's beautiful, new, blue and gray bedspread.

Aghast, Marty looked over to his mom and listened in awe as she said in a clearly audible stage whisper, "Shit!"

Marty felt a mixture of shock and fascination. Jean Mayes did not swear, at least not that he had ever heard in his own fourteen years. As his father once said with a smile, "When you hear your mama cuss, stand back because the sun'll go black, and the desert'll freeze! When your mama cusses, boys, it *means* something!"

It was one of the perhaps a hundred ways Andy and Jean Mayes were complete and total opposites. It was in their upbringing. It was in their genes.

ONE

Jean Marie Holloway grew up the youngest of three siblings in Donelsburg, Illinois, population just under 20,000. She, her brother, and older sister were all born and raised in Donelsburg, where they went to school during the week, attended church every Sunday, and divided any time that was left between helping Mama at home and Papa at Holloway's Hardware Store. It was a good life, she supposed: simple and sensible, almost happy.

Donelsburg was founded as a small village in 1811, where it grew a bit and faded a bit only to grow a little more over the years. All that changed in the early 1900s with the arrival of the Smithton Coal Company. The population immediately exploded with the establishment of two very productive mines, known simply as Smithton Numbers One and Two. By 1925, the year of Jean's birth, Donelsburg had become the largest producer of coal in Illinois. And the small village grew. The coal industry brought the trains and, in turn, the trains brought more people.

So it was coal that caused Barbara and Jimmy Mayes to move with their ten-year-old son to Donelsburg in 1935. The couple were virtually children themselves when they married in Dearing, Alabama. Jimmy was eighteen and Barbara, a mere sixteen. They struggled as their parents had before them, good people all, who held an unswerving belief in the values of faith, hard work, and sacrifice. But the only industry in Dearing was cotton. And the only thing a poor family with nothing could do was pick.

That was the lot of Jimmy Mayes, his father, mother, and two brothers. They, along with most of their friends, were sharecroppers, tenant farmers working hard in the field only to give a goodly portion of their earnings to the landowners. It was a hard life, bitterly hard to Jimmy. He worked in the field from an early age, and it was a constant struggle. The cotton dust irritated his nose and throat, often throwing him into a spasm of coughs.

Jimmy's discomfort only increased as the brothers grew older. Jimmy was the middle child, yet both his older and younger brothers were larger and stronger, tormenting him as weak and lazy, accusing him of just trying to get out of work whenever he needed to stop to cough or catch his breath. He began to hate his brothers and even his father, who seemed to agree with their assessment of him. His mother, fearful of her husband, never dared confront Jimmy's tormentors.

The older Jimmy grew, the more he yearned to leave this wretched life. He had to find someplace else, something else, though he had no idea what it might be. He did know that, whatever that something else was, he didn't want to do it without his beloved Barbara.

Barbara Hartley and Jimmy Mayes grew up on adjoining plots of land, each in a decrepit shanty too small for their large families. Each family farmed land that belonged to the same landowner, Kenneth T. Harris, who had portioned off his property and built a humble shack on each section long ago.

Their families never owned the land they farmed, the houses in which they lived, or much of anything else. Everything belonged to Mr. Harris. They had an agreement with the landowner to give him a quarter of their crop at harvest and keep the rest as their own. It never worked that way.

Mr. Harris provided supplies, tools, seeds, fertilizer—all they needed – for a price. At harvest, the landowner sold the cotton they picked and kept his 25% plus what he said they owed him plus interest for all he supplied. That figure always came to more than another 25%. Receiving payment of less than half of what the crop sold for, the families then had to settle with Dearing merchants, from whom they bought food and everything else they needed, all to be paid with interest after the harvest, all with the hope there would be enough to cover the debt. Debts would too often be carried over to the next year and the Mayes, the Hartleys, and all who worked the landowner's fields found themselves in an unending cycle of abject poverty.

That was Jimmy and Barbara's life in Dearing. They both knew what it meant to work in the fields from an early age. Many children of sharecroppers began laboring with their families as early as age five. There was a one-room schoolhouse in Dearing which was in session six months out of the year. Children of sharecroppers seldom attended beyond fifth grade, and most on Mr. Harris' property never made it past two or three years.

Jimmy liked every aspect of his school experience. It was, of course, an escape from his physical and emotional struggles at home. But, more than that, Jimmy was eager to learn. And he met teachers there, adults who authentically cared about him. He discovered children there who treated him with friendship and respect, so unlike his brothers. Talking to those children over time gradually unveiled another important revelation. There were families unlike his own, where children felt safe and loved. Jimmy yearned to be in such a family.

Time away from home and fields, encouraging relationships with teachers, and close friendships with students; those were all reasons school was important to Jimmy. But most of all, he looked forward to school because it was there that he really got to know Barbara Hartley.

Jimmy was in his third year when he saw her, really saw her for the first time. Little Barbara, daughter of Isaiah and Leotie Hartley, was beautiful. She had the kindest eyes, big and brown, that seemed to look into a person's soul. She was only six years old, but to Jimmy, her eyes held the wisdom of the ages. Her hair was black, jet black and shining, and her skin, smooth, brown, and so beautiful.

She noticed him, too. How could she help but notice this boy watching her at every opportunity. They never talked that first year, neither knew what to say. But one year grew to the next, and the two children grew with it, growing up together. They gradually became friends, then best friends, and finally, far too soon in their early teens, lovers.

Jimmy was blue-eyed and blonde, with fair skin that was mostly burned bright red from his hours in the sun. He was short, a bit on the skinny side, and oh so very serious. Even as a youngster, he seemed to be carrying the worries of the world.

Barbara also was small for her age, short and thin, but that was where their physical resemblance ended. Barbara was quite dark, with deep brown eyes and long black hair. She was half Cherokee on her mother's side, a fact that brought more than a little brutal bullying for all the family in their rural Alabama town. But something in Barbara's inherent emotional makeup kept her positive through it all. While Jimmy saw every problem, Barbara directed him to every potential. And, as they say, opposites attract. They were drawn to each other from childhood, and their love only grew with age.

So when Barbara informed Jimmy that it had been two months since her last period, neither had any doubts about what they would do. They talked to their parents, and a preacher came to the Mayes' home the next week, tying the knot in front of their house with only the two families present.

TWO

The wedding was short and sweet. It seemed only moments from "dearly beloved" to "you may kiss the bride." The preacher made his exit, and the two families, now also supposedly joined by this same ceremony, stood staring at each other. Jimmy's younger brother spoke first.

"So. Where you two gonna live? Guess you should probably be gittin' there."

Jimmy and Barbara looked at each other, speechless. They had never even considered this. They had no place to go and no money to pay for it, even if they did. Jimmy had assumed they would move in with his parents until he could find work, perhaps in Dearing. He would not permanently be subject to a landowner as a sharecropper. That much he knew. But what about now?

"Well, you sure ain't stayin' here," his little brother continued, speaking directly to Jimmy. "We don't have no room for you, much less your squaw wife'n'red-skinned baby."

Isaiah Hartley started to move toward the boy, but his wife thrust out her arm to stop him.

"Right," his older brother chimed in. "And we don't need no screaming papoose messin' up our house!" Jimmy's father concurred, and his mother, looking sadly on, said nothing.

"I was thinking of no such thing," Jimmy said, forcing a smile. "You think I'd bring a poor little baby into this shit-house?"

"Watch'cher mouth, boy!" And his father brought the back of his hand hard across his son's right cheek. Jimmy stormed away from the others, followed immediately by Barbara and her entire family. He stopped several yards away, breathing rapidly with gasps, trembling in anger and hurt. Barbara, her mother, and father circled Jimmy, wrapping their arms around him.

"Come live with us, Jimmy," said Mr. Hartley.

"Yes," Mrs. Hartley agreed. "We've always loved you, and it would be such an honor to have you as our son. What joy it will be to have a beautiful little baby to love once again!"

So Jimmy considered himself as adopted, joining Isaiah, Leotie, and Barbara's older siblings, Matthew and Kate. Each welcomed Jimmy as family. He felt especially close to Isaiah, who was the polar opposite of his fault-finding, belittling father. At last, he felt like a true and wanted son.

Jimmy even experienced unexpected satisfaction when his birth father came by to say that his family needed him to work in the field. Jimmy opened his eyes wide in feigned surprise and said, "Why, sir, I am shocked you want me around! I'd never think of ever bothering you." And with that, he vowed to never set foot in his parents' house or field again.

Jimmy Mayes had dropped out of school after sixth grade, laboring with his father and brothers in the field in spite of ever-increasing respiratory issues. He often went into the field by sheer willpower, but he had little capacity for the long days, sweating in the humidity and the heat. Truthfully, he hated those cotton fields and dreaded the thought of bringing a child into the unending cycle of poverty that came with sharecropping.

He had already developed a plan to create a new life even before his marriage. With his marriage and separation from his father's demands, Jimmy knew it was time to act.

Word was spreading amongst his neighbors about Jimmy's natural ability in carpentry, both building and repair. He would use Isaiah Hartley's tools at their house and neighbors' tools when helping them. But the skill was all his own, and no one, including Jimmy, knew where it came from. His mother-in-law said it was a gift of God.

Whatever the source, there was nothing broken Jimmy could not fix, nothing needing to be built he couldn't design and construct. Further, he loved this work. It used his hands and mind, his intellect and creativity. And so, immediately after his wedding, Jimmy took initiative to spread the word to any who would hear: Handyman Jimmy Mayes was at your service.

He was disappointed but not surprised at the response. All were happy for Jimmy to offer neighborly help, but no one Jimmy knew was able or willing to pay for it. However, Mr. Harris soon discovered Jimmy's skills, increasingly calling him from the field to do odd jobs around his property. One day, Mr. Harris handed him a metal box with a latch on the side and a handle at the top. Jimmy was told to open it and found a small supply of tools inside: a claw hammer, Philips and flat head screw drivers, measuring tape, a small carpenter's square, and so on. Jimmy looked up, questioningly.

"They're all yours," said Mr. Harris. "You're going to be needing them. I've let my friends all know about your skill, Jimmy. You can walk some places and, when it's too far, they'll pick you up or I'll have an employee drive you. I want what's best for you, boy. You're gonna be okay."

Jimmy couldn't believe Mr. Harris' kindness and thanked him again and again. It wasn't until later that Jimmy learned that the cost of the tool kit and its contents (though they were all used, from Mr. Harris' own tool shed) had been deducted from the Hartley family's profits that harvest. He also discovered that Mr. Harris expected his usual twenty-five percent of Jimmy's earnings.

Jimmy continued to labor side by side in the field with his new family, looking forward to those times he would be summoned by Mr. Harris to work for the landowners of Dearing. Everyone praised his skill, whether building, restoring, or repairing, so he wondered why he was not called on more often. Jimmy was not aware of the increasingly failing economy of that time, but he soon realized that his hopes to make a living for his new family would not be realized

That family now included Andrew who, even as a toddler, had the seeming spiritual depth and striking physical attractiveness of his mother, with thick, dark brown hair and olive skin, stunningly contrasted by his father's deep, blue eyes. The boy also seemed to have inherited his father's skillful hands. He loved to accompany Jimmy on various jobs, amazing everyone even at age seven with how well he could handle his father's tools.

Jimmy carefully taught his son how to address his elders with courtesy and respect. "Always listen and don't speak until someone talks to you first. And when we're working at their homes, you always call them Mr. Harris or Mrs. Johnson and answer with 'Yes, sir' or 'No, ma'am.'" Andy listened well and followed his father's rules. The landowners looked forward to seeing him, rubbing and mussing his hair, calling him, "Little Chief." Jimmy cringed inside when he heard this nickname but said nothing. Andy would grin in delight.

It looked like the young Mayes family would settle down permanently in Dearing. But both Jimmy and Barbara knew better. They often talked quietly at night, long after others were asleep, about the gaping gulf between Dearing's few rich and the many poor. Mr. Harris clearly favored him, but that favor always worked to the landowner's advantage and had its limits. There was very little chance of Jimmy possessing any land of his own while in Dearing. This was something that had become increasingly important to him. He hated the poverty of his family and friends, along with the prejudice of the entire community.

The white sharecroppers scorned Negro sharecroppers, which struck Jimmy as odd, since neither owned a thing and both worked in the fields, barely scratching by a living. Why, even his own wife and mother-in-law, angels on this earth, were treated with contempt because of their culture and darker skin.

Jimmy's mother-in-law was the most spiritual and godly person he knew. He could not think of a more fitting description of her than her given name of Leotie, which means "flower of the prairie" in her native Cherokee language. *Such a beautiful name,* he often thought. *Such a beautiful person.*

Leotie's grandfather was an influential elder in the Cherokee tribe of northeast Alabama, a converted Christian, and friendly to the United States. When Andrew Jackson forced the removal of the Cherokee from their ancestral homes to so-called Indian Territory in present day Oklahoma, her grandfather was dismayed. Indignant at this seeming betrayal, he rose to leadership of those who refused to join the majority of their tribe on the horrific journey later known as The Trail of Tears.

Andy loved to hear tales of his great-great-grandfather, who became chief of this brave and independent tribe. Barbara would nod and laugh when he proudly boasted, "My grandma is an Indian Princess!"

He was captivated by the stories of their proud heritage, often shared by his mother as she tucked him in bed at night. She shared her own mother's beautiful synthesis of her Native American faith with Christianity, pointing out that the God of the Bible is one and the same as the Great Spirit of her people. But there are also ancestral spirits, she said, like Andy's own great-great-grandparents who had passed over before him. "They watch over you. If you are quiet and listen carefully, you can feel them guide you to the right path."

Jimmy and Barbara would often talk together about the wonderful experiences each shared with their son. There was something very special about him, something very gifted, spiritual and deep beyond his years. "One thing I know," said Jimmy one night, "we can't wait much longer to leave this place. I can't bear to raise our son here."

They would leave. But they didn't know where they'd go or how they'd get there.

THREE

There was one landowner who called on Jimmy's carpentry skills several times. Jimmy grew to like him very much. His name was Mr. Jacobson, and he gave Jimmy the biggest building assignment of his brief career in Dearing: to add a room onto one of Jacobson's houses occupied by a sharecropper.

Jimmy was amazed that Mr. Jacobson would be so generous with one of his sharecroppers. He told Jacobson this, which elicited a warm smile.

"My farmer and his wife have two sons that live with them, and all four work the fields," he said. "One boy's married now and got a baby on the way. They need another bedroom."

"That was really kind of you, sir."

"If you say so, Jimmy. But I see it as good business. I need that family to work my fields; won't have no crop without 'em. I'll take care of them. They're takin' care of me."

Jimmy turned those words over and over in his mind as he began that addition for Mr. Jacobson. It gave him hope. It also gave him an idea.

Mr. Jacobson drove him back to Mr. Harris' house at the end of the workday. Jimmy thanked him for the work and for the ride, then headed straight to Mr. Harris' home. He knocked on the door and, invited in, he stood as Mr. Harris sat in the living room chair.

"I sure appreciate all you have done for me, sir. I do have something I'd like to ask, though. My family works hard for you, Mr. Harris, and this would help my family greatly."

"Go ahead, boy."

"You know, it's getting mighty crowded with all my family in the house you kindly let us use. I'd like to add a bedroom on. I could do it myself, and my boy, Andy, and my wife could help some. We can do it evenings, take nothing away from our work."

"Where you getting the materials for this project?"

"Well, like I said, I'd do the work and—"

Mr. Harris laughed out loud. "Why in the world would I want to pay for such a thing?"

"Well, I thought of that, sir. It's really your property, and you would benefit, too. It would raise the value of —"

"Hold on, there, boy. I have no interest at all in raising the value of that property. Why, you fix that place up and, next thing you know, I got all these tenants knocking on my door saying, 'Look what you did for the Hartley folks. I need this, and I need that. What about me?' No, boy, you just go home and be glad you got it so good."

Jimmy was stunned, but the shock quickly passed. "Yes, sir. I understand completely, sir. I'll go do just that. Thank you for your time."

He moved toward the door when, looking up, he saw Mrs. Harris standing in the kitchen door out of the sight of her husband. She gazed sadly at Jimmy then slowly nodded her head. He wasn't sure what she was saying, but her look was so kind that Jimmy felt a strange connection with her in that moment. He turned and began his walk home.

Jimmy continued helping on his in-law's field and whatever carpentry work he might get around Dearing. But it would never be the same after that conversation.

One thought plagued Jimmy's mind after Mr. Harris' response: *I have no control!*

It was an ever-repeating thought. *I have no control over what I can do with the property. I have no control over my income; not as long as Kenneth Harris is in charge of the books and tells us the percentages. I have no control.*

He spoke of it to Barbara late one night, as they lay side-by-side.

"I remember how surprised I was, when my school friends told me about their loving families," he said, quietly into the dark. "I remember wishing I had a family like that, but I had no power to do anything, to change anything.

"That's exactly how I feel with Mr. Harris. He decides what I'll have and what I can do. I have no power to change anything. He's like the adult, I'm like the child, and I hate it, Barbara. I hate it."

"I never thought of it that way," Barbara said, "but I understand what you're saying."

There was a moment of silence.

"I've found that family I wanted, right here with you and your family," Jimmy said. "It made me think about trying to have us all work for Mr. Jacobson, how much better that might be. But, even if that could happen, the landowner still has the power. It just isn't enough, Barbara. I want better for us."

"You deserve better, Jimmy."

"We all do," he added. "I want Andy to be able to grow up, really grow up into an adult, who decides for himself who he can be and what he can do. And that won't happen here, Barbara. We have to leave. And it has to be sooner rather than later."

***

Some weeks had passed, when Jimmy again was dropped off at Mr. Harris' house. Andy had joined him at work, and they were about to walk home together when Mrs. Harris stepped to her door and waved them back. She stepped away from the house, hopefully out of earshot from her husband.

"Hi, Jimmy, Andy. Good day, today?"

"Yes, ma'am."

"Well, thanks for stopping before heading home. I'm sure you're tired. But I've something important to tell you. I want to tell you about my favorite cousin. He's a good man and doing pretty good for himself in spite of this horrible, awful economy. Did you know we're in a horrible depression, Jimmy? Probably not, because your life has been horrible anyway. It's bad. But my cousin's doing all right. He's pretty high up in this company called Smithton located in Illinois.

"Smithton's got two coal mines in a town called Donelsburg. Now, coal's been hit harder than anything else, with miners not working and some mines shutting down. But Smithton mines are big, and they're going to make it. I know they are."

Jimmy was confused, but he nodded and listened politely. Where's this going?

"I wrote my cousin. I told him about you and your good family, what a hard worker and how smart you are. He said if you can get there, he could use you. It's hard work. You'd start out at the bottom, do all the grunt work. But you're smart, Jimmy, and determined. You'll work your way up. He says they've got company houses to live in, but Donelsburg was there before the mines. They've got neighborhoods; you could buy your own place someday. It could be your future, Jimmy, if you'll take it."

Jimmy was getting excited, but he was also painfully aware of his situation. "Thank you so much, ma'am. I want to do that. I do. But how? I got no way to move all the way to Illinois."

"You tell me when you want to leave, and we'll find a way."

"What about Mr. Harris?"

"You let me worry about Mr. Harris."

Thanking her again, Jimmy and Andy headed home. Andy asked his father, "What's it mean?"

"I think, son, it means we're gonna get the hell out of here."

FOUR

Mrs. Harris had all the arrangements made before her husband even knew of Jimmy and Barbara's plans. Jimmy had a job and a house waiting for him. Train tickets had been purchased. Arrangements had even been made for the family's transportation to the depot. All was set.

The day before they left, Jimmy walked to the Harris' home to say his final thank-yous and goodbyes. Mrs. Harris came to the door. Jimmy just stared a moment. He couldn't help it. Her lip was badly swollen. A large bruise covered her left cheek just below the eye. Jimmy began to feel sick.

"It's okay, Jimmy. You just go find a new life. This'll blow over. But you better get on home. This probably isn't the best place for you to be right now."

Jimmy's shock moved to guilt. "I'm so sorry, ma'am."

"I made my choices, and I'd do it again. Now, go."

It was his longest and saddest walk home. But each step he took brought Jimmy further from remorse and closer to red hot anger. For the first time in his life, he knew what it meant to hate, to truly despise another human being.

Jimmy was a gentle spirit, someone who looked past his own disadvantages to concentrate on how to overcome. Others might slight him, but dwelling on it accomplished nothing. Revenge never occurred to him, only how he could work things out to move ahead. Now for the very first time, Jimmy wanted more than anything to hurt someone, to cause Kenneth Harris some modicum of the misery he heaped upon the lives of others.

Jimmy stopped both his steps and his thoughts as he came to his family home. Awash in an emotional tidal wave, he stood and looked at the sad, old shanty. Suddenly, he was overwhelmed with guilt at leaving behind his family. However they may have treated him, however unhappy his life had been in that house, this was his family. They did the best they could with what they had.

He continued to walk. His pace was slow, but his mind was racing. Jimmy realized that he had been so focused on getting Andrew and Barbara away from this place that he hadn't even considered the people he'd leave behind. Would he see his parents and brothers again? And what of Barbara's family, who had accepted him as their own? He thought of Andy, who had completely bonded to his grandmother Hartley and would likely be lost without her.

What was he doing? How could he be so selfish? And what of Mrs. Harris? How much more would she be battered because she dared show him kindness? Mrs. Harris. Did she have to live with that monster? If she could help him escape, why couldn't she break free, too?

Jimmy was jolted from his thoughts by the sound of his name. His eyes focused on Barbara, who had seen him from the house and was walking his way.

"Jimmy, are you okay?"

"Sure. I'm fine."

"Mama and Papa invited everybody over tonight for supper."

"Everybody?"

"Sure. Our two families all together to say goodbye. I've got us all packed and ready to go today. We're just going to spend this last night with family. It'll be good."

Jimmy went in to clean up. Maybe, this would be a chance to heal wounds. He hated to leave his family with so much shared hurt. He resolved to do his very best to make things as right between them as possible.

Supper time came, and there was no word from Jimmy's family. Minutes passed into an hour. Barbara stepped out of the kitchen. "Mama says there's lots of food, and it's getting cold. Let's eat."

The food was delicious, but the silence at the table seemed deafening. When the table had been cleared and the dishes all washed, Jimmy took Leotie Hartley's hands and looked into her eyes.

"Thank you so much for everything. We're all going to miss you." He paused a moment, then added, "I'm going to miss you."

Leotie smiled and brought her son-in-law close. Embracing him, she said softly, "You just take care of my daughter and my brilliant, gifted grandson. I have total trust in you, Jimmy. I couldn't ask for a finer son-in-law."

It was a beautiful, touching scene, filled with love. Leotie and Jimmy did not notice Barbara by the kitchen door, watching with a tear and a smile. And none of them noticed, outside the house, looking in a screened window, Jimmy's mother also watching. She had only tears.

The next day, Jimmy, Barbara, and Andy were driven to the depot and boarded a train for a new life in Donelsburg, Illinois.

FIVE

Jimmy knew nothing about mining, but he was industrious and smart. He had never in his life worked so hard, got so incredibly dirty, or hurt so much at the end of the day. But he persevered. His body adjusted over time and he became one of Smithton's hardest workers. Soon, he was bringing home a decent living for his young family.

It was all for family. Jimmy and Barbara were completely devoted to each other and to their beloved Andrew. They were so devoted to family, in fact, that they did virtually no socializing after work. They just tended to their own business and figured others would do the same.

It seemed to Jimmy and Barbara that this "minding one's own business" was exactly what was happening. Actually, the opposite was true. Much was said in the community about this new family, beginning with the awareness of the wife's dark skin.

"What is she?"

"I hear she's an 'Injun.'"

"Worse! Nothin' but a half-breed!"

So the family moved in incremental steps away from their poverty, but prejudice was waiting in their new home. And the people talked, but no one came by. Jimmy and Barbara did not hear their whispers. Andy heard far more than he wanted.

It began his first day in school, when children laughed and told him he talked funny. It continued each day after that, as he was forced to return and face the children's stares, hearing taunts that he knew the children were learning at home.

'Hey look! It's Injun Andy!"

"His family's a bunch of stupid hillbillies."

"The father's a little, weird klutz."

"The mother's a squaw."

Andy loved his family and virtually worshiped his father, but he wondered why they would bring him here to such a cold, hateful place. Each advancing year brought a greater distaste for the town, its people, and the coal mining company that seemed to own their lives.

Yet, his parents both spoke of how much better things were in Donelsburg. Jimmy had never heard of a union before his move but was now a member of the United Mine Workers of America. The UMWA was founded in 1890 and was established very early in Illinois. It was chartered in Donelsburg shortly after the arrival of the Smithton Company mines. The union did not have a great deal of power in the 1930s, but they could openly meet and freely discuss their conditions, a stunning new reality for the son of a sharecropper.

Jimmy knew for a fact that things were better here. His family had moved into a company house on arrival in Donelsburg, but this truly was a house not a shack. And they could choose whether or not to buy at the company store, with enough income to trade with the town's other merchants. In time, Jimmy was able to buy his own modest home in Dearing and, his greatest acquisition, a 1925 Ford Model T, purchased from his shift foreman.

Barbara knew that their family had finally "made it" into modern life when they actually connected with the world through their very first telephone. Who cared if it was a party line that rang several homes in their neighborhood simultaneously? As far as she knew, that was true for everyone in the United States, and all you had to do was listen for your personal ring. And, of course, you were expected to keep all conversations to under five minutes out of courtesy to your neighbors (hoping no one was eavesdropping on your call).

While Jimmy realized there was prejudice in Donelsburg, it was nothing compared to prejudice in Dearing. He had witnessed it there until it sickened him: prejudice against Barbara's wonderful family because of her mother's Native American heritage, prejudice against Negroes who worked in the fields, sharecroppers just like his own family and friends. In Donelsburg, he loved the fact that Negroes and whites worked together in the mines. He knew he was in the right place when he heard a fellow coal miner say, "Hell, we're all black down here!" And it was true. Jimmy left the coal mines as black as his good friend, Beau Davis. Beau also belonged to the UMWA and earned the same salary as Jimmy, at least what Jimmy was paid when he first started work there.

He and Beau worked first shift together at mine number two. They took an instant liking to each other, quickly discovering a surprising number of ways they were alike. They were both married and completely devoted to beautiful wives. They both had one child and both boys were the same grade in school. And they both were at the very bottom of the Smithton Mining Company hierarchy.

For his part, Jimmy was the new guy, insecure and awkward. While he tried to be careful and methodical, he fell prey to accidents on the job and became known as a bit of a clumsy dolt. This reputation started honestly enough from his very first day, when Jimmy began work as Beau's helper.

"You watch me," Beau said. "Do what I do." Jimmy watched as Beau shoveled coal that had been broken loose by picks and pneumatic drills, scooping and carrying it to a rail car for extraction from the mine. Jimmy nodded and plunged his shovel into the pile of coal. As he spun towards the rail car, he immediately tripped, propelling both his shovel and its load forward, as he tumbled face first onto the mine floor.

Beau checked on Jimmy and, discovering the only major injury was to his dignity, bellowed a hearty laugh that rang through the mine and up the shaft. Word of the incident spread, and Jimmy was soon the target of multiple cruel and biting jokes. But they passed and were forgotten as he caught on to the work.

For his part, Beau was loud, boisterous, and black; qualities that did not change. Nor were they forgotten, however capable Beau was at work.

The racial prejudice was subtler in the mines than the cotton fields, but it was there. And part of the prejudice was that the miners preferred a quiet, humble Negro. That was not Beau. He never lowered his head and looked away when he was approached by his white co-workers, something Jimmy had seen other Negro miners do. Beau stood tall and confident. And Beau could exchange verbal taunts with the best of them.

It didn't happen every day, and it was always at lunch or before work as they gathered by the elevator to be lowered into the mine. One of the miners would direct an insult Beau's way, something outlandish, personal, and harsh about his work or intelligence or appearance. Everyone would laugh, and Beau hit back hard, followed by a loud, howling laugh of his own. It could go on quite a while with still others joining in, always laughing at Beau.

Jimmy was shocked and then fascinated, as he quickly realized that it was a time of release for the men, entertainment during the break in work.

At the heart of it, these men liked Beau. And they respected him. Beau was without a doubt the hardest worker among them. When the breaks were over, all nonsense was put aside. Coal mining was brutal and dangerous work, and Beau took that more seriously than any of them. If there was a problem in the mine, every miner knew that Beau would have his back.

Beau was a dedicated, capable worker. But Jimmy was sure that Beau would never advance beyond his present status. Yes, he was liked and respected by his coworkers, but Jimmy knew not one of them would openly acknowledge as much or venture to associate with him outside their shared work shift. It was sad. It was wrong.

Jimmy felt confident that his own low social standing would eventually rise. He knew Beau's never would. And it was true. Despite Beau's years of experience, Jimmy advanced in both rank and pay. Beau never did. But somehow that injustice never damaged their relationship. Even after they stopped working side by side, the two made a point to eat lunch together and exchange greetings when possible before or after work.

Their times of sharing brought changes that would dramatically affect their lives and the lives of their families.

SIX

Two years passed for Jimmy, as he worked day in and day out in the mines. It was a Tuesday, and he had finished his shift but had not been fully focused on work that day. He needed to talk to someone, as family issues weighed on his mind. He was heading into the company showers, a ritual after each work day that was both required and welcome, and met Beau, who was on his way out. Beau started by him with a wave and, "See you tomorrow."

"Just a minute, Beau," Jimmy said. "Can we talk a minute?"

Beau saw immediately the heavy load his friend seemed to be carrying. "Sure. What's on your mind?"

Jimmy led him away from the door to the showers and over to the grounds at the side of the building. "It's my wife," he said softly. "I know she seems so strong and, in so many ways, she is. But physically and, well, in her mind, she's in horrible shape right now."

Beau took a step closer. "I'm sorry," he said.

"You know we only have our one boy. Barbara had so much sickness with her pregnancy and a horrible time in the delivery. I didn't really know. I mean, I was just a kid myself! I didn't know anything. I only knew the midwife said it was a harder than normal delivery, something to do with Barbara's pelvic girdle. She told us both that. But she only told Barbara that this childbirth went well, but the next might not. She recommended no more children.

"But Barbara's always wanted a big family. She never told me about that warning. And she was so excited about a year later when she told me another baby was on its way." Jimmy stopped a moment, eyes stinging as he fought back tears. "She carried that baby only a few months when she lost it. It broke my heart, but it almost killed Barbara, emotionally and physically."

Jimmy took a deep breath, looked around nervously and continued. "It's happened again," he said. "Barbara was excited when she first realized we were having another baby. She was hopeful. I was just scared." Jimmy paused and looked from Beau to the ground between them. "It's been three months and, well, she—" Jimmy's voice broke. "—she miscarried this weekend."

Beau laid a hand on his friend's shoulder. "I'm so sorry, Jimmy."

"I'm worried about her, Beau. Barbara's so frail right now. I learned about a midwife here in Donelsburg. She came by and spent time with Barbara, examined her. She said bedrest. And she said Barbara needed someone with her. I can't take off, Beau. I don't know how long it would be. Andy's just twelve. He's got school, and he's scared for his mother. He doesn't understand. I don't know what to do."

All was silent for a moment, and then Beau turned his friend so they were eye to eye. He spoke directly to Jimmy, slowly and softly.

"Let us help, Jimmy. I know my wife, Lorrie, would love to help. She could spend time with Barbara, do whatever she needs. She'd need to bring Bill, but he's the same age as your boy. People don't like us coming to your side of town after work unless we're help, you know, like paid maids or gardeners or nannies. Let them think that. But we'll know, it's 'cause we're friends."

Jimmy was shocked at the offer and unsure, but he was also desperate. Barbara's health was in the balance. "I don't know what to say."

"'Yes' would be a good start. And 'thanks' would be pretty good, too," said Beau with a smile.

"Yes, and thank you, but only if Lorrie really wants to do it."

***

Lorrie did, and her relationship with Barbara blossomed into the closest friendship either of them had ever known. Each day, Lorrie would drop Beau off at work and stop by to see Barbara. They would enjoy coffee together and talk. Then, Lorrie would do whatever Barbara needed that day, knowing that, whatever task was awaiting her, Barbara's greatest need was being met in their coffee and conversation.

Lorrie would go home each day right after lunch, to give Barbara time for a nap. Then, she would return after Bill came home from school to help prepare dinner and let the boys get acquainted. It was a schedule that the four of them faithfully kept, Monday through Friday, for several months. And Lorrie was paid, although she objected at first. Jimmy and Barbara insisted, saying it would help if anyone questioned how much time they were spending together, knowing the unspoken taboo on friendships across racial lines in Donelsburg. Beau and Lorrie had to agree. There could surely be problems and they should be prepared.

The strongest bond within this relationship was formed between the two boys. They wanted to continue to see each other after the formal "contract" ended. The women agreed and set "checkup" appointments for Lorrie and Bill to look in on Barbara at least twice a week, sometimes more. These visits continued for well over a year, and the boys managed to stay in touch after that. Neither was very social within their own communities. They found all the friendship they needed with each other.

Time passed. Andy and Bill's friendship grew. And their deepening bond made the rampant injustice of the town all the more evident to Andy. Yes, blacks and whites worked together in the mines, but any relationship ended there. Any time the Mayes and Davis families spent together, beyond the clear employer-employee relationship, they broke unspoken but established social norms.

One such visit forever burned itself into Andy's memory. Bill and Andy were both thirteen years-old. It was the summer. Lorrie and Bill had been visiting with Andy and his mother most of the day, one of Lorrie's periodic "check-up appointments" that extended beyond its usual couple of hours. Lorrie called to Bill. "It's almost three," she said. "Your father will be home from work soon. Let's get going."

Andy followed them out the front door and watched in surprise as his friends suddenly stopped, silent and frozen on the porch. He followed their eyes and saw old Mrs. Winthrop, their gossipy neighbor from three doors down. She stood there, bent over her cane, facing their house, scowling and nodding for a good, long moment. Then, she looked directly at Andy, pointing a twisted, arthritic finger his way.

"Their kind don't belong out front," she muttered, her voice low and shaking, barely audible. Then, more loudly, "Help uses the back door!" With that, she abruptly pivoted on her heel and continued on her way.

Lorrie and Bill said a quick goodbye and left Andy on the porch, moving from shock to anger. The anger grew into a fury that was unleashed on his unwitting father some twenty minutes later on his return from work.

Jimmy had barely stepped in the door, when Andy stopped him with the story of Mrs. Winthrop's menacing look. "I'm sorry, Dad," he said, "but I just hate Donelsburg! It's not one town, it's two: Donelsburg and Colored Town. And people like the Winthrops will do everything to keep it that way."

Jimmy nodded. "Mr. Winthrop warned me we were headed for trouble," he admitted. Then, he looked at his son and smiled. "But it's all talk, Andy. No one's ever done anything to stop us from seeing our friends."

"They will. You watch," Andy said. "One of these days, they will. That's who these people are."

The two walked together into the living room and sat down facing each other. Jimmy, sensing his son had more to say, leaned forward, forearms resting on his knees, and waited.

"Bill told me that, years ago, Donelsburg had a thing called the Sundown Law," Andy said after a few moments. "If Bill's dad came to our side of town after sundown, he could go to jail or worse. Just being here made him a criminal!"

Jimmy nodded. He'd heard of the law.

"Well," Andy continued, "there's no written law now, but there's rules just the same, dangerous rules. Bill told me that, right after they moved to Donelsburg, his dad accidently walked into a white neighborhood. A whole gang of those decent, Christian white folks circled and jumped him. They kicked him and beat him up good. That's where we live, Dad." Andy's voice broke with emotion. "That's the good, happy place we live." With that, Andy rose from his chair and left the room.

Jimmy sat a moment in silence then leaned back into his chair. He saw Barbara step from the kitchen, where she had apparently been listening to the entire conversation. She shook her head, sadly. Jimmy looked away from her and up to the ceiling.

"I never said Donelsburg is good," he said softly. "I only said it's better."

SEVEN

Andy was not usually looking for trouble. Somehow, it often seemed to find him, especially during his seventh and eighth grade years. Part of it came because Andy was naturally attracted to people on the edge, including a couple of fellow students who were labeled misfits and troublemakers.

Some of their handiwork remained classics for years to come. Sure, most stories gained some embellishment as they were told and retold. But the first narrator of the following tale witnessed it personally – from behind a fence – and immediately squealed the story to everyone she knew, finally calling Jimmy Mayes to gleefully rat on the boy.

It was Andy's seventh grade year, a beautiful spring day. Andy and his chums, Jerry Owens and Don Walsh, were out enjoying the day, when they walked in front of the home of another junior high student. Andy stopped and sniffed. He turned to the other two. "Hey! You guys smell that?"

Don lifted his nose high into the air and dramatically inhaled deeply. He coughed. "Smells like shit."

"Sure does," agreed Andy. "It's Tim Williams' house, and he's got a yard full of shit!"

Andy went up to the door, knocked and invited Tim to come out for a visit. With more than a bit of hesitancy, Tim concurred.

"Hey, Tim," Andy said. "Your yard's got some powerful smells here."

"My dad's fertilizing the yard. You smell fertilizer."

"Smells like shit," said Jerry.

"Well, it is. It's manure. It's fertilizer. What's your problem?"

Andy took it from there.

"You got a box anywhere we can borrow? Just a little one, you know, like a gift box?"

The neighbor next door was watching, listening to the whole interaction from her backyard, dropping as needed behind her five foot privacy fence. She did one of those drops as the four boys, led by Tim, stepped inside his family's garage. They came out with a small box, some transparent tape, and a roll of gift wrap.

She watched and dropped, careful not to be detected, as Andy walked around the yard, kicking the manure into the small box, filling it to the top. Then, he took the gift wrap and tape, wrapping the box. He did it quite nicely, the neighbor noticed. Andy then placed it in the street, and all four hid behind a bush, watching and waiting. They didn't need to wait long.

A car passed the box, stopped, and backed up. A man got out, looked around, and walked over to the box. Looking around again, he picked up the gift-wrapped box, hastily put it in his car, and drove off.

"And the boys, egged on by your son, laughed and laughed like they'd done something just great!" the neighbor said when she told Andy's father about it on the phone. "Well, I just thought you should know!"

Jimmy had to cover the phone's mouthpiece to hide his chuckle. *Yes,* he thought, *the boy's a problem. But he's creative!*

***

Andy's parents didn't always find humor in the reports from school and around town. Things were hard for their son, and they knew it only too well. Andy was actually quiet, even introspective, and remarkably philosophical at a very early age, despite the pranks he liked to play. But his ruminations could sometimes grow dark and then angry. When that happened, his fuse could grow short, ready to detonate at the least provocation.

The worst such occasion, one that shocked all who witnessed it and shook even Andy to his core, happened his seventh-grade year, one month after the gift wrap incident. It was early May, and Andy was in English class. By that time, Andy's reputation as a fighter, a strong fighter, had long been established. Most people gave him a wide berth, and he liked it that way. But, for some strange reason Kenny Moore, the student who sat next to Andy, decided to poke the bear.

The class was working quietly as their teacher, Miss Clark, had requested. Before each student was an English grammar worksheet, which some were painstakingly completing, some were staring at blankly, some were not even looking at, and all were hating and wondering, what's the point of this? But they were quiet as the teacher demanded, all obediently quiet.

Miss Clark was standing at the front of the classroom, surveying the students, when she noticed Andy slip Kenny a note, which the second boy read and then laughed hysterically. The teacher scowled. Passing notes was completely out of character for Andy, but she also knew there was a history between these two boys. Everyone knew.

Miss Clark had gotten between them before. She lectured them about getting along and forced a very unenthusiastic handshake. Then she had the bright idea of placing them next to each other in class, warning them to behave. Maybe that was a mistake, but so far things seemed peaceful enough. Maybe it worked too well, and they had become partners in mischief, the teacher thought.

Miss Clark walked quickly to the boys, intending to confiscate the offending note and embarrass the two of them as much as humanly possible. But what followed was a surprise to all, including both boys, and gave poor Miss Clark nightmares for weeks after.

Miss Clark had moved quickly and quietly to retrieve the paper, arriving by Kenny's side as the boy let out his loud war whoop of a laugh. She was barely conscious of the arm being lifted high before her, the pencil in Andy's hand like a dagger. In fact, everything that followed was unconscious reflex, as Miss Clark watched her own hand shoot out before her, grabbing Andy's arm as it was poised above Kenny's shoulder.

The moment seemed frozen in time, as the full impact of what just happened slowly dawned on the three of them. Only a few others actually saw the attempted attack, but virtually all looked up in time to see the disturbing tableau before them, with Andy's arm held by Miss Clark, pencil aimed downward at Kenny and the astonished, incredulous look on each of the three faces.

Miss Clark made the decision in that instant not to send the boys to the office. This was too huge to let go until she got to the bottom of what had happened. She trembled as she released Andy's wrist. She had to lean over to hold Kenny's desk just to steady her shaking body. After several deep breaths, and in spite of strict rules to the contrary, she decided to leave her class and escort the two boys outside, closing the door behind her.

"What just happened?"

Both boys looked down. "I don't know," Kenny said.

Miss Clark snapped, "What do you mean - ?" She caught herself. Another deep breath, then she said, "Okay. Give me the note."

Actually there were two notes. The first was handed by Kenny. It read, "I hear your mama's a squaw."

When Andy read it, his jaw started to tighten. He clenched a fist and then relaxed it. It wasn't worth it. He turned the paper over and scribbled on the other side, then passed it back.

"My mother is an Indian princess."

A deep, inconsolable sadness filled Miss Clark as she pieced together the story. She decided again not to take the boys to the office. She instructed them that they were to remain in her class after school, hoping she could somehow be of help to them. But their parents must know. She would call them herself.

This was Miss Clark's first year in Donelsburg. She was one of very few teachers who were unaware of the boys' hostility the previous year, which pitted them as sworn enemies ever after. Had she known, she would never have placed Andy and Kenny in adjoining desks.

***

It was Andy's sixth grade year. Lunch was over, and he was walking from the cafeteria along with other students, heading to their afternoon classes. Mr. Bennett, the assistant principal, was disdainfully monitoring the halls, taking seriously his duty to keep these young hooligans in line.

Bennett observed the parade of young people, mostly ambling along, chatting and laughing together in clusters of two or three. He noticed that Andy Mayes was walking alone until Kenny Moore stepped up his pace to join him. Bennett watched the boys closely, both perpetual troublemakers.

Kenny, who stood a head taller, said something to Andy as he walked up, bumping the smaller boy to the side. Andy seemed to ignore him and kept walking. So he repeated the action, saying something else to Andy, who suddenly spun in a fury, knocking Kenny backwards. Then, Andy rushed him, hurling Kenny hard onto the floor, leaping on him, and lifting his right fist high to strike.

Bennett barreled down the hallway to intervene. Andy's fist remained hovering above Kenny's head just a few beats before lowering as Andy stood, straddled above the bewildered boy.

Bennett pulled Andy back, holding him firmly by the shoulders as Kenny managed to stand up, shaken but unharmed. The assistant principle clutched both boys by their arms, forcibly ushering them to his office.

Mr. Bennett rather enjoyed his role as chief enforcer of school discipline, especially when he had the opportunity to bring a couple of young punks like Mayes and Moore down a few pegs. He unceremoniously stood them before his desk and sat down in his artificial leather office chair, authority-in-chief.

"I don't know exactly what brought that on and, quite frankly," he asserted, "I don't care. You two are in big trouble, no matter what. I can tell you this for certain: you can both plan on at least one week's suspension for that little outburst. That's a done deal. You both could be expelled outright for any one of the offenses in your files."

He paused to let that sink in. The boys looked straight ahead, saying nothing.

"That may come later but, for now, count on a suspension." He paused again. "But just for the record," he continued, "why don't you tell me what incited this latest provocation."

Again, the boys stood erect and silent. So Mr. Bennett asked again to which Andy simply shrugged and said, "Nothing to be said, sir. It sounds like it doesn't matter."

Andy and Kenny were both indeed suspended from school, which created an enduring enmity between them. Kenny nurtured his hatred because he blamed Andy for getting in trouble. Andy, for his part, would never forget the loathsome insults that spewed from Kenny's mouth before he was slammed to the ground. Andy had heard it all before and had resolved to ignore it. But Kenny's verbal assault marked once too often, at the wrong time, in the wrong place, and aimed at all the wrong people.

"Hey, Mayes," Kenny taunted as he nudged him to the side, "you know you don't belong here."

Andy said nothing. He just looked straight ahead as he walked, thinking, *Yep, can't argue with that.*

Kenny wasn't finished. "So why don't you do us all a big favor and crawl on over to Colored Town? Your daddy's a pansy, your momma's a half-breed, and your best friend's a nig –" And at that split second, fire flamed through Andy's being, exploding through his arms onto Kenny's unsuspecting frame.

EIGHT

More than a few times, Barbara would get a call from the Donelsburg School, usually to report Andy was in yet another fight. It was terribly frustrating, not only that her son was so often in trouble, but because she felt helpless to do anything about it.

Barbara felt confident that she understood the source of the problem. It was two-fold. First was Andy's heartfelt, righteous indignation over anything he perceived as unjust or the vicious maligning of his family or best friend. The sixth grade incident with Kenny Moore was not the first time such disgusting verbiage exploded Andy into action. Further, several fellow students had reported that Andy had been escorted to the principal's office after he had stepped between a bully and his victim. But the teachers very seldom saw the start of the fight and quite frankly didn't care. Some gained satisfaction from seeing Andy in trouble, since more than once his stand on behalf of a student involved confronting a teacher.

Barbara knew that the other reason for her son's aggressive behavior stemmed from how unhappy he was living in Donelsburg. Andy was quite happy with their life in Dearing. His two memories that overpowered all others were accompanying Jimmy on his carpentry jobs and the unabashedly doting love of Grandmother Hartley. He never felt the downside of living in Dearing.

There was an unbreakable bond forged between Andy and his grandmother. He began asking about returning home to Dearing from their very first week in Illinois. But even at ten years old, Andy understood that they could not afford train tickets to Alabama. So he finally stopped asking and outwardly contented himself with the regular exchange of letters between his mother and grandmother. Inwardly, he fantasized about leaving this nightmare of a new home and returning to the sanity and love of Dearing.

Andy finally got his wish for a trip home the summer before entering Donelsburg High School. Letters from Grandmother had begun to slow during his eighth grade year. They ceased altogether for several months until a letter came from Barbara's sister, Kate. Actually, Kate had written all the previous letters as well since neither Grandmother nor Grandfather Hartley could read or write. She would read Barbara's letters and then write down Grandmother's replies.

Kate's letter said that her parents had not been well, Grandmother especially, as she had stopped eating and lost considerable weight. Barbara was asked to come home for a visit. Her mother had been asking to see her, Jimmy, and Andy.

It was a long train ride home. Andy's intense anticipation of seeing his wonderful home and family was met with shock and disappointment. The dilapidated shack, unpainted and loosely nailed together, looked like it would blow over in a strong wind. Heat came from a single wood-burning, potbelly stove, and there was no indoor plumbing. And was it really this small? Andy's Uncle Matthew had married and found work in Dearing. Only his grandmother, grandfather, and Aunt Kate still lived there and it didn't seem big enough for even the three of them. How did they all fit in it before?

But it was so wonderful seeing his beloved grandparents again. And the visit most definitely lifted his grandmother and grandfather's spirits. Andy felt he could see the energy reviving within them as they hugged, laughed, and spent time together.

The Mayes family stayed for several days. Jimmy and Andy set to work on the Hartley house during their second day there. The porch bowed in several places with one open hole. A number of boards were loose on the sides of the old house, with light shining through in several places. Jimmy and Andy laughed and talked as they worked. It felt good to be working side by side.

Every now and then, Jimmy found himself looking toward his parents' house. Should he just drop in and see what happened? He decided against it, at least for that moment. He brought the subject up with the Hartley's that evening.

"I'm sorry, Jimmy," Isaiah said. "Your whole family just keeps to themselves. I see the boys out in the field and sometimes your father's there, but no one ever speaks. I believe they think we stole you away or something."

Jimmy laughed. Then, another thought struck him.

"Mr. and Mrs. Harris, do they still own this land?"

"Oh, sure," Isaiah said.

"But Mrs. Harris ain't here no more," Leotie answered. "She left Mr. Harris about a year ago. I heard she just got fed up with his abuse. She moved to Mobile and got herself a good lawyer."

Jimmy smiled. "I'm glad to hear it. Mr. Harris didn't deserve her." Then, after a moment, he added, "I think I'll try to see my folks tomorrow. All they can do is not answer the door, right?"

Actually, that's exactly what they did. Jimmy was surprised how apprehensive he felt as he stepped onto the rickety porch and tapped his fist on the front door. He was surprised again at his relief when no one appeared. As he turned to leave, he heard a familiar voice speak softly behind him.

"Jimmy."

"Mother?" Jimmy looked back around to see his mother standing, smiling with tears streaming down her face.

"Jimmy, I was so afraid I'd never see you again."

Jimmy stepped forward and took her extended hand, covering it with his other hand. He smiled.

They stood there several moments, neither knowing what to say nor feeling like they needed to. It was good just to see each other. It was good just to touch. Then, Jimmy winced as he heard a second very familiar voice yell, "Alice! Get your ass back in this house! Now!"

Both smiles faded. Jimmy lifted his mother's hand, leaned forward, and kissed it.

"Goodbye, Jimmy," she said. "I love you."

"Goodbye." And Jimmy Mayes started to leave, but paused. "Mother."

She stopped and faced him again.

"Mother, come with me. Leave this, this life, and come back with us."

She smiled and gently shook her head. "You go. I'm happy now just to know you're all right. This is where I belong. And this is where you never belonged. Go."

Again, the voice from the house, louder now, "Alice!"

Jimmy watched his mother go inside and turned, stepping off the front porch of his childhood home. And he walked. He didn't know where he was going. He just walked. He walked, and he cried.

NINE

No one spoke on the long train ride back to Donelsburg. For one thing, Jimmy and Barbara were both completely exhausted from the trip. Their energy had been in a steady downward spiral, and the week sapped the strength that remained. They were both very glad they had made the visit. It was deeply satisfying to know they had helped Isaiah and Leotie. But each returned to Illinois, not only extremely tired but with a profound sadness.

Barbara felt a longing for the incredibly strong, vigorous parents of her youth. It hurt to see their health slip so much in just four years. She wondered how soon they would need to make this trip again to say a final goodbye.

Jimmy was heartbroken to realize how much his mother had suffered all these years. He felt unspeakable guilt that he had interpreted her quiet, submissive presence in the background as consent to all his father and brothers had said and done. He made a silent vow to go see her again someday, to tell her he was sorry, and respond to her statement of love with his own.

Andy, too, was lost in thought, trying to sort out all that had happened these past several days. He knew that something deep within him had changed with this visit, though he wasn't exactly sure what it was. He would still miss his Dearing family and cherish the childhood he had with them. But he now realized that he could never go back. He would indeed leave Donelsburg someday, but it would be a going forward, entering something new. He had no idea what that something was, but that's okay, he thought. It would come. And, whatever it was, it would include Jean.

Andy smiled as he remembered the first time he saw her. It was shortly after their arrival in Donelsburg. School hadn't yet started, and he had gone with his father to pick up some needed supplies at the hardware store.

Andy saw the pretty girl in the next aisle, smiling and talking to a customer. She led the customer to the aisle Andy and his father were in, directing the man to a box of three-quarter inch bolts, just a few feet from where Andy was standing. The man thanked her, took several of the bolts, and walked to the cash register.

She smiled at Andy, and he watched in shock as she walked away. *Does she work here?* he thought. *How could that be possible? She doesn't look any older than me, ten or eleven at the most!*

Andy saw the girl again his very first day at Creekside Elementary School. He spotted her right away in her desk on the other side of the classroom, but she showed no recognition of him whatsoever. *She smiled at me,* he thought. *I'm sure she'll remember me.*

They often laughed about that in the years that followed: how Andy boldly walked up to her during recess and introduced himself, reminding her of how they "met" that summer in the hardware store. She had no memory of it, she said.

"But you smiled at me," Andy insisted.

"I smile at everyone," she answered and walked away with a giggle. Andy liked that giggle. He decided that it meant she liked him. And he was right. Their relationship grew from that beginning, growing through the years into something very special.

Jean's parents had no patience with this budding romance, however. It was their eighth grade year when it fully dawned on her father where this relationship was heading. Andy's reputation as a prankster and troublemaker preceded him, and Jean was told plainly, and bluntly, it just wasn't going to happen.

Jean told Andy about her father's decree and also her response. "You don't really know him, Papa," she had told Mr. Holloway. "Let me bring him to the store. Just meet him. He's nothing like you're thinking." So Jean worked her charm, and her father agreed to one visit. Andy held out both hands, shaking his head with a clear "no way" when she told him of the agreement. But he too finally gave in.

It began just as awkwardly and miserably as Andy had expected. But Jean was confident. It would all be wonderful. And in a strange, uncanny way, it was. After some painfully uncomfortable "Hi's" and handshakes followed by way too much silence, Jean stepped in with the first thing that came to her mind.

"Papa's doing some work around the house now. He's redoing the walls in the living room and bedrooms."

Andy immediately perked up. "What kind of work, sir, if I may ask."

"Oh, nothing you'd care about, son. All very boring. Just some drywall."

"I'd be glad to help you, sir. I've helped my father with nailing, hanging sheetrock, spackling, painting, and everything back in Alabama. I've handled a hammer since before I was ten. I've helped with repairs all around the house since we've been here, too. It'd feel good to help you if you'll let me."

A bit shocked, Jean's father said he'd give it a try. Andy knew what he was doing. He was a great help. The guys talked and laughed. As they say, the rest was history. Gradually, steadily, the Holloways became Andy's second family.

Jean was so amazing! Andy marveled at how she not only brought him together with Mr. and Mrs. Holloway but even introduced them to his best friend, Bill Davis. She was a master negotiator, that Jean. She was bold but thoughtful and careful.

Her parents prided themselves at being "educated and enlightened," and therefore "open-minded and accepting" of other cultures. They were quick to let Jean know that they had no problem with Andy's Native American heritage. They said that they thought it was wonderful. But Jean sensed they would be less open and accepting of a friend from Colored Town. And she was right. But she had become friends with Bill through Andy and felt that this couldn't be hidden from them forever.

She first reminded them of how proud she was of their lack of prejudice, so unlike many in their town. Then, she told them of Andy's wonderful friend and all of his positive traits. It was a leap from Bill being Andy's friend to the three of them spending time together, but she navigated it with expertise and charm. When the time felt right, Jean's parents met Bill and were maneuvered into living out the liberal acceptance they professed.

Yes, Jean was truly amazing. It's no wonder he was attracted to her from the very beginning. She was smart, pretty, confident, and kind. *But what does she see in me?* Andy wondered.

He had thought about that question a number of times, especially as their acquaintance moved to friendship and on to something more. He finally drew the courage to actually ask her. He had walked to Jean's house the night before he left with his family for their visit to Dearing. They sat together alone that evening on the Holloway's front porch swing, and she surprised him by saying, "I'll miss you while you're gone. I'm so glad you're my boyfriend."

"I'm glad, too," he said, "but I really don't understand it, Jean. You're the perfect girl! I don't get why you'd care for someone like me. Honestly, Jean, no one does."

Jean smiled. "I remember the first time you spoke to me at school," she said. "You were so cute and funny."

"Funny?" Andy said with a mock tone of hurt.

"And handsome," she added with a smile. "I mean it, Andy. I was attracted to you, right from the start. You have those blue eyes that seem to look right through me and . . ." She reached over and flipped the hair on his forehead. ". . . that beautiful, dark brown hair."

Andy felt his face begin to flush, and Jean laughed. "Sorry. Guess I got a little carried away." Andy grinned and shrugged. Jean wasn't done. She looked deeply into his eyes.

"That caught my attention, but what really drew me to you was something deeper, something I'm just now starting to understand. You care about things, Andy, important things. You care when you see someone bullied. And other people might just see you getting in trouble for fighting at school, but I could see how you were standing up for someone." She smiled. "And I loved you for it."

They sat quietly a moment, and Jean smiled again. "And you make me laugh. You're a fun, wonderful guy, Andrew Mayes. You make me happy."

***

Andy closed his eyes and sighed, losing his thoughts into the rumble of the train. He was actually eager to return to Donelsburg and especially to Jean. Yes, whatever the future might bring, he knew one thing with certainty: that future would include Jean.

TEN

So many things had converged in Andy's young life that summer before high school. His friendship for Jean was maturing into what he knew would be a life-long love. His drive to break away from Donelsburg was also intensifying but, at the same time, he felt compelled to stay. He was beginning to grasp just how incredibly fragile both his parents were at the moment.

That summer, his father had told him for the first time about Barbara's two grievous miscarriages. The first was when Andy was only two years-old. He had, of course, no memory at all of that traumatic incident. However, Andy was twelve at the time of the second. He knew something horrible had happened to his mother and had been frightened by what he did not understand. Now, his father had explained it all, and Andy was heartbroken by what his mother had to endure.

"I'm so sorry," Andy said to his father. "I do remember Mom being sick and Lorrie coming by to help her."

"Lorrie was a great help, Andy, but no one could change the fact that your mother lost that baby, and we almost lost your mother. She carries the wounds, physically and spiritually, to this day."

"I'm so sorry," Andy whispered again. "I never knew."

"Well, I'm telling you now," Jimmy said. "I want you to know what an amazing mother you have and why she struggles sometimes. I want you to know that you're the reason she has stayed as strong as she has. You're her life, Andy. She loves you more than life itself. You've been a blessing to your mother, son. You're a blessing to us both."

Andy knew that his mother was not in the best of health. She was always thin and never terribly strong, but the emotional and physical ordeal of losing a second child intensified her frailty.

Andy's father was not doing a lot better. Jimmy was never suited for the extreme manual labor of the cotton field or the coal mine. Moreover, Andy had noticed a troubling increase in his father's chronic cough and an ever more persistent wheezing as he breathed. Andy knew. The coal mines were slowly killing his father.

Jimmy knew the mines would take their toll but never thought it would be so soon. He was only thirty-two the summer before Andy entered high school. Breathing had been an issue off and on for much of his life, but he was too young for it to bother him this badly.

He came to Donelsburg with a plan B in case this happened. Jimmy noticed breathing issues his second year in the mines and decided to try once more the work he loved. He would work on the side as a handyman, building up his clientele and, when the opportunity presented itself, go full time as a carpenter. He gave it his all for a year and never could make enough to support his family. Jimmy was surprised and completely disheartened to discover how little the townspeople thought of him, how much undeserved disdain Donelsburg could express for his family.

It broke Andy's heart to see his father, the finest human being he had ever known, mistreated and hurt. A number of townsfolk helped support his efforts, but it became clear the only thing his new business could do was be a tiny supplement. Jimmy finally dropped it altogether and decided it would be the mines for the rest of his life.

Andy's parents were so wonderful to him. They had given him everything that was important: his life, their love and, above all, values that taught him the truth of what really matters. He had not only learned about kindness and family, he had experienced it. Because of them, he knew that money and things are not the first priority. And because of them, he learned that people are people, regardless of education or possessions or color. His mother was half Cherokee. His father's best friend was Negro. Andy's parents in intentional and unintentional ways had shaped him, molded his life.

How could he leave? But how could he stay?

Of course, Andy shared none of this with his mother or father. But he talked at length with Jean and Bill. And, friends that they were, they let him talk; they listened and cared. He told Jean that, whatever happened, he never wanted to go anywhere without her. She smiled and replied, whatever happened, he'd better not. They laughed together as Bill chimed in, "Hey, don't leave me behind!"

So Andy stayed in school, entering his ninth-grade year worrying about his parents and about what he would do after graduation. Jean said, "Don't worry so much, Andy. Just watch and pray. Your answer will come when it's time."

And Jean was right. The answer came at the close of his senior year in the form of a letter, dated Friday, May 28, 1943. At the top of the letter was the seal of the Selective Service System. And beneath the seal were the words in capital letters: "ORDER TO REPORT FOR INDUCTION."

Andy was surprised that he was surprised. After all, America had been part of the Great War in Europe for four years. He was eighteen years old, and he had, as law required, registered for the draft after his eighteenth birthday. His first thought was, "Of course, I'm being called."

His second thought was, "Jean was right. This is what I'm supposed to do."

His third thought was, "I wonder if Bill got a letter."

Andy went immediately to Bill's house and learned that, no, there was no letter. "But you can believe that I'm gonna enlist!"

"What? No, Bill! You don't have to!"

"I want to! It's my country too, and we gotta stop these fascist, imperialist pigs from takin' over the world! And I told you already, man: where you go, I go!"

"Oh, God, Bill. I haven't told Mom or Dad or Jean. What about Jean? How can I do this? What will I say?"

ELEVEN

Andy left immediately for home. He had to go there first. He'd left the house for Bill's without even saying a word to his mother about the letter. That just wasn't right.

She was in the kitchen getting everything ready to cook dinner. God, how he loved his mom. She was so beautiful, so wonderful, and so perfect.

"Hi, son! How's –?" She stopped, her hands hovering over the pot handle near the stove as she took in his grim expression. "Andy, is something wrong? What's wrong?"

Andy said nothing but just walked up to his mother and held her close. Without releasing her, he said softly in her ear, "I love you, Mom."

"I love you too, Andy. But, uh, what - ?"

Barbara pulled away from her son and looked deeply into his eyes. "I love you, but there's something you need to tell me. What is it?"

"I got a letter today, Mom. Selective Service. I guess I'm going off to fight Hitler."

Barbara pulled back more, putting her hands over her mouth. Quickly, she composed herself, and Andy could tell she was searching for what to say. She was working so hard to be strong. Andy knew a terrible evil was going on in this world, and other sons were leaving to fight it, including many from Donelsburg. Andy understood that Barbara knew that, as well. But he also realized how different it must be when it's one's own son.

"It's okay, Mom. I want to go. I need to go. I just hate leaving you and Dad. I think you need me right now."

They embraced again. Barbara had no words. She wasn't even sure of her feelings. She sensed pride. And fear.

Andy headed to Holloway's Hardware where he knew Jean would be working. He was surprised by a strange surge of emotion, as he approached the storefront with its two massive display windows. So much had happened in that place, from the first time he saw Jean, to meeting her father, and countless conversations with this family he had learned to love. That love seemed to fill his very soul as he rehearsed one more time all he planned to say, all he prayed they would accept.

He walked through the glass doors and saw Paul Holloway standing alone in aisle six, clipboard and pen in hand.

"Hello, Mr. Holloway. Sir, I need to talk to Jean just a bit, if I might."

"I'll get her, son. And I'll give you a little privacy."

"No, I think I want you to hear this, too. Please stay with us."

"Okay. Jean's in the office. If it's okay, I'll bring her and Mrs. Holloway, too."

"Please."

The Holloway family before him, Andy took a deep breath. "I'm entering the army soon," he began. "I've been drafted, but I want to go. I want to serve my country."

Mr. Holloway nodded. Mrs. Holloway sat silent. Jean stepped over and put her head on Andy's shoulder and began to sob quietly. Andy put his arm around Jean's waist and continued. He'd planned out and practiced this speech in his head as he walked to the Holloway Store. He wasn't about to hesitate now.

"I'm eighteen now, and it seems to me that I'm pretty much a man. Anyway, I'm going to war."

Andy paused from his rehearsed speech. Hearing himself say those words momentarily stunned him. *I am going to war!* He took a deep breath and continued.

"I'm going to war, and I bet, if I'm not a man now, I'll come back as one. And I already know what I want, and I know that won't change in one or two years or however long it might take. So when I do come back from all this, if Jean will have me and if you give your blessing, I'd like to ask Jean to be my wife. I love her, and I'll take care of her and provide for her the best I can, I promise. I'll be good to her, you never have to worry about that."

Jean's light sobs broke into a full bellow cry as she grabbed Andy so tightly around the neck he momentarily feared for his life. "Yes! Yes! Yes! Of course, Andy! Yes!"

Andy looked to her parents and saw all smiles from both and a flowing of tears from Mrs. Holloway. Mr. Holloway extended his hand. "Welcome to the family, son."

Andy cherished his time remaining with his family. It went quickly. On Monday, August 2, 1943, Andrew Mayes boarded a train for basic training at Camp Grant in Rockford, Illinois.

One week after Andy's train departed for Rockford, Bill Bradley enlisted in the United States Army. His first destination was Fort Huachuca near the Mexican border in Arizona. It was a military base, appropriated for training Negro servicemen in the then segregated armed forces. For the next year, Bill did little besides what he felt were odd jobs he was daily assigned, along with regular training drills. But then, in the summer of 1944, he was on his way to Italy as a member of the 92nd Infantry Division (Colored), where he got his wish to fight the fascists.

Andy was deployed to fight the Japanese in Papua New Guinea. He had never heard of this island before it was introduced during training, but he would go where he was sent. He would fight as he was commanded. And every day, every day, he would write to Jean.

Each week, Andy also wrote a letter to his parents. He looked forward to their letters as well, which most often were less than newsy. What was there to say about life in Donelsburg? The big exception was a letter he received in January of 1945. Barbara wrote that she had received word that his beloved Grandmother Hartley had died of pneumonia. She was only sixty years old.

Then came a second shock when Barbara wrote in this same letter that she doubted Jimmy was healthy enough to travel for the funeral. What? One month later came yet another blow. Grandfather Hartley had followed his wife, his very love and his life.

"They are home now," wrote Barbara, "together again."

TWELVE

On May 8, 1945, families across the United States sat expectantly in front of their living room radios, hearing the long-awaited news: Germany had surrendered. War in Europe had ceased. It was a time of ecstatic celebration in Europe, yet the battles raged on. Japan did not declare defeat until August 15, with a statement of unconditional surrender to follow on September 2, 1945.

Still, families waited as the military had to be demobilized in a slow, systematic way. Too slow for Jean and all Andy's loved ones. Too long.

But Andy was one of the lucky ones, one of the first to be discharged from the military at the end of World War II. It was Friday, December 14, 1945 when a smiling, laughing, overjoyed crowd of family, friends, and well-wishers mobbed their own Andrew Mayes as he stepped from the train in Donelsburg, Illinois.

Andy, for his part, never talked about his experiences except for a funny or strange anecdote now and then. He did his duty to the best of his ability. Beyond that, he had nothing to say. He didn't want to think about it. He wanted to look to the future. And he wanted to enjoy the present. That's what he told his friends and family again and again that first week back, adding, "I'm just glad to be home."

But Andy did need to think and, most of all, talk about his experiences the past two years. At least, that's what Jean thought. She could only imagine what he had seen and experienced, but she felt sure he needed to talk it out.

"I loved the letters you wrote me, pretty much every day these past two years," she told him as they walked hand in hand together one moon-lit evening. "They were all so sweet, so full of love. I'll keep them all forever."

Andy squeezed her hand as they walked. "And I loved yours as well. I still have them."

"You wrote about how much you loved me and missed me," Jean continued. "And, for a while, you told me what you were doing in your training. You wrote about some of the soldiers you met. It was nice. But it all changed after your training. I mean, it was nice and all, but that's just it. You never talked about what was happening anymore. I got worried."

"I don't understand. Why were you worried?"

Jean stopped and turned, looking into the eyes of her fiancé.

"I worried because you were at war, Andy. You'd tell me about the guys in your unit and how tough the weather was, so hot and humid, raining and muddy all the time. And then, sometimes, you'd just mention that you were on patrol in the jungle. I was worried and scared because I wasn't sure what that meant. You wrote nice letters, Andy. Thank you. I loved everything you said. But I worried about what you didn't say."

Andy smiled. He leaned over and kissed Jean gently on the lips.

"All that matters is I'm here. You're here. We're together, and we're going to be married. And, Jean, I have never been happier in my life."

Jean nodded. She never broached the topic of Andy's war experiences again. She felt confident that he would eventually share what he needed as he needed and changed her focus to looking, along with this wonderful man, at their future together.

For the time being, that future would be in Donelsburg. It's where they both grew up and the place Andy meant when he said, "glad to be home." But Jean knew Andy never did feel truly at home in Donelsburg. And not every aspect of his homecoming was entirely happy.

Andy was shocked when he first saw his parents after his return home. Jimmy and Barbara were incredibly frail, especially Jimmy who, at thirty-nine years old, looked and moved like a man twice that age. Andy could not believe his father's health could slip so far in just two years. It was the mines. Andy knew. They all knew. It was the mines.

Yes, Andy was home. For now, that meant Donelsburg. For now, home also meant working each day at Holloway's Hardware Store. For the near future, it meant working around Donelsburg doing carpentry, both building and repairs. And eventually, when Bill was discharged from the army, it would mean his best friend helping with these weekend and evening jobs, steadily increasing his own already proficient skills.

Andy was home and seemed to be content with that. But Jean noticed a hopeful look with renewed energy when he reminded her about one of his army buddies, Donnie Winston, from Arizona.

"Remember? I wrote you a couple of times about Donnie. Great guy. And you should have heard him talk about Arizona, wide open spaces surrounded by mountains. And it's growing like crazy, lots of homes and business buildings going up everywhere. Donnie's from Phoenix, and he worked for a builder there. He told Donnie his job was waiting for him when the war was over, and Donnie said he knew his boss would hire me, too. No question! But don't worry one way or another right now. Just think about it, Jean. We'll just think about it.

THIRTEEN

The year 1946 was momentous for Andy and his family. It was the happiest year in his life thus far. It was also definitely, beyond question, the saddest.

After the most amazing Christmas celebration of their lives, Andy and Jean set about their wedding planning. They both wanted something small and simple. Of course, Andy knew the Holloways expected it to be in a church officiated by a minister. Since church for the Mayes family pretty much meant Christmas and Easter, he figured the wedding would be held in the Holloway's home congregation. That was fine with Andy. He just wanted Jean as his bride however it happened. And he wanted it soon.

Soon it would be, as they married less than a month after Andy's return to Donelsburg. On Saturday, January 12, 1946, Andrew Michael Mayes and Jean Marie Holloway were united in marriage at the First Methodist Church with the Reverend Vincent Edwards officiating. The service was indeed simple, traditional and unpretentious. Everyone said it was one of the most reverent, beautiful ceremonies ever.

The young couple decided to postpone any honeymoon trip as they were excited to complete all the paperwork and processing needed to buy their home with the help of President Roosevelt's new GI Bill. It wouldn't be long and, until the day they could move in, Mr. Holloway had a small, two-bedroom rental that he was happy to let them call home.

Their first week of marriage was perfect. Although, Jean had noticed Andy was a restless sleeper, seemingly struggling with troublesome dreams. Though concerned, she said nothing. Then, he startled her one night in their second week, shouting loudly in his sleep and then waking abruptly. He sat up in bed for a moment before lying back down as carefully as possible, embarrassed, and hoping he hadn't awakened his wife.

Jean gently placed her hand on his shoulder. "Are you all right?"

"Sure. I'm fine, really. Must have been a bad dream or something."

"Could you tell me about it?"

"Yeah. I will, as much as I can remember. But not right now, okay? I think I just need to get back to sleep."

"Okay. I love you."

"I love you, Jean. More than you can know."

They held each other. Andy lay awake a good while, afraid to reenter the dream. And it would be quite some time before he shared it with his wife.

It was the happiest year.

Andy and Jean had been married several months when they learned two pieces of wonderful news. The first was the impending return home of their dear friend, Bill Davis. The 92nd Infantry Division (Colored) had been inactivated in December of 1945. But the demobilization of America's military following the war was painstakingly slow because of the massive number of enlisted men and women. As eager as he was to return home, Bill was grateful to be discharged as early as he was.

The other great news came to Andy from Jean. He was going to be a father. On October 16, 1946, family joined Andy as he and Bill paced side by side in the hospital waiting room.

There was only one hospital in Donelsburg, and it was thus integrated but with floors designated specifically for

Negro patients. Andy noticed the hospital volunteer nervously staring at Bill, apparently wondering if she should ask him to leave. Andy decided he should put her at ease. He walked over to the attractive lady in her mid-fifties.

"Hello," Andy said with a smile. Then, gesturing toward Bill, he added, "Don't worry about that gentleman over there. He's my brother."

The doctor joined them at 10:25 p.m., smiling broadly and extending his hand to the new father. "Congratulations! It's a boy!" he said, before escorting Andy for his first sight of Michael James Mayes, all head, hands, and feet with a generous supply of his daddy's brown hair.

It was the happiest year. It was the saddest year.

Andy joined his wife as an employee of Holloway's Hardware. Jean had begun working part time at the store while still in high school and moved on to full time after graduation. She had a natural gift with numbers and soon took charge of all things financial, including tracking inventory and bookkeeping. Jean only stayed home with Michael a couple weeks after his birth. She actually brought him with her to the store each afternoon so her mother could spend time with the baby while she caught up with her work. If pushed, she had to admit that she enjoyed working outside the home. But, more often, she just said, "I don't want you to forget what an asset I am!"

Each day after work, Andy and Jean would bring Michael for a brief visit with Grandma and Grandpa Mayes. Both were always home because, by September of that year, Jimmy could only walk a few feet before needing to stop and catch his breath. The doctor called it pneumonia. It was a diagnosis often given out of consideration for miners. Every doctor in a coal mining town knew that a miner with the diagnosis of black lung disease would never work the mines again. But it didn't matter. Andy knew Jimmy's mining days were over. How could he work? The man could barely breathe.

It was mid-November. Andy and Jean were already talking about how they would maneuver Thanksgiving meals between their two families. They were chatting about that very thing this chilly November day as they headed from the Holloway Store to visit with Andy's parents with month-old Michael in his father's arms.

The day was Monday, November 18, 1946. It was a date Donelsburg, Illinois would record and remember forever after. It was the day of the Great Donelsburg Mine Disaster.

Things were quite normal that afternoon for most in Donelsburg, certainly for Andy and Jean Mayes. All that concerned Andy as he stepped into his parent's bedroom was that his father seemed worse, much worse than usual. Normally, Jimmy would be sitting in his living room chair, waiting expectantly for their visit. Today, he was still in bed, smiling quietly as he watched his son and grandson enter.

Andy brought Michael over to the boy's grandpa as Jean and Barbara moved to the other side of the bed. There they were, all quietly, lovingly admiring their beautiful baby boy when they heard voices outside. Men were running down the street, past the house, shouting:

"The mines! Explosion in the mines!"

Jimmy tried to sit up in bed but fell back with a gasp. Andy and Jean stood together. "Love you, Mom, Dad, Jean," Andy said. "I gotta go." And with that, he hurried out the door.

FOURTEEN

Coal mine fires and explosions were appallingly common throughout the United States, often with several happening each year. Andy had heard of deaths in the teens and twenties from single mine disasters that took place during his own lifetime. Older miners spoke of coal mine explosions that killed hundreds of miners at a time in the years before that. That's what Andy heard, but never did he imagine he would witness it.

The Donelsburg mine explosion was nothing short of horrific, snuffing out the lives of 122 miners. They were people the Mayes and Holloway families knew well: friends, neighbors, classmates, and coworkers. Yet, even as he grieved the loss of so many, Andy could not help being thankful for one fact: his father's shift of 7 a.m. to 3 p.m. had already left the mine. Jimmy's coworkers survived, including his best friend, Beau.

Rescue workers, some two-hundred in all, worked all afternoon and through the night, ever hopeful someone would be found alive, but not one was. Those who survived the explosion died of asphyxiation from the huge amount of carbon monoxide, methane, and coal dust.

Searches continued through the next day, followed by the arduous work of bringing bodies out of the mine and the gruesome task of identification. Many were burned and/or dismembered beyond recognition. Identification tags, provided to the miners by Smithton and required to be on their person at all times in the mine, helped rescuers with the grim task of identifying victims.

Federal and state inspectors later reported that, without a doubt, it was the methane that caused the explosion in the first place. Pockets of methane gas build up in the walls of every coal mine. It's the primary cause of most coal mine explosions. The Donelsburg explosion was the worst-case scenario with the easily ignited methane forming a huge fireball that flamed through the mine, igniting the much more volatile coal dust. The explosion was catastrophic.

The horrible shock wave of the mine explosion was only intensified by the inspector's report. It ended with six words that rocked Donelsburg and the nation: "This disaster could have been avoided."

This disaster could have been avoided!

Further, the report contained documentation that previous inspection had warned Smithton Company of breaches in established guidelines, including designated methods for controlling methane gas. Specific recommendations had been given and were completely ignored. But the federal Bureau of Mines had no authority to enforce any established codes. Inspectors were assigned for research to gather information and, at best, make recommendations. That advice could be ignored, which Smithton chose to do.

Donelsburg was in shock as their horrendous grief was increasingly interlaced with growing rage. Andy felt the grief that grew to rage. He realized he'd been harboring this fiery anger throughout much of his life. The hatred of most things Donelsburg had become microscopic, almost invisible, with his marriage and the life-giving presence of Jean and Michael. But the rage exploded along with the mine. It burned as hot as ignited coal dust. It reverberated with the revelation of a negligent company that slaughtered 122 loyal employees and would very soon cause the death of his father, the most kind and wonderful man he had ever known.

Andy was ready to fight to take down Smithton Mining. But he had no idea where to start or even what to do. And then, he thought of the other miners and their families, the whole community of Donelsburg that depended on the mines to survive. He suddenly felt exhausted, helpless.

Jean noticed that her husband's restlessness and recurring dreams both increased and intensified. He had gone to the mine after leaving his parent's house that dreadful evening. He had watched as miners assembled into teams of rescue workers, descending into the mine, searching for survivors, bringing what remains they could to the surface. He helped to move those bodies to a number of makeshift morgues housed in several buildings around the town. And, for weeks after that, he could not shake the grisly experience, not wanting to go to sleep. The sleep that finally came would be short-lived, with Andy startled awake from the dreams that constantly haunted him.

Finally one night, fresh from the horror of recurring vision and sounds, Andy opened his heart to his wife, sharing his nightmare as she held him, shaking, in her arms.

"We were marching, soaked in rain and sweat, rifle held ready. We marched through the mud, deep enough to pull at our boots, straining to walk, straining to watch. I had soldiers, my buddies, there marching with me, straight ahead, straight behind, marching, watching."

Andy paused, breathing quick and shallow.

"Allied planes had made strikes on a Japanese air strip hidden deep in the jungle. Most of their planes and buildings were destroyed, but you have to finish the job on the ground. Some of the enemy would be left. So we marched, and we watched. And we came to the air strip and saw nobody, just rubble, no people."

Jean suddenly realize that Andy had moved from sharing his dream to remembering aloud the actual event that provoked it. Then, she watched in shock as a look of terror crossed her husband's face.

"Barry! You remember Barry from Indiana. We talked about the little nothing-towns in the mid-west that we called home and the people in those little towns. I think I liked Barry most of all. He was a good man, had a wife and two kids at home he always talked about, showed me their pictures, beautiful family. You remember me writing about Barry."

Jean nodded, there beside him in their dark bedroom. "Sure, Andy. I remember Barry."

Andy looked into the dark, eyes wide as he relived the moment.

"There was no one there, Jean. And then one shot, one goddamn shot! And then Barry! Barry was right there in front of me, and he went down. The bullet, the bullet struck him and, my God! Barry! The side of his head! Oh, God!"

Andy curled forward, grabbing his legs and pressing his face into his knees. Jean reached over, wrapping her arms around her husband. After a moment he looked up, staring straight ahead. When he spoke again it was soft, almost a whisper.

"It seemed like everything stopped, just for a split second when Barry fell, but then all hell broke loose. There were shots, gunfire all around us. I dropped and crawled behind a barrier, all that was left of a bombed building. I started shooting toward the gunfire and I saw that they were in the jungle ahead of us, in the bushes, behind the trees. They were in the trees! We all worked our way forward and started spotting them there. We fired and lobbed grenades and started picking them off. Oh, Jean, I hated them like I never hated anyone. I wanted to kill them all."

Andy was silent again. When he spoke, his voice was sad but calm, matter of fact.

"I don't know how many I killed that day, Jean. But I know too many men, good men I loved like brothers, too many died that day. The army called it our victory, said we were heroes. But I saw too many die that day and many other days."

Andy's voice was almost breath, a whisper Jean could barely hear as he spoke once more.

"Death. Death. And now I'm home and – How much more, Jean? How much more?"

Andy was still sitting up in bed, arms grasping his legs which were bent before him. Jean was beside him, facing him on her knees with arms wrapped around him, her head resting on his shoulder. Here they remained in silence for several moments. Finally, lying down together, they lay in each other's arms until they embraced together in blessed sleep.

FIFTEEN

It was the saddest year.

The very town of Donelsburg seemed to have faded silently in mourning.

Meanwhile, there were high level meetings at Smithton Company. Mine number two was seemingly destroyed. Executives at Smithton talked earnestly about the need to keep a full crew working at mine number one. For once, however, the leadership chose to follow wise counsel.

The town was already dangerously hostile after learning details of the federal and state inspections. The company simply must be cognizant of their grief, temporarily shutting down all operations out of respect for all who had died. Smithton didn't like it but did just that, publicly expressing condolences and calling the fallen miners "heroes."

The townsfolk desperately needed that freedom from work, not only to mourn together with family and friends, but for time to attend the overwhelming number of funerals in the weeks ahead. There had been passing discussion of the town holding a mass funeral with all the slain miners named, prayed over, and buried in a mass grave.

The families were horrified at such a suggestion. Each would make arrangements for its own loved ones with their own church, pastor, and tradition. Yet most had lost multiple family members or such dear friends they were the same as family. Thus, loved ones gathered, laying to rest three, four, or even more deceased within a single service.

All townsfolk knew some of the miners and most knew a large number very well. People felt the need to be with their grieving friends, but the number of services was staggering. Most citizens of Donelsburg could be found either in church, at a graveside, or in their homes.

Andy and Jean had been to churches and to gravesides, many churches and gravesides. Tonight, they were home, side by side in bed, both emotionally and physically exhausted. They had been to funeral after funeral. Probably the worst were with families who lost multiple members and held one service for, say, three siblings. But none were easy and there were so many; so much grief. Now, they would have time to rest, to have a blessed moment to just be together away from all the pain.

But it was not to be.

It was only 9:30. The lights were out; Michael was sound asleep. Andy and Jean were in bed, awake, mostly silent and just thinking, sometimes talking quietly. It was one of those rare, almost holy, moments that give birth to questions of meaning and conversations of things eternal.

Jean was a committed Christian, baptized and confirmed in the Methodist church. Andy had been baptized in a creek at the tender age of eight by a Baptist preacher he knew only as Brother Jed. His family were members of Dearing's Ebenezer Baptist, attending services there two or three times in a good year. But Andy had an abiding faith, shared and nurtured by his mother.

That faith was in God, Jesus, and the promise of eternal life. His faith did not require a building or any structured organization, trappings that seemed so important to the landowners and merchants of Dearing, who worshiped on Sunday then cheated the poor through the week. But their hypocrisy did not mean that the Spirit wasn't real, that God wasn't good.

Barbara taught Andy of the Great Spirit, a name she used interchangeably with Jesus, the Son, and God, the Father. She told him the Bible too spoke of the Spirit, the Holy Spirit who is the Presence. The Spirit is God present in nature. The Spirit is God present within us. The Spirit is always with us, always here, she said. But there are times when you could feel the Presence. These were the holy times.

Andy had shared these things before with Jean. But as Andy spoke of his mother's teaching again, in this time when they both so needed that Presence, she was filled with a beautiful peace.

"Feeling the Presence is a gift," Andy went on. "You can't make it happen. It only happens in those special holy moments. Oh, some people experience the Presence all the time. But they are the holy people and there are very few. Most of us don't, not here, not in this world. But, one day, we will know and feel the Presence completely, every moment, the day we pass over."

Jean sighed deeply and pulled close to Andy, her head on his chest. She said softly, barely a whisper, "That's our hope, isn't it? It's the hope for all those miners' parents and wives and children."

Andy gently kissed her forehead, filled with such love for his beautiful wife.

His serenity was abruptly shaken. A loud knock. Andy got up, slipped into some overalls and stepped to the door without shirt or shoes.

It was Shirley, his parents' next door neighbor.

"I'm sorry, Andy. I didn't know you'd be in bed, but I had to tell you. Your mother sent me. She said for you to come now. Your father's not doing so good."

Andy thanked Shirley and said he'd be right there. He closed the door and headed back to the bedroom, slipping on a shirt, shoes and a coat as Jean got dressed and carefully lifted Michael, still sleeping, from his cradle. It was Sunday, December 15, one year after Andy's return home from war. They stepped into the cold, dark night with Michael snuggled in a baby blanket and walked together the two blocks to Andy's parents.

His mother was there, sitting in a straight back wooden chair several feet from the bed. By the bed was Doc Bentley, standing tall, looking down calmly at Jimmy Mayes who was lying on his back, eyes closed, arms resting at his sides. Jimmy seemed to be asleep, but his breathing was irregular, sometimes pausing his breath for several seconds before taking a shallow breath only to pause again.

Doc extended his hand, and Andy took it with sincere appreciation.

"I'm so sorry, Andrew. You're dad's a good man, decent to everyone." Andy thanked him.

"I'm going to go for a while and give you all time together. You talk to him now. Tell him how much you love him. It may not seem like it, but I'm convinced he'll hear every word, and it'll mean a lot to him if you do that – and to you, too. I'll be back soon."

Andy thanked the doctor again. Then, he stepped to the bed. Barbara and Jean stayed back with a peacefully sleeping Michael.

Andy knelt by the bed and took his father's hand. He wanted to talk. He had so much to say, so many words, but nothing seemed to come. He laid his head on the hand he held and felt hot tears, burning his eyes as he tried in vain to hold them back. Jean handed Michael to her mother-in-law and walked beside Andy, placing a hand on his shoulder. Andy looked up.

"Dad, you're such an incredible man. I love you so much."

Jimmy took a deep breath, a gasp for air. Andy heard a rattle from deep in his father's chest. Then, all was quiet for a moment. Andy held his breath and listened. His father inhaled again.

Barbara rose, carrying little Michael to the bedside. She gently laid the boy by his grandpa and, keeping her hands on Michael, knelt by her son.

They all felt it. They all knew. This was the holy moment, the holy place. And they all experienced the Presence that was beside them, around and within, the Presence who would comfort and strengthen them, the Presence who would soon lead their beloved husband, father, and grandfather home.

Andy was aware of the Presence. He was also increasingly aware of the ever-widening space between his father's breaths. The breaths grew shallower, the rattle deeper. Andy was surprised to feel his own lungs suddenly spasm with a noisy gasp. Jean knelt by him and reached around him, gently holding him close. And they listened together.

Breath. Long pause.

Breath. Longer pause.

And then.

Silence.

And to their amazement, Michael woke and began to cry.

SIXTEEN

Another funeral. Another heartbreak.

Andy, Jean, and Barbara sat with heads bowed as Reverend Edwards offered the prayer, committing their beloved Jimmy's body to its resting place and his spirit to eternity with God. They stood and received the warm embraces and condolences. Andy appreciated the kind words but was ready for them all to go away, to be undisturbed in his emptiness for just a little while.

Andy was surprised by the depth of his sadness. But, as he reflected on this incredible angst, he realized it was more than grief over what had happened, horrible as that was. He was also grieving over what he knew was to come.

There would be yet another funeral. Perhaps soon. His mother was frail; she had been since he could remember. But the physical drain of caring for her husband during his long illness, the emotional toll of watching the man she loved slowly diminish before her eyes had consumed Barbara, body and spirit.

For Barbara and Jimmy, it was much more than symbolic when the preacher pronounced them husband and wife, saying, "The two have become one." They were one with a unity that grew increasingly stronger over the next twenty-one years. Barbara could not imagine life without Jimmy. So Andy had to watch over the last year as his mother faded from life each day, right along with her husband. When Jimmy passed away, most of Barbara was gone too.

Andy and Jean insisted that Barbara come live with them. It would be just for a while, they said. They would love having her there, and she would be a great help watching Michael. That last rationale was all she needed. Barbara moved in.

Jean had already begun some modest decorating for the holiday. Barbara was surprised how much helping her daughter-in-law put final touches on the Christmas decor lifted her spirits. She was also buoyed by the frequent visits of her dear friends, Beau and Lorrie. Bill often came with them but, more often, stopped by alone and shared precious time with Jean and Andy.

During the first month after Jimmy's funeral, a surprising number of other townsfolk also came by to visit, mostly miners and their families wanting to express sympathy to Barbara, Andy, and Jean.

"Jimmy was about the nicest guy I ever knew," said one.

"He never had a bad word for nobody," said another. "I'm so sorry for your loss, ma'am. Jimmy's gonna be missed by us all."

Andy was surprised how touched he felt by each visit, how much he appreciated every word. These were people who had snubbed his father before, who never had a kind word for any of his family at any point in time. Now, they dared to come to their home with compassionate words of condolence when he's gone.

Andy should have cringed at the hypocrisy. But he didn't. Why? Partly, he decided, because every word they said was true. Jimmy Mayes was indeed the kindest, most generous man he had ever known. Andy could see that the townsfolk not only spoke these words of truth, but they honestly believed them, and he was grateful.

The other reason Andy was not cynical about Donelsburg's kindness was the magnitude of every citizen's loss. Each person who stopped by to share a kind word was doing so while overwhelmed by grief of their own. There was not one person in all of Donelsburg that had not lost a loved one in the horrible mine disaster, whether a relative or dear friend.

Each resident was struggling with profound grief. Yet, these people made the time and effort to personally visit Barbara and her family in their loss. It amazed Andy, and he said as much to Jean. She smiled and hugged him close.

"They're good folks at the heart of it, Andy," she said. "In fact, deep within their very center, I think every person is good."

Andy stood quietly with her for a moment, and his thoughts turned to Smithton Mining Company.

"It's a nice thought, Jean. But I'm not so sure."

SEVENTEEN

Christmas in 1946 was far from festive in the mining town of Donelsburg, but it may well have been the most religious Yuletide in anyone's memory. Not only were the town's churches full throughout the month of December, families were regularly praying together in their homes, many for the first time. Then, January began with a handful of preachers, many of whom would never consider associating with each other before this year, actually talking together about revival.

The year also began with work resuming at mine number one. It was just one week into the New Year when the first shift arrived, and the crews took their places. Downtown, stores and businesses were preparing for their day. Laborers were on their way to their jobs.

Everything was back to normal.

No person was back to normal.

For this generation that personally witnessed that horrific catastrophe, who personally experienced the incredible loss, nothing would ever really be back to normal. But it was a new year, and they would have to move forward to discover their new normal, whatever that might mean.

For Andy, Jean, and Bill, it meant spending as much time together as they possibly could, remembering their years together, catching up on years they had missed, and looking forward to years yet to come. Some of the time was spent with Jean listening, occasionally interjecting a question or comment, as Bill and Andy talked of their different experiences in the war.

Jean suggested that they have their conversations in a small meeting area in the back of Holloway's Hardware. The room adjoined the store's office and was out of view of curious onlookers. It became a favorite gathering place for the friends, meeting for a couple hours every Sunday for the first few months of 1947. Jean was pleased at how comfortable they all seemed to be whenever the three were together. She was thrilled how both men talked more and more openly about their military years.

She sensed that even Bill was surprised when he carried much of the conversation at their third "Sunday Stopover," as they came to call their visits. There, she learned that Bill was assigned to a segregated division, as were all Negro enlisted men. Most would never see action, as America's armed forces did not believe "colored" soldiers were fit for battle. They were assigned to various grunt projects involving manual labor, sorting and transporting supplies and so on.

"There were two divisions that were actually able to go overseas and fight," Bill said, "the 93rd Infantry in the Pacific Theater and the 92nd in Europe. I was in the 92nd. We fought, and we fought bravely. I think we served our country proud."

Jean could indeed hear the pride in Bill's voice. She smiled, but then was a bit surprised at what Bill said next. "It's interesting," he said, "that both these divisions trained together in Arizona."

Jean looked over to Andy. He was smiling broadly.

"What did you think of Arizona?" Jean asked.

"Hoo! It's one hot place! Desert, dirt, and rocks!" Bill said.

Now, it was Jean's turn to smile. "So you didn't like it?"

"Oh, I didn't say that. It took some getting used to, and some of the men just hated everything about it: no trees, no grass. And that's what I thought at first. But then, I started really looking at things. No trees maybe, but I saw some wildflowers there in the spring that'd take your breath away. No grass, but the stars at night, why Jean, I never once saw stars so dense and bright as I saw in Arizona.

"One night, I was gazing at the sky, truly never feeling so full of peace and hope, and I thought, 'it can never get more glorious than this!' Then, I saw this shower of shooting stars all across God's heaven. I've never seen anything like it, Jean. Never."

"Sounds awfully nice," said Andy. But Bill wasn't done.

"There were mountains close to Fort Huachuca, ranges of gray, rocky mountains. Honestly, I think that's what I miss the most now that I'm back here in Donelsburg. Here all we know are holes, huge tunnels down into the ground. I don't know. It kind of pulls me down, too. You know? It pulls down my spirit."

Andy nodded. "I think I know what you mean," he said.

"The Bible says, 'I look up unto the hills.' Well, I saw those mountains, and I looked up, and I felt my spirit lift, too."

Andy looked with wonder at his friend. "That's amazing, Bill. It sounds like you really loved it there."

"I think you can learn to see the good if you try. It's there somehow, wherever you are. Camp was hard, Andy, really hard. You know. You did it. And there's a hardness to the desert, too. Some of my buddies, that's all they saw. I guess I was blessed to see other things."

"It's just a surprise to hear you talk that way about Arizona," Andy said. "I told Jean about a guy in my division from Phoenix. It's a big city with lots of growth and lots of opportunity. I don't know when, but I want to check it out. Maybe, we'll move there someday."

Jean chimed in, "Maybe."

Andy smiled.

"I'm just saying check it out for right now. So, good buddy, how'd you like to check it out with us."

Bill looked surprised. He thought for a good while before answering.

"I did like Arizona," he finally said, "but I'm going to have to give that some thought."

***

Bill and Andy had discussed the possibility of launching a company as building contractors, bringing Jean on board with her outstanding financial and bookkeeping skills. Yes, they had the skills, but prospects were few. Donelsburg, once bustling and robust, was shrinking before their eyes. No new houses were needed. People were needed to fill the ones that were increasingly vacant.

Andy and Jean continued to work at Holloway's. Bill had no desire to work for Smithton, even if jobs had been available. He finally found work at Anderson's Market, living at home with his parents.

The grocery store was just a few blocks from the Davises' home, a fixture in Colored Town throughout the years. But Jeremiah Anderson, the seventy-two year-old owner, could no longer keep it up and neither of his two children wanted anything to do with it. Enter Horace Cline, the owner of HC Grocery and Meat in downtown Donelsburg. He made an offer and, with no other buyers, Jeremiah accepted. In 1944, Anderson Market officially came under white management.

Jeremiah and Horace both took considerable heat for the sale in each of their respective communities. But Anderson's customers needed their groceries, and H.C.'s customers certainly didn't want to shop side by side with "coloreds." When the dust settled, it seemed that little had changed. Other than the white manager Cline placed on site, the new owner made sure locals were employed to deal with the public.

Bill Davis, however, felt stifled in his new employment. He found himself thinking more about Andy's invitation to investigate opportunities in Arizona.

EIGHTEEN

The year progressed and, as it did, so did an increasing appearance of normalcy in Donelsburg. Beau was hard at work in mine number one. Number two had still not reopened. There simply wasn't enough staff between the men killed in the great disaster and the number of miners who decided it was time to leave, usually at the urging of their spouses.

The wives, of course, were most concerned about their husbands' safety, but the miners could see even bigger reasons to move on. Most of those who moved lived in company housing. There was no ownership in the town to keep them there. And the economy was improving, even as it seemed Smithton Company was slipping away. How strange that both Smithton mines were moving at capacity during the Great Depression and now, as everything else in America seemed to be turning around after the war, Smithton could barely keep both shifts at work in one mine.

Beau and his fellow miners were ready to go back to work. Sure, they carried a huge weight of resentment for all that had happened, but work was work, and you had to survive. Feelings were being somewhat cooled by meetings of UMWA on the miners' behalf both in Washington and with Smithton. Promising news was coming out of the capital about new federal safety standards for America's mines, with hints of laws that had the teeth to enforce them. Smithton Company, for its part, was watching these developments carefully while keeping a vigilant eye out for any intimations of a potential strike among its workers. None ever came.

Barbara continued to live with her son and daughter-in-law. She loved caring for Michael, such a handsome and happy little guy. He reminded her so much of his father at that age. But she was also feeling incredibly tired of late.

She had never really recovered from the absolutely debilitating ordeal of Jimmy's illness and death. Then she immediately launched into helping Jean with her Christmas preparations and, though she truly enjoyed her time with her daughter-in-law and family, she left the holidays more exhausted than she entered them.

Andy and Jean both worried about how weary Barbara looked. But she insisted that everything was fine. Nonetheless, the couple asked Jean's parents about rescheduling their shifts so that each went to work on alternate days, the other staying home so Barbara could rest and build up her strength. The Holloways were fine with the idea. Barbara protested. But that was the plan for the next several weeks.

February came and went. Still, Barbara's energy waned. Her strength was enough to care for Michael during the day. But when his parents returned home, she headed for bed and a long nap before dinner. After dinner, she would lie down again, often sleeping through the night. This pattern continued most days through the month of March.

Andy phoned Doc Bentley, who called at their house early that very evening. The doctor reported that he couldn't find anything medically wrong beyond a lower than normal blood pressure. Bentley then gestured for Andy to follow him outside.

"Andy, to be honest, I think Mrs. Mayes is mostly exhausted and depressed. She's been through a lot. You all have."

"This whole town has, Doc."

"Yes. Yes, it has. But I never knew a couple as close as Jimmy and Barbara Mayes. Your mama is sick with exhaustion and a broken heart. You give her rest, all right, but she also needs you to show your love any way you can. Take walks together. It's warming up soon enough; have a family picnic. She just loves you and the family so much, I think that time will be better'n any medicine I could ever prescribe."

"Sounds like wise words, Doc. We'll do it."

NINETEEN

The next week, on the first Sunday in April, the Mayes family headed to Rotary Park. It was spring. The grass was green, flowers were in bloom, and Andy was ready to join with Jean and Michael to be the best medicine possible for his ailing mother. Barbara did seem to enjoy the picnic and thanked them for sharing this beautiful day. But shortly after they enjoyed their sandwiches and potato salad, she said she felt tired and asked if they could return to the house. A few days later, when Jean and Andy approached her about an afternoon stroll, she thanked them but declined, saying she would rather stay in. And so it went through the month of April.

One evening, when Barbara had gone to bed for her after dinner nap, Andy mentioned to Jean that his mother seemed to be losing weight. Jean replied, "She definitely is, and it's really no wonder. She hardly eats anymore, picking at her food and saying she's not really hungry."

"I've been thinking," said Andy. "Maybe, she needs a change. Everywhere she looks, there's a memory of Dad. I think change might be a good thing."

"Uh-huh. You're talking Arizona."

"Well, it might be good. I mean, Doc says it's depression, and what's more depressing than Donelsburg? Do you think I should just run it past her, tell her a little bit about Phoenix?"

Jean thought a moment. "No. I don't. It's too much change and too sudden. She really didn't do that well going out to the park for a picnic. I think taking her all the way to Arizona isn't a good idea."

"You're probably right. But let's just let it rest a day or two and talk some more. We won't do anything that big without a lot of thought and a plan. But let's not drop it altogether yet."

That's where they left it. Nothing else was said through the spring and into summer. Barbara's health was declining to the point that Andy feared she could not survive the stress of such a journey. Doc Bentley stopped periodically on his rounds and he, too, was troubled by her continuing deterioration. She had no interest whatsoever in food and ceased to get out of bed to hold and read to her grandson, the thing she loved most in the world.

Then, one Sunday afternoon on a sweltering hot August day, Barbara got out of bed. She put on her robe and walked slowly, quietly to the bathroom where she washed her face and patted it dry. Then, Barbara walked to the living room. Jean was relaxing on the sofa, watching delightedly as Andy crawled around on the floor, laughing and playing with his son.

Barbara watched too, standing in the hallway, smiling. Andy saw her first and moved quickly to his feet.

"Mom! So great to see you! Please come sit with us."

Barbara walked over to a chair and, grasping the chair arms tightly, slowly sat down. She still looked desperately tired, but she was up. Jean and Andy were thrilled.

"Please forgive me for being such a weight on you both all these months," Barbara said. "I just wanted to apologize and to tell you how wonderful this year has been, living here with you."

"Oh, Mom, you're not a weight, you're a joy! I'm so thankful we've had you here, and we'll keep having this time together, more time to share that's better than ever."

"We love you, Barbara," said Jean. "It's been a wonderful year for me, too. I cherish this year with you."

"Well, I sure do appreciate that, both of you. I just needed to let you know how much being with you has meant to me. I wanted to tell you both how very, very much I love you. And, I guess as much as anything, I wanted to hold my little Michael and read him another story.'

"He's a bit squirmy today," Andy said. "I guess that's my fault. I got him riled up a bit, but let's give it a try."

Andy picked up Michael and placed him on his grandmother's lap. She snuggled him close in her arms, and he smiled his most radiant smile. Barbara looked across the room and spotted Michael's favorite book.

"Andy, please bring me *The Three Little Pigs*." And she read the story with great animation, directing Michael to the book's pictures and changing her voice for each character. Michael listened, enraptured, giggling with delight as his grandmother deepened to her best bass reading of, "I'll huff, and I'll puff!"

When the story was over, Andy took Michael's hands and helped him applaud. Jean was watching Barbara who had a look of blissful peace on her face but whose body seemed limp and weak. She was completely, physically exhausted by the effort.

"Barbara," Jean said, "you have so blessed us today. Please let me know what you'd like for dinner. You just name it, and we'll see that it's ready for you. I can see you might want to rest and, when you're up, dinner will be served."

"I do need to rest, dear. You just do whatever you think is best, and it will be perfect, just like this afternoon was perfect. It's just exactly what I wanted, exactly what I needed. Thank you."

Andy carefully lifted Michael and placed him back with his toys. Then, he offered his mother his arm to help her out of the chair. He was surprised how much she was leaning on him as they slowly made their way across the living room and into the hall. He helped her into bed and gently covered her with the blanket.

"I am so blessed, Andrew," she said. "I cannot remember when I felt so blessed."

"I love you, Mom. You have been the blessing."

"That time we spent just now, that was a holy time. Do you feel the Presence, Andy? The Great Spirit is always with us but, if you listen and watch right now, you'll feel the Presence. The Spirit is here. The Spirit is in our love."

"Yes, Mom. I do. I feel the Great Spirit here with us. I do." And he did.

Barbara closed her eyes. "Thank you, Great Spirit God, for such a wonderful son."

Andy kissed his mother on her forehead and, as he rose, reached down to wipe a tear from her cheek. Then, he noticed: the tear was his.

TWENTY

Andy found both Jean and Michael in the kitchen where Jean was already seeking ingredients for dinner. Later that evening, the entire house was filled with the tantalizing aroma of eggs and wild onions with a side of fry bread.

Jean was excited to prepare this dinner for Barbara who had introduced her to the traditional Cherokee meal. But the meal sat at the table uneaten. When Andy couldn't awaken his mother for dinner, he called Doc Bentley. But Andy already knew. Really, he knew as he kissed her before her nap that he was kissing her goodbye.

Barbara was indeed blessed by those months with Andy, Jean, and Michael. But her spirit yearned to be with her beloved Jimmy. She loved her children, but this was not home. Home was with Jimmy. Home was with the Great Spirit. Home was where she prayed to each night, where she hoped the Great Spirit would allow her to be.

And it was time for her prayers to be answered. She knew on that Sunday afternoon, half awake, half asleep, as she became aware of the beating of distant drums and the voices of her ancestors, chanting the ancient prayers. She sensed the Presence within and around her, closer than she had ever known. And she opened her eyes to see the faint form of one that she knew instantly was the spirit of her great-grandfather, chief of the rebel Northeastern Alabama Cherokee.

He was here, she knew, to escort her home. And she was ready, so very ready. But she prayed again, a prayer to her grandfather's spirit, a prayer to the Great Spirit. "Give me one more hour," she prayed. "I only ask for one more hour with my family, to touch my son, to hold my grandson. One more hour and then, Great Spirit God who is with me always, I want to be with you."

Doc Bentley offered to request an autopsy, an official post mortem to determine the cause of death. Both Jean and Andy declined, saying they didn't feel it would be respectful. But the real reason they refused his offer was that they already knew why their loved one was gone. She chose to leave. Barbara Mayes had essentially willed herself to die. And she was at peace now with her husband who was her life.

To his surprise, Andy was at peace, too. He really never expected that. He had seen the death of so many who were close to him and was dreading the passing of this woman he dearly loved. But the past months with her had been an incomparable gift of grace. His spirit was filled, overflowing, as he watched the joy she and Michael brought to each other and into their home. He had the amazing opportunity to share with his mother deep conversations about life, their family, and faith. He knew that their shared faith and convictions of all things spiritual gave him incredible strength for this and every challenge life might bring.

Moreover, he understood the enormous contrast between his mother's passing and the horrific losses of the past several years. As much as Andy would terribly miss his mother, as deeply as he regretted that Michael would never truly know this extraordinary human being, he was grateful that she was home and at peace. Her life was not tragically snuffed out like his friends in the war or those in the mine explosion or even his own father. She had yearned to be set free, to be reunited with love and life. She was home.

Months passed. Even with his deep convictions of faith and the spiritual understanding of his loss, Barbara's passing had left a gaping hole in Andy's being. He found himself returning home each day looking forward to sharing an experience or passing thought with his mother as he had almost daily through the previous year. He would walk through the front door, ready for their conversation, only to remember she wouldn't be there.

But the expectation and the sorrow which followed lessened in both frequency and severity as time went on. Sadness gradually diminished and, in its place, were all the good memories and thanksgiving for the blessing of wonderful parents.

Andy was increasingly released from his grieving to become ever more focused on his immediate family and their future together. And ever since his discharge from the army, he had a growing conviction of where that future would take place.

TWENTY-ONE

It was Thanksgiving Day, November 27, 1947. Paul and Margaret Holloway hosted their traditional family meal at their home. Guests were welcomed by the aroma of turkey roasting in the oven, homemade pumpkin pie, and logs crackling in the fireplace. Many commented on the delightful fragrances as they were entered the Holloway home. "It smells like fall," declared one.

At Andy's request, the Holloways also invited Beau, Lorrie, and Bill Davis. Guests also included the Holloway's son and older daughter along with their families, so it was quite a crowd even with Paul and Margaret Holloway's spacious dining area.

There was chatter around the big table since all were part of the family and knew all the inside jokes. All but the Davis family, of course. They smiled and nodded politely but never felt comfortable adding to the conversation. They, along with all the Holloway family, wondered why Andy insisted they be included.

Lorrie ventured her first words as dinner came to a close, complimenting Jean's pumpkin pie. "Thank you," said Jean. "It's my mother's recipe. And your green beans were so good. I'd love to have the recipe."

"You'll have it," said Lorrie, grateful to be included. "But nothing can compare with your mama's turkey and dressing."

All smiled, and Paul chimed in, "Yes, indeed. It was all so good, I just couldn't stop eating!"

"Uh-huh, you got that right, dear," Margaret added with a wink, followed by laughter that spread around the table.

When the laughter settled, Andy decided the mood was perfect to share what was on his mind. "Excuse me," he said. "If it's all right with you all, I'd like for us to go ahead to the living room. We can worry about clearing the table later. Right now, I want to share some news."

With that, Andy rose from the table, lifted Michael from his high chair, and headed out of the dining area. The others followed. When they were seated, all eyes were on Andy who was still standing with Michael. He handed his son to Jean and moved to where he could see each person. He looked first to Beau and Lorrie.

"Beau, Lorrie, I want to share with you something I've already run past my family and Bill, and I want to bring the rest of them up to date with some new information."

Andy's eyes panned the room as he smiled. *I hope I don't look as nervous as I feel,* he thought. Andy took a deep breath and continued with a speech he had practiced in his mind throughout the previous day.

"I have a good friend named Donnie Winston who lives in Arizona. He was with me in New Guinea and was always talking about Phoenix, how it was growing with all kinds of opportunity. We exchanged addresses before shipping home, and I wrote him last week to catch up and ask about opportunities there right now. He wrote right back and said I definitely should come out there and soon. Here's how he said it, and I quote, 'Construction in Phoenix is hotter now than ever (PUN INTENDED).'"

Andy grinned, and Jean groaned.

"Andy loves that line," she sighed. "He must have read it to me half a dozen times and laughed every single time."

Beau fidgeted. He could see where this was going and decided to help it along. "So you're saying you're planning to move?" he asked.

"Well, I don't know. I'm saying I'm planning to check it out and see. Nothing's going to happen right away. But Jean and I love you all so much, and we've always been so close. I knew a move that far away would be hard on all of us, and I wanted you to all hear it at the same time, you know, get all the same information and have a chance to ask any questions. It's kind of a big deal."

The room was silent. Lorrie stood up and walked behind Bill's chair, laying a hand on his shoulder, as she addressed Andy. "You know we love you and Jean, Andy," she said. "Of course, we'd miss you. But we want what's best for you. I know Bill will really miss you." She looked down at her son. "You're like a brother to him."

"Well, that's just it, Lorrie. I, uh, we're asking Bill if he'd look into going with us, at least making this trip out for a visit."

Beau stood up. "You say what, young man? Bill, did you know about this?"

"Well, sir, Andy had told me about it, but it was just some possibility. I told him I'd have to really think on it, and this is the first I've heard about an actual visit."

Beau sat back down and looked slowly around the room. "It seems we're the only ones here that didn't know a thing about all this. Am I right?"

"We're in the same boat as your son," Mr. Holloway responded. "Didn't think it was any more than a pipe dream. And I can say, I'm not excited about my daughter and grandson moving so far away." He paused and took a deep breath. The rest waited, sensing he had more to say.

Lorrie moved back to her chair. Paul Holloway continued as Andy found a place to sit.

"It's been a while since Andy told me about Arizona. I gotta say, I was a bit upset at the thought, hoped it would all just go away. But I've had some time to think about it. I decided, if it did come up again, I'd let the kids know it's their life to live. I mean, really folks, there's no real opportunity here beyond the coal mines, and that one's fading fast. I've seen Andy's skills, and he's a builder, talented and smart. I think he should look into Phoenix, and we'll just maybe have a winter vacation spot when we retire."

Mr. Holloway looked at his wife and shrugged his shoulders. She smiled, proud of her husband's kindness and wisdom.

"Fine for you," said Beau. "I'm happy for Andy, and I admire what you say; you love your kids to pieces, I know that. But Bill –" He looked at his son. "Bill, you're my only child and, well, when did you become a carpenter?"

"When did I become an adult flunkey doing nothing but stocking a small-town grocery store?" All looked at Bill in silence. He shrugged and said, "I'm sorry, Dad. I didn't mean to be disrespectful. But, honestly, sir, there's nothing for me here. There's never been anything for me here beyond you and Mom and Andy. I can saw a board straight across and hit a nail on the head every time. I work hard, and I learn fast. I don't know if I'll go to Arizona, don't know if I want to. But can we just do what Mr. Holloway said and wait and see?"

Again, there was silence. Andy was regretting his great idea, wishing he had heeded Jean's warning that it was probably not the best way to wrap up Thanksgiving. He had successfully transformed a happy family gathering filled with laughter into a dark circle of silence.

Good job, Andy, he thought.

Lorrie Davis broke the silence. She had not spoken, initially out of shock, learning her son was considering moving far away. But that initial shock was overpowered by the pain in Bill's voice as he spoke about how lost he had felt all these years in Donelsburg. First and foremost, she needed to address that pain. She spoke directly to her son.

"I think the hardest thing for me as a mother was the day you boarded that train to go off to war. It pretty much broke my heart. I cried all that night and prayed every day for you to stay safe."

Bill nodded.

"You came back safe. I was so thankful. But then, it was hard all over again, Bill. I had to watch you feel less than you are. I mean, you told me how you made a difference in the army. You were proud to serve with good, brave men who cared about you, and you cared about them. And you were somebody together: strong, black men who proved themselves worthy, disciplined, proud. And I watched that pride slip away. You go do what makes you proud, Bill. You're never so happy as when you're with Andy and Jean. If that's what's best for you, you do it." Then with a smile, added, "I can take care of your daddy."

Andy smiled and thought, *I sure do love that Lorrie.* Then, he decided it might be a good time to share the first part of his plan.

"Thank you, Lorrie. Thank you, Paul, and each of you for all you've said. This isn't easy and, like I said, I don't even know what's going to happen for sure. I do know that the next step will be a short trip to Phoenix. Jean says she wants to stay here with Michael and keep helping at the store while I make this first visit. So what I'd really like is for Bill to go with me."

Beau stood up again. "Hell, no!"

TWENTY-TWO

Andy looked at Beau in shock. But Bill nodded. He understood.

Beau paced back and forth in the middle of the circle of people. He couldn't believe what he had just heard. Finally, he stopped and stared at Andy.

"Are you crazy, boy? A white man and a black man, side by side in the same damn car? Driving together across these United States through places where if the KKK don't kill you some renegade, racist cop will? Are you completely out of your mind crazy? Hell, no!"

"But we'll be careful, Beau."

Beau laughed, and Bill shook his head.

"Be careful how, Andy?" asked Bill. "My father's right. You just don't know how it is. We took a risk just coming here for dinner tonight. Did you know that? Right here in Donelsburg, the town I've lived in all my life, I could get the life beat out of me just because I dared to come to this part of town and have a Thanksgiving meal with a white family." He paused a moment to let that sink in. Then, he added, "You'd be at risk, too, Andy. No, I can't do that to you."

Andy sat silently looking at the ground. Then, he looked at Bill. "Okay. You're right. I don't know how it is. But I know what you said just minutes ago. I heard you say there's no opportunity here. So where will you go? And how are you going to get there, how are you going to get anywhere, without any risk? You can face that risk alone or you can face it with me. If I'm at risk, so be it. I believe it's worth it. And we can do it, Bill. There's got to be a way."

After another moment of silence, Lorrie looked at her husband and spoke in soft, measured words. "Beau, this whole idea is insane. It scares me to death. But I was just thinking about my little brother, Jake." She looked around the room and continued.

"Jake. That boy knows no fear. But he's careful. Jake came to my mind when Andy said that, and I thought, 'yes, it is possible to be careful.' Jake has traveled some. He's told me about it. Had some real adventures, that boy." Lorrie chuckled and shook her head.

"Yeah, Jake is fearless, but he's smart. He don't have much money, but he saves, and then he travels. He's been all up and down that Route 66 road."

"That's the way we'd go," said Andy, getting very interested. "That's how we'd go to Arizona."

"Jake told me about it," Lorrie continued. "Said you gotta be mighty careful out there, but there's some help. He buys a book every year that tells him where to stay. He said, let me think now, he said it's 'The Negro Motorist Green Book.' It's printed out new every year with places it's safe to stay, 'cause Jake says you pick the wrong place, and you could end up in jail, beat up, or dead."

Beau faced his wife. "Woman, you need to hush! Ain't no Green Book gonna keep a white boy and a black boy together in the same car safe! What happens when the police stop you and say, 'what business you two got together? What you up to'?"

"That's where you gotta be smart," Lorrie said, waving an index finger in the air. "Andy says something like, 'I know it seems wrong, sir, and I wouldn't have it at all except my Uncle Joseph K. Jones has this ranch in Arizona and he needs himself a good nigger ranch hand. He sent me all the way to Illinois to fetch him this good boy who knows horses and cows. And I'm a-haulin' him back to my uncle. Ain't he a strong, good-lookin' nigger, officer? And right smart, too!'"

Andy was aghast. "Oh, I couldn't say that, Lorrie!"

"You could if it kept you from being hauled to jail or shot!"

Beau was shaking his head. "Good Lord, Lorrie! Where'd you come up with that?"

Lorrie tapped her forehead with the same right index finger. "You gotta be smart," she said, smiling.

Paul Holloway was enjoying this. He decided to put in his two cents. "I could order you a driver's hat, Andy. Bill could wear it, drive through any towns with you in the back seat. Anyone stops you, just say he's your driver. They'd believe that."

Andy laughed. "Great idea, Paul. Have you seen my car? No one would believe it!"

Bill was looking at his mother in amazement. "I remember Uncle Jake," he said. "I was just a kid last time I saw him and thought he was the neatest person I'd ever met. How do we get this Green Book?"

"I don't know, but I bet we can find out. Listen Bill, Andy, I don't like this. I don't like it at all. I think it's crazy and reckless. If you take this long drive together, I promise I won't sleep but a few hours a night, I'll be so busy worrying and praying. But you boys have lived through war. You're grown men; good, strong men. If you go, well, I can't stop you, but please be careful and be smart. And if you don't call and check in with me every day, I'll personally give you both a whipping when you come home. I'm a mama, and I can do it!"

Andy got up, walked over to Lorrie, got on his knees in front of her chair and hugged her. "I love you, Lorrie

Davis," he said. "Whether we go on this trip or not, I will always be thankful for what you've said here tonight."

Andy stood up and looked at Beau. "If we go, sir, it would sure mean a lot if it was with your blessing."

Beau shifted in his seat. Finally, he said, "Can't stop you. If Bill says yes, I guess he'll go. But my blessing?" He paused and frowned. Then, he looked at Andy and said, "Hell, no."

TWENTY-THREE

Bill gave no answer that Thanksgiving night other than, "I'll have to think about it."

"It's okay," Andy said. "I understand, and we have time. Donnie wrote that the toughest drive will be from a town in Arizona called Holbrook, heading south through the mountains. He said there's already snow there now, in late November. It could be a really dangerous drive until spring. You think about it and, if you say 'no,' I'll understand."

Bill was walking to Anderson's Market early the next morning. He was scheduled for both Friday and Saturday that week and dreaded it. His relationship with the store's manager was awkward, to say the least. It was clear to Bill that Bruce Bailey was shoehorned into an assignment he never wanted. He was not happy there and didn't care to pretend otherwise, nor did he put forth any effort to hide his contempt for each of his employees.

Bill paused a moment as he approached the market's old, frame building. Its appearance had improved considerably. Mr. Cline sent workers to replace some of the damaged siding, and the exterior had been completely repainted. The wooden sign was again placed over the door, still hand-painted, with "Anderson's Market" in large, block letters. Bill was glad for that. It seemed to preserve at least some of the warmth that had vanished with the departure of Jeremiah.

Bill walked into the market, bracing himself for another day on a job he detested, a day that would be accompanied by boredom and humiliation. Something had to change. But he put in his hours on Friday and Saturday. Sunday was spent pondering his plight. On Monday, he called Andy.

"I've thought about it," he said. "Let's go."

It was good to wait for the trip, they both decided, so that they could put in some extra hours at work and set aside gas and food money. They had both been banking most of their handyman income already. Andy was fairly confident his 1940 Chevy would be up to the trip. This was really going to happen!

Their anticipation mounted as the months passed.

It was a rainy April morning and still dark at 5 a.m. when Andy kissed his wife and son goodbye and climbed behind the wheel of his Chevy. He had loaded his suitcase the night before and Jean had prepared a large box with food and water for the first day. Roadmaps for the seven states on the trip were stuffed into the glove compartment. He knew that was hardly necessary since they would be on Route 66 all the way to Arizona, but one never knew when they would need to journey off "The Mother Road," and Andy hated the thought of getting lost. They just didn't have the time.

Bill was waiting on the porch with a small suitcase beside him. He hurried in the rain to load the suitcase in the trunk then took his place in front seat of the car, laying a small paperback book on his lap.

"Ready for an adventure?" Andy asked.

"Yes, sir, my friend! Yes, sir."

They had talked at length about the logistics of the trip, towns where they might stop for gas, food, and supplies. They even had discussed if they should try to find lodging at all or sleep by the road in the car or even take turns behind the wheel so each could sleep while the other drove. The topic came up again as they drove the highway into Missouri.

"I've brought some help for that because, believe me, Andy, we don't want to stop just anywhere." Bill held up the thin, green paperback book and read aloud from the front cover: *The Negro Motorist Green Book*, 1948 Edition, Victor H. Green, Publisher.

"You got it! Where did you find a copy?" Andy glanced at his friend then back to the road.

"My mailman, Joe, heard about our trip. He said this could keep us safe. I never even told him I was looking for one. He just said, 'You need this.'"

Andy knew that the Donelsburg Post Office had added one token Negro mail carrier after the Roosevelt administration made racial discrimination in hiring federal employees illegal in 1941. Joe Monroe was doing a great job, with his route covering a few streets in white neighborhoods along with all of Colored Town.

Andy shook his head. "It sounds like everyone knows about this thing but me."

Bill laughed. "You gotta be kidding, man! What would you need with this book, at least before this week? I mean, you can call Route 66 America's Mother Road, but face the facts, Andy. It's not that great for all Americans. I can tell you that I won't be welcome or safe on most of it, and you won't be either 'cause you're with me. People who need this book know about it. Right now, you need it, so, right now, you know."

No one spoke for the next several miles. Bill was right. Andy hadn't worried about finding supplies along the way. He knew that, over the past several years, innumerable gas stations and shops had appeared in every town on this incredibly popular highway. But if you're black, your options are limited at best. The majority of places would refuse you service. More than a few could be outright dangerous.

Andy appreciated having the Green Book, but the fact that such a book was needed by anyone filled Andy with a painful mixture of sadness and indignation. And he wondered: *would it ever be different? And what reception will we find in sunny Arizona?*

Andy was surprised how quickly they drove Route 66 out of Illinois and into Missouri. He handed Bill a list he'd drawn up of towns they'd be passing through. "I guess the passenger's job is to look through the Green Book for friendly folks along the way. We'll probably be needing to stop for gas before we get out of Missouri. I think we have enough food and drink for our first day so that's no problem. But we will need to find a place to stay or else sleep in the car. I don't think we'll be able to drive through the night."

"I'll watch for Esso stations," Bill said. "They'll be okay."

Andy felt the familiar anger build at the age-old blasphemy. That's what his mother used to call it. Blasphemy.

"The Great Spirit made all people," she would say. "The Great Spirit lives in all people. To hate or belittle any person, Andy, is blasphemy against the Great Spirit who made and lives in that person."

Blasphemy. Well, whatever you call it, Andy thought, it's wrong. It's evil. Andy had seen far too much of that evil in his life. Things were new and different in the West. Surely, it would be better in Arizona.

TWENTY-FOUR

Andy shook his head and sighed. Bill grinned. "Hey! What's your problem, my friend? We're off for a great adventure!"

"We've grown up in Donelsburg living in different neighborhoods because some stupid rule says we can't be together. Good people are divided up and told that the other side's worse because of the way they talk or the color of their skin. You can't live here or eat there or buy over there. I'm just sick of it, Bill. I can't wait to get away from it, that's all."

"Oh, Andy, haven't you been listening? Why do you think Joe gave me this book? It covers the whole United States!"

"I was hoping Phoenix would be different."

"Sure, it will be different. It'll be desert and mountains. That'll be different. And we'll be in a big enough place with lots of growth and opportunity. I'm looking forward to it! But there will still be people who hate anyone who's different, Andy. That's everywhere."

There was an uncomfortable silence, and then Bill went on. "You want to leave Donelsburg for something better. That's fine. Just remember that your parents and mine both came to Donelsburg looking for something better. And they found it."

"Your folks came from Chicago, right? They were looking for something better?"

"My family's history is looking for something better, Andy. Granddaddy Davis took the train to Chicago from Louisiana, just him, my grandma, and a couple of kids. He was like every one of our people coming north just trying to get away to something better. My grandparents were both children of freed slaves, struggling just to live. Granddaddy was a laborer back home and moved north with pretty much nothing but the clothes on his back. But, before long, they had a home on the Southside, and he was making some money in a factory. It was hard, but he was harder, one tough guy. That's where my daddy got it, I think. It missed me somehow."

"Stop that, Bill! You're one of the strongest guys I know."

Bill shrugged and then continued his story.

"As you know, I was born in Donelsburg. My father met my mother in Chicago, and they got married and moved there so he could make big money at the coal mine. How's that for a laugh? They moved here in 1920. I was born in '25, only child."

"Just like me."

"Just like you. And like your father, my father found work. And they both found places they weren't supposed to go and people they weren't supposed to be with. A lot was different, but some things never change, Andy, things like people afraid of people because they're different. Some things never change."

"I hope and pray you're wrong. But, yeah, I guess there's a reason we need that Green Book of yours."

They had moved deeper into Missouri, and Andy glanced down at the gas gauge. "Speaking of your book," he said, "I think you should take it out now. We're coming up to a town pretty soon, and we'll need to start looking for one of those Esso stations."

"What's the town?"

"Waynesville. We could go on if we have to, but I really don't want to risk it."

"Nothing listed, Andy. What do you want to do?"

"Stop and get some gas."

They pulled into town and looked around. Andy spotted a gas station and pulled in. A station attendant in his mid-twenties stepped from the building wearing a completely tan uniform of slacks, long-sleeve shirt, tie, and cap. He walked to the driver's side of the car and peered in the open window, speaking to Andy but with eyes fixed on Bill.

"Yes sir," he said. "Fill 'er up?"

"That's right," Andy replied, adding, "And where are your restrooms?"

"Men's is over on the west side of the building, sir. But there ain't none available to the boy there."

Andy cringed but continued in a calm voice. "Well, sir, the boy as you call him is the same age as me. Fact is, he's the best person I know and my best friend, pretty much my brother, you might say. So my brother and me, we've been on the road close to four hours. Car needs gas. We need a restroom."

"Sure, that's true, but them's the boss' rules. I'll be happy to fill up your car, clean the windshield, check the oil, take care of you right good, sir. Can't let the boy use the facilities, though. Just can't do it."

"Then, you can keep your gas and your bullshit with it." And with that, Andy drove off.

"Hey, Andy," Bill said. "Pull over the car a minute. I got something to say."

Andy pulled over to the side of the road and stopped.

"Now, that was real nice of you. I mean it. But, I'm telling you, that's the best we're going to get just about anywhere on this trip. If you keep pulling away, we're gonna have to walk to Phoenix. So I say you better go back there or find someplace else here before we drive out of town. You coulda actually got gas back there, brother. I'm telling you, the next place just might pull out a baseball bat or something."

Andy sat fuming. "I hate this, Bill. It's not right."

"But it's life, my friend. It's life. Welcome to my world."

TWENTY-FIVE

Andy sat a moment then made a U-turn. He pulled into the same gas station and, again, the same attendant came to the car. He smiled and said, "Welcome back, sir. Fill 'er up?

"Yes, and do check under the hood, too. You're a very polite young man. Just doing your job, right?"

"That's right, sir. Boss says we gotta take care of our regular customers. Folks are 'fraid of contamination, ya' know?"

Andy was shocked, sickened. He wanted to scream then squeal his car out of this station and this town before they contaminated him! It took a moment to get as much composure as possible.

"Is this boss man of yours around today?" he asked.

"No, sir. It's a Saturday. He'll be in on Monday, though."

Andy mused to himself that it might be worth coming back. He smiled and said, "You go ahead and take care of my car. We'll be on our way." He looked over at Bill and knew exactly what his friend was thinking. *No*, Andy thought, *I won't do it. I refuse to use the bathroom here.*

"They insult my friend and brother, I'm sure not honoring them with my pee," Andy said out loud.

Bill laughed. "Ah, they got no idea how they missed out!"

Andy paid the attendant and pulled onto Route 66 with a clean windshield, a full tank, and a badly complaining bladder. After they drove on through the small downtown area, he turned onto a narrow dirt road that disappeared into a grove of trees. Turning out of sight of the main road, he stopped. Both men took care of their business and got back on their way.

The drive went amazingly smoothly following that significant bump in Waynesville. Andy was feeling pretty good about it all, especially congratulating himself on how accurate his estimated times between stops had been. Another three and one-half hours, and they were just outside Galena on the Kansas state border.

"You about ready for some food?" he asked Bill.

He got a hearty, "Believe so." Andy pulled over to the side of the road and put the car in neutral.

"I'm going to leave this running for a minute while we get out the fixin's for lunch. Everything's in the box in the back floorboard. Let's put together some sandwiches and get on our way."

They finished their lunch in the car before moving into Galena for gas. No stations were listed in the Green Book, and their experience was very similar to the last stop, minus Andy's angry departure and U-turn.

They switched drivers before leaving Galena. Bill was actually eager to get behind the wheel for the rest of the trip. He'd gained a great deal of experience as a truck driver during the war, both stateside and while in Italy. Andy leaned back, closed his eyes, and sighed, his mind on their experiences in Missouri and Kansas.

"That's two for two," he said "I never knew whole towns could treat another human being that way."

"Come on, Andy. We live in a Sundown Town."

"I'm so sorry, Bill, and embarrassed. That stop in Galena went way too easy. It's like I'm getting used to it! I don't want to ever get used to that."

"Probably won't. I've been at this a lot longer than you, right? I never got used to it."

Bill's words hit Andy hard. He'd always hated the way his Negro friends were kept segregated and suppressed, but he'd never witnessed it from the other side. And it was a superficial experience. When this trip was over, Bill would still be living with this absurdity. He would not.

Bill glanced over at his friend and then back to the road. "Hey, it's okay. It's a messed-up world, but we're doing fine. You bless me, brother! Just watch that temper. It's always been your downfall."

"I'll try," he replied. "I'll try." Andy smiled as he said it, but his thoughts were still troubled. He hoped with all his heart that he'd never get used to what his mother so rightly called blasphemy.

Bill was surprised when he saw the sign, "Welcome to Oklahoma." Andy explained that Route 66 just clips the southeast corner of Kansas.

"I figured we'll hit Oklahoma City about seven," he said. He opened the Green Book and shouted, "Hey! We've got a place there! What ya' say we stop at an actual café for dinner?"

"Let's do it!"

And they did. The gas station and restaurant were not right on the highway and took a bit of searching to find, with Andy worrying as they searched that the café might not be open that late. But Lyon's Café was open. Andy waited in the car while Bill conferred inside about his white guest. He was told it would be no problem. Andy did get a few nervous looks at first from other diners, but he and Bill were able to enjoy a warm meal together undisturbed.

As they walked to the car, Bill asked, "Okay, my brother, what now?"

"Let's get some gas, and then I vote we put on some miles before we stop for the night. It'll be really late, but I'd like to make it to Amarillo, Texas and head out from there tomorrow morning."

"How late?"

"Midnight, I think. I'll be glad to drive."

"No," Bill said. "I'm feeling fine." He unlocked the driver's side door and reached across to let Andy in. As they drove toward the highway Bill said, "Midnight, huh? Hope we can wake up a clerk or somebody to give us a room!"

Andy said he just hoped they felt as welcome there as they had in Oklahoma City. After a moment of silence, he added, "Honestly, though, getting so freely served there only made me more embarrassed by the way you were treated."

After stopping for gas, the men drove out of Oklahoma City and on into the night. Their conversation continued in spurts, dropping off considerably as the night wore on. Andy felt the silence surround him and began to doze. He was awakened by Bill pointing to the right side of the road and saying, "Texas state line."

Andy looked up to see the sign posted on the side of the road. "Texas state line," he repeated. "No 'Welcome to Texas' or 'Sure glad you're here.' Hope that's not an omen of things to come."

Bill laughed. "You're a funny guy, my brother, a real funny guy."

TWENTY-SIX

It was indeed around midnight when the two drove across the Amarillo city limits. They somehow found their hotel in short order, Watley's Hotel on Van Buren Street. Bill walked up to the office door. It was locked. There was a knocker on the door and a lever to twist for the doorbell. Bill did both. After a moment, a voice called from inside. "Yeah, yeah. I'm a-comin'!"

Another minute and curtains were pulled aside from the window. An elderly black man peered out. Seeing Bill, he opened the door. He pulled back as Andy stepped up beside Bill.

"It's all right, sir. It's all right," Bill said with a smile. "My friend and I have been driving all day and all night. We sure could use a nice place like this to sleep."

The man, bent with a bald head framed in thick, white hair, looked suspiciously at Andy without saying a word. "Yes, sir," Andy said softly. "We're mighty tired, and, you know well, not every place is all that friendly. We'll be on our way tomorrow morning. We're on our way to Arizona to find some work there."

The man nodded, backing up and gesturing for them to come in. "Come on in, and we'll get you a room," he said. "Sorry I was slow about that but, well, ya' just don't see white folks 'round here that much, ya' know?"

"I understand," said Andy. "Thank you so much."

They'd overslept, and it was already 8:30 when they stepped out of the hotel office into a warm, April morning. The clerk, Samuel, recommended the Harlem Grill for breakfast. They could drive or walk, as it was only a block away. They opted to drive rather than return for the car. "And what about gas stations," Bill asked. "There weren't any recommended for Amarillo in the Green Book."

"Ah, the Green Book," Samuel smiled. "Sell them here myself. It brings me a good deal of business," he said, adding with a wink, "though most choose to check in before midnight."

"So sorry about that," said Andy. "But thanks for your hospitality. Now, um, a gas station?"

Samuel made his recommendation, and the two men walked to the car with breakfast on their minds. "Ah, sizzlin' crisp bacon and two eggs over easy," Bill sighed.

It had to have been the best breakfast Andy ever had, perhaps the best ever in all the world, he thought as they walked out of the Harlem Grill to their car. Andy climbed into the driver's side to take his turn behind the wheel. One request to "Fill 'er up" and they would be on their way to their next gas stop in Santa Rosa, New Mexico.

"You know that crack last night about 'an omen of things to come'?" he asked Bill as they pulled out onto the street. Bill nodded. "Guess I gotta take that back. Have to say that Texas has been all right."

Andy drove north and then west onto Amarillo Street, following Samuel's directions to a service station. From there, he would go south on Western Street to Route 66. It all sounded easy enough. He spotted a station on the right and pulled up to the pump. The attendant approached their car. He was white.

Andy quietly sighed. "I think maybe we're at the wrong place."

Bill laughed. "You did great before, and I already took a leak. It's fine."

Things did go fine. They both stayed in the car while the attendant worked. Still, Andy found himself nervously glancing around the area.

Looking to the right, a sign read, "Gas, 16 cents a gallon."

To the left, an occasional car driving down the road.

To the front, the hood was up, and the oil was being checked.

To the rear – Andy's gaze froze on the rearview mirror. Three white men stood side by side behind the Chevy, glaring through the back window.

The man on the left was probably 6' 4" with a massive build. He had short-clipped red hair and a long, red beard flowing to the middle of his chest. *You're one scary guy, Red*, Andy thought. *Yep, scary Big Red.*

The man Andy decided to call Red noticed his stare and began walking toward the open driver's side window. The other two men had made their way to Bill's side of the car. Both were much smaller than Red but still intimidating. One, blonde hair and pale, Andy named Blondie. The other had a deep scar across the left side of his face from eyebrow to earlobe. *Scarface,* Andy thought with a frown. *I really don't like this.*

Andy turned to Red and smiled. "Beautiful mornin'," he said.

The man laughed, a hearty laugh. A bit too hearty, Andy thought.

"Welcome to Amarillo! Amarillo's a good little city, and we like to keep it that way. See by your plates, you're all the way from Illinois. Passin' on through, I guess."

"Yes, sir. Heading out and on our way. But it is a nice place. Been real friendly so far."

"Well," the big guy said, "it don't look like you'd like it here all that much. You and your friend wouldn't fit in. Everybody has their place around here and stays in it, like the good Lord intended."

Andy began to feel a twinge in his neck. *Relax,* he thought. *It's not worth it.* What he heard himself say was, "Like the good Lord intended?"

"It's the order of nature, but your kind don't understand God's natural laws, do you? So take your nig – Oh, excuse me." The man's upper lip curled into a mixture of snarl and smile. "Take your neeee-gro and get the hell out of my town while you can."

Andy noticed the attendant standing by the left front fender, shifting side to side nervously. Andy waved the young man over. He walked to the car window slowly while keeping his eyes on Red.

"How much I owe you?" The attendant told him. Andy averaged the change upward and gave him all bills. "Keep the change, buddy." He shifted the car into first, keeping the clutch pressed to the floor.

"And real nice talking to you, Red. You don't need to worry about us messing up your natural order here. We won't be back. Town is nice, at least the colored part of it. But you're right. We wouldn't fit in here. And you know, I don't think the good Lord does either, if the white section's filled with ignorant dipshits like you." With that, he calmly drove away.

"Jesus, Andy! You gotta stop this! One way or another, you're gonna get us killed!"

"Now, that hurts, Bill. I thought I was very calm," said Andy. Then, he added, attempting to sound sophisticated and perhaps a little British, "And really most proper and polite."

"Very funny. Seriously, that guy was twice your size, Andy. And his two friends were waiting for me."

Andy glanced up at his rearview mirror. "Well, I guess maybe I did rub 'em wrong."

Bill looked back. A big, blue pickup truck was following them, matching their speed. The first thing Bill noticed was the gun rack attached inside the truck cab. Then, he focused on the three men, one behind the wheel and another on the passenger side. Standing up in the truck bed, holding onto an open window with his massive left arm, was a third. He appeared extremely large and menacing, peering over the truck cab. His long, red beard was whipped by the wind.

TWENTY-SEVEN

"Nice truck," Andy mused. "1941 Chevy, I'd guess. Maybe they just want to escort us to the city limits."

"Maybe," said Bill. "And maybe the big guy wants to personally thank you for calling him a dipshit."

"Well, that truck there has one massive engine. No way for us to outrun it. We'll just keep it calm and easy, see what happens."

"You'd think there'd be people on this street. We're just a little north of 66, and there's nothing here."

"It's the desert, my friend. Not much up here off the business strip. Here's my turn."

The truck followed them left onto Western then sped past them, swinging in front of the car and slamming to a stop. Andy hit his brakes hard. The Chevy dipped forward just enough that its bumper completely missed the truck's rear bumper. Andy stopped the car just as the truck's bumper touched the Chevy's grill, caving it in at its center. There wasn't a scratch on the truck.

Bill had been thrown forward, striking the metal dashboard. Andy looked over and saw his friend in shock, blood on his forehead.

"You okay?"

"Yeah," Bill said. "I think so."

Andy looked out the windshield. Red was on his way. "Hold that temper," he whispered as he quickly rolled up his window. "Think."

Red slammed his huge fist onto the car's left front fender leaving a good-sized dent. "Hey! You sons-abitches wrecked up my truck! You gonna pay with money or skin?"

Andy spoke softly as he looked straight ahead. "Hey, Bill."

"Yeah?"

"How much hand-to-hand training did you do in the army?"

"Some. I did some."

"They're gonna open our doors and drag us out. We gotta beat 'em to it. Get your feet up to the door, grab the handle and, when one of them walks up, you smash him. You open that door and kick it for all your worth. Got it? Then, fight like a demon, man. Go eyes, slap ears, kick balls. No mercy."

"No mercy," Bill whispered as he moved into position. With those words, everything happened in a flash of fury. A man had been knocked backward on either side. Bill leaped out and forcefully lifted his right foot between the legs of the second man, the one Andy had silently named Scarface. He then swung that same leg to the right, twisting his torso and bringing the full force of his body into his left fist, as it slammed into the right cheek of Blondie.

Bill shouted, "No mercy," and landed a powerful right cross on this same man, who fell backward at the side of the road, out cold.

At the same time, Red, barely fazed by the force of the door, had grabbed Andy in a suffocating bear hug. The man was a giant, lifting Andy's slender five-foot seven-inch frame completely off the ground in a vice grip that emptied Andy of air. His eyes blurred, and his head swam. Andy thought for a moment he might pass out.

But, instead, he reacted. Andy thrust his head forward with every ounce of force he could muster, slamming his forehead onto Big Red's nose. Blood spewed onto Andy's face. He then broke free from the powerful arms as he gasped frantically, filling his lungs with precious oxygen. After two loud, rapid breaths, Andy buried his right fist deep into Red's solar plexus with all his might. The huge man lunged forward and dropped to his knees, head down. Andy sliced an open hand karate chop, full force, onto the back of Red's neck. Big Red fell face forward onto the ground.

Bill looked from Red who lay unconscious by the road over to Scarface who was still on his knees from the well-placed kick. Gasping, the man pulled a large hunting knife from a sheath on his belt. Without hesitation, Bill leaped beside him and kicked the knife from his hand before kicking the kneeling man in the head. He too lay unconscious on the ground.

Bill turned to check on Blondie. He wasn't there. He was closing the door of the truck and lifting a hunting rifle to his shoulders, aimed at Bill.

Bill dropped to the ground, yelling, "Andy!" Both men hit the pavement, expecting to hear a gunshot. What they heard was a siren. Blondie heard it, too, lowering the rifle only slightly.

"Drop the goddamn gun, Joe," came a yell from behind Andy's car. Bill, still on the ground, spun around and looked behind him. He saw a police car with lights flashing and two uniformed officers both standing behind open car doors with guns aimed at Blondie.

"I mean it, Joe. Drop it." Blondie dropped the rifle.

One of the officers walked to the truck. He spun Blondie and handcuffed him, leading him back to the police car. The other officer surveyed the scene. Scarface and Red were both awake, awkwardly trying to stand.

"Stay down, boys," the policeman said. He then turned to Andy and Bill. "You two, get up. Face the car. Okay, now put your hands on the car and spread your legs. I need to frisk you for any weapons." As the two complied, the officer shouted, "Hey, Sam! Call for another car. We need to take these two in for questioning. And get these two vehicles towed to the station."

By this time, the first officer had secured Blondie and was walking Red and Scarface to the police car. "Yes, sir," Sam said as he directed the two men into the back of the police car and closed the door.

"One more thing, Sam. Get the camera out of the car. I want shots of the scene, especially the skid marks from both vehicles. I think we got ourselves an ambush here."

TWENTY-EIGHT

Andy and Bill soon found themselves seated across a table from Sergeant Donaldson, the policeman who had brought them to the station.

"Okay, boys," said the sergeant. "Thanks for your statement. It all checks out. I saw the tire marks there on the corner. It shows they peeled around you and slammed on the brakes. Besides, we got a call from a very scared young man at the gas station. He told us what happened there and that he was worried for your lives. He had reason to be. Those three have quite a history with the law."

The sergeant folded his hands and leaned toward Bill and Andy.

"I don't want you to judge our little city by what just happened. It's a fine town. Those three and a few like them are a carryover from some bad history. The KKK had a big presence in Amarillo some twenty years back. There's still some meetings, but they stay low for the most part. Then, we have a few outlaws like Joe, Wyatt and Red."

Andy smiled. "His name is Red?"

"Well, that's what folks call him. Big Red. You can see why."

"Yes, sir."

"Well, they're trouble. They troll our colored part of town looking for easy targets to terrorize. We've got them on everything from vandalism to assault, but this is the first time we've caught them with gun in hand, ready to shoot. Saw it with my own eyes. I'd like to put these thugs down, boys, and would really appreciate you two staying around long enough to testify for me."

Bill and Andy looked at each other and then back to the officer. "Sir," said Andy, "we're on our way to Phoenix to check out work and maybe a move. Friends are expecting us there, and then we've got jobs and families waiting for us back in Illinois. We're behind schedule now. Is there any way-?"

"Boys! These guys wrecked your car and threatened your lives! You're just going to walk away from that?"

"We really need to get on the road," said Bill. "You have our written statement, and you saw the rifle."

Andy jumped in. "How long would we need to wait here in order to testify?"

The sergeant thought a moment. "When you fellas coming back through on your way home?"

"We're staying in Phoenix till Friday and heading home. We're staying with friends there, Sergeant. I'll give you their phone number in case you need to get in touch with us."

Donaldson gave Andy a business card with his name and contact information.

"I'll check it out with the captain, but I think we can make this work for you. We'll get our prosecutor in here to meet with you today, maybe even in the next hour or so. You tell him what happened, and we'll arraign these bastards. The trial will be, I don't know, a week? A month? You work with me. We'll get it together to finally get these thugs off the street. Meanwhile, tell Deputy Stephens here what kind of sandwiches we can get for you."

TWENTY-NINE

It was 2:00 p.m. before Andy and Bill drove onto Route 66 en route to Santa Rosa, New Mexico. They drove in silence, still in shock from all that had happened to them. Luckily, damage to the Chevy was minimal. The grill was slightly crumpled in, but the radiator was not touched, and the headlights were both functional. All in all, they both felt incredibly fortunate, considering how the morning might have gone.

Bill felt blessed to be back on the road with his best friend, but he could not shake concern about a future trial. *I just want to be rid of this whole day,* he thought. *I don't know if I can look at those three again, much less talk about them while they're staring at me.*

Bill's reflections were interrupted by Andy's cheerful voice. "Hey, my brother! You handled yourself pretty good back there. I mean, two against one, and they didn't stand a chance."

Bill didn't answer so Andy followed his lead and drove on silently. It was Bill who broke the silence after several minutes, saying, "I really hate it, you know."

"What's that?"

"The fighting. I think you hate it, too, no matter what people used to say. You know, you even had a reputation in my school. Kids would say, 'that white boy, Andy Mayes, would rather fight ya' as look at ya'.' But I knew better. You have a big heart, Andy. You care."

It was Andy's turn not to answer for a while. When he did speak, it was so soft, Bill had to strain to hear him.

"Do you know who I envied in the war, Bill?"

"The people not in it?"

Andy laughed. "Yeah, them, too. But, I thought, how great to be a fighter pilot. I'm sure it's not true, but it seemed to me that it had to be better. I mean, they never had to see the people they had to kill. So many times, the planes would bomb a camp or an airport, and then we'd go in to finish it off. We'd use grenades or spray bullets with machine guns, but lots of times it was one man at a time. And sometimes, I'd wonder about that kid I just killed. He was somebody's boy, maybe a husband and a dad. Then, you'd see your buddy next to you go down, and suddenly they were just Japs, you know? They were the enemy, and they were killing us. I'd hate 'em, Bill! I'd hate them and shoot to kill."

Andy paused a few beats. "Then, back at camp that night, I'd lie down to try to sleep, and it'd all come back. I killed sons and husbands and fathers. And sometimes at night, I'd think back to my mother, telling me how the Great Spirit lives in every person and I'd think –" He paused a few more beats. "I'd think, Jesus, forgive me."

Andy's voice started to break. He took a deep breath. "Yeah, Bill. I hate the fighting. I hate it, too."

Another quiet time and Bill spoke. "Andy?"

"Yeah?"

It took Bill a moment more to speak. "I never told anyone this, but I have nightmares."

"Yeah?"

"I mean, they're more than nightmares. It's like I'm still there, you know? I hear the gunfire all around me and the bombs; I can feel the explosions. I'd see a buddy fall and the blood, and I jerk awake, sweating and shaking."

"I know," Andy said.

"You know?"

"I know. I have them, too. You say you never told anyone?"

"I'm ashamed. I've always felt weak. I mean, my whole life. My father's so strong, so fearless. He already thinks I'm weak. And I mostly agree, Andy."

"That's bullshit, Bill. I don't think your dad believes any such thing, and I know for a fact you can whip two men at the same time, knock 'em out, and never get a scratch. No, man. You're not weak."

"I saw guys lose it in the war, and everybody pitied them. They called it 'shell shock,' but as far as I could tell, shell shock just meant weak." A pause, then Bill looked intently at his friend. "Did you say you have dreams, too?"

"Gut-wrenching,   wake-up-sweating,   screaming nightmares, buddy. And I know exactly what you're saying. It's more than a dream. You're back there. You're honest to God back there. And I didn't tell anyone the same as you. Then, one day, I woke up, and there was Jean, all worried and everything. I finally told her that particular dream. I didn't tell her there were others and how they were not dreams at all but what I really lived through. But I told her the dream, Bill. And it helped. She kept saying I need to keep talking about it, and now I see she was right."

"But you can't just talk to anyone, Andy."

"That's true. But you talked to me, buddy. And you helped me. But I was just thinking about what you said about not liking to fight."

"Uh-huh?"

"You're right, Bill. I hate it, too. But I still say there's some things so wrong in this world that we have to stand up to them, like it or not. I'll do my best to do that without going crazy with my temper, but sometimes you just have to fight."

"I'm with you, brother. You keep slaying giants, and I'll take on a couple of the little ones."

"Ha! You got it!"

THIRTY

They drove into Santa Rosa around 4:30 p.m. Andy was welcome to buy gas at a service station there, but Bill was again refused use of the restroom. Andy bought food at a grocery along with some needed supplies, including toilet paper. He saw a hardware store nearby and picked up a small garden shovel.

The two men drove Route 66 out of town and turned onto a side road to an isolated area. They searched for a place to dig latrines (a skill both learned in the army and neither thought they would ever need again in a million years).

Back at the car, Bill said, "Think it's still my turn to drive. Let's move away from here a ways and have some lunch." They ate lunch side by side in the front seat of the Chevy, neither saying a word.

Bill drove onto the highway. "Okay, Andy. What's our next gas stop?"

"Gallup, New Mexico. I figure about five hours." Andy pulled out the Green Book and checked where they could be served. "There's a restaurant there, but I don't see any place to stay. It'll be between 9:30 and 10:00 when we get there. It's only another hour and a half to Holbrook, Arizona, but there's no place listed there either." Andy threw the book onto the car's floorboard. "This is bullshit, Bill. No human being should be treated like this just because of the color of his skin."

"Got that right, Andy. But we're not gonna change it by tonight. So what you want to do?"

"We'll get ourselves a meal at the Fred Harvey Restaurant and see what they might know."

"I like how you think, brother. Let's just hope they're open late on a Sunday night."

They arrived in Gallup at 9:30 and found the Fred Harvey Restaurant. To their amazement, it was indeed open. The food was wonderful and the service the best either of the weary travelers had ever experienced.

The waitress introduced herself as Anna. She was young with beautiful skin that Bill decided was the color of dark cinnamon. Anna was happy to tell her customers about Fred Harvey, who established the Fred Harvey Restaurants and motels, called Harvey Houses, throughout the southwest. Anna told them that these were the first such establishments to hire and serve people regardless of the color of their skin.

"Well, that is one of the best things I've heard since we started this trip," Andy told the attractive young waitress. "You mentioned Harvey Houses. Is there one here in Gallup?"

"Why, right next door," she said. "It's named the El Navajo Hotel."

She smiled and laid the check on the table between the two men. "They'll be happy to give you nice gentleman a room for the night."

Bill thanked her for her wonderful service and kind help. Andy left a generous tip on the table and stepped to the cash register to pay. Turning, he looked back to their table and smiled. Bill was still chatting with Anna, laughing as they talked. Bill glanced over, shrugged his shoulders and grinned.

The exhausted men were sound asleep minutes after checking into their room. Bill was awake first the next morning, rising around 5:30. Andy woke up just a few minutes later to the sound of Bill humming Nat "King" Cole's "Sentimental Reasons."

"My, but you're mighty cheerful this morning," said Andy, grinning broadly.

Bill grinned back. "You suppose Anna has some bacon and eggs for us this early?"

Andy's grin split into laughter. "Well, it probably won't be Anna, but someone will serve us some breakfast. They'll start early. These folks cater to travelers, remember?"

Andy had taken the Arizona road map out of the glove compartment the night before and opened it up to chart the remainder of their trip.

"Another hour and a half, and we leave Route 66. That's where things could get tricky," he told Bill. "Let's get a good breakfast and gas the car here. Then, we'll stop in Holbrook and see what they can tell us about our trip south."

The time seemed to speed by, the farther they drove west out of Gallup. Andy began to notice the terrain, seeing a surprising beauty in the desert all around them.

"Look at the colors in those mountains! Isn't it beautiful, Bill? Who knew the desert could be all those different shades of red and gray? And look at the sky! I never saw sky that blue in Illinois!"

Bill would just smile and nod. He had to agree that his own energy was building as they grew closer to their destination. Then, he saw the sign shouting, "Welcome to Arizona, the Grand Canyon State!" It was his turn to get excited.

"Look at that sign, Andy! It's beautiful! Never saw one like that, all full color with mountains and trees and cactus. Yeah, just beautiful!" They both joined in a full voiced laugh. This would surely be worth all they had endured so far.

Andy pulled into the first gas station in Holbrook but parked away from the pumps.

"What can I do for you, sir?" said the uniformed attendant as Andy got out of the car.

"Well, what I need is information. I'm on my way to Phoenix. I have a road map and know I take the 77 to Globe and then 60 west to Phoenix. But I've never been on these roads and wondered if you had any advice for the trip."

"Yes, sir. My name's Arnold, sir, and I've been on those roads dozens of times. I can sure help you, sir."

"All right, Arnold. I'd appreciate it.:"

"Well, sir, first and foremost, stay alert. It's a beautiful drive. You'll go through desert with cactus and mountains with thick pine forests and, best of all, the Salt River Canyon. Now, that's just amazing and you'll want to look around. Don't do it! Especially as you go into and out of the canyon. It's steep with lots of twists and turns. You look at the canyon and just when you're saying, 'ain't that pretty,' the road turns, and you'll go over the side for a real close up look! Don't do it! And don't speed through the turns or lose control going down. And don't ride your brakes! You won't have no brakes!"

"Well, Arnold, thanks. It sounds scary. Many accidents?"

"Oh, sure. But just watch, and you'll be fine. Let your friend there describe the scenery. You just drive. Your main problem probably won't be an accident. It'll be getting hot."

"Getting hot?"

"Oh, not you. Your car. Radiators lose water. Cars overheat. You need extra water. Now, lucky for you, we sell these really nice desert water bags. You hang them from your front bumper. Ours are flax, and they need to be soaked before use, but we keep a batch treated and ready because people need 'em for the mountains and desert. If I were you, why, I'd get two for sure and fill 'em with water. Now, they'll seep a little 'cause they're supposed to. It evaporates and keeps the water cool to drink and ready for your radiator if your car overheats. Yes, sir, I'd take two, sir. I'll help you attach 'em and show you how to use 'em."

Andy smiled as he thought, *This guy's smooth. I think I've just been conned.* But he bought the two bags anyway. No sense taking any chances. Arnold then offered to check his radiator, topping it off.

They were ready to head south.

THIRTY-ONE

Arnold had directed them to Navajo Boulevard, which he said would become State Route 77. Andy was ready for the worst. He kept saying to himself, even before they left the town, "So far, so good. Not too bad, yet. Not too bad." Then, he noticed himself thinking that again as they continued for several miles down the two-lane highway. It made him smile. Maybe, this won't be so bad after all, he thought. But he stayed watchful, nonetheless.

The drive was everything Arnold promised. It was beautiful. There were amazing changes in topography as they continued south on Arizona State Route 77. But Andy did little more than quick glances as he drove, afraid to take his eyes off the road. He followed the young man's advice and was glad that he did.

The descent into Salt River Canyon was truly spectacular, but Andy missed most of it because of his intense focus on the road. Bill also missed much of it because he kept covering his eyes. Andy had to smile at the gasps from the passenger's side when the Chevy maneuvered between a mountain wall on the left and a gut-wrenching drop-off to the right.

They both gave a sigh of relief when they ended their descent, and then it occurred to Andy: now they would have to climb. "I think this may be where we'll need our water bags," he said to himself. "But I sure hope not."

To Andy's great relief, they made it out of the canyon without the car overheating too badly. They did see cars pulled over with hoods up at the occasional shoulders in the road and scenic viewing areas. Many drivers did have the desert water bags in hand.

The road began a slow descent after cresting out of the Salt River Canyon. "That was a long stretch," Bill finally said. "How much longer to Phoenix?"

"I think we've got over an hour to a town called Globe. Then, we head west about eighty-seven miles. I don't know. Three more hours, maybe?"

"Whoa! I'm beyond ready! Say, you had quite a drive back there. You want me to go the rest of the way? You look like you could use a rest."

"Let's stop in Globe and stretch our legs. I'll let you know then."

They topped off the gas tank in Globe and headed west. Bill took over driving while Andy quietly perused the Green Book. He looked over to Bill. "I was just looking at Phoenix in your book. I guess I shouldn't be surprised, but somehow I never thought about places being listed in Arizona."

"What do you mean?"

"Well, if Mr. Green bothered to list places we'd be welcome, that would probably mean we're not welcome at other places."

"So you thought those good Phoenix white folks would just say, 'Hey, ya'll come'"?

"I was hoping."

Bill just laughed.

It was mid-afternoon when Bill drove into Phoenix. "I'll watch for a payphone and give Donnie a call," Andy said. "I've got an address but not sure how to find it."

Bill spotted it first. "There at that gas station," he said and pulled in. Andy made the call while Bill waited in the car. It was a woman's voice that answered.

"Hello?"

Andy looked again at the piece of paper with both Donnie and his wife's names by the phone number.

"Hello! This is Andy Mayes. I'm calling for Donnie Winston. Is this Betty?"

"Yes! We've been expecting you, Andy! You're all Donnie's been talking about for weeks now! He's at work, but he'll be home in a couple of hours. Please come on over! We have a guest room all ready for you. I'll give you directions."

"I guess Donnie told you that I was bringing a friend. His name is Bill, and he's thinking about moving here, too."

"Sure, no problem. You'll just have to share the guest room or put him on the couch."

"Oh, we've been sharing rooms for two days now. I'm looking forward to meeting you."

Andy's initial excitement began to wane as they made their way through city streets to Donnie's home. Perhaps, it was just exhaustion setting in after the three-day ordeal of their journey. Perhaps. But he knew it was more. It was the city itself: the downtown, urban mass of concrete, and cars that seemed to close in on him as they drove.

What did he expect to see? A paradise with giant tropical flowers and palm trees swaying in the breeze? No, of course not! But what was it? He couldn't quite decide until Bill gave him the words.

"Sure ain't as pretty as the mountains," Bill said.

"What?"

"This city. I liked the road getting here better. It was wide open desert and forests and mountains. I really liked the mountains."

"You know, Bill, I did too. But this is downtown. We won't be living here." Andy looked at Betty's directions. "Looks like you need to head north at the next street," he said. And from there, he navigated while Bill drove until they came to a neighborhood of houses and finally the home of Betty and Donnie Winston.

Bill parked in front of the tan stucco house and followed some distance behind as Andy walked to the front door. The woman who stood before them was just what Andy had pictured for Donnie's wife: young, attractive, and perky with a big smile and infectious laugh.

The laugher began as she saw her husband's friend, Andy. And it suddenly stopped when she looked from Andy to Bill, her eyes widening in surprise.

THIRTY-TWO

"Hi, Betty. I'm Andy Mayes, and this is my good friend, Bill Davis."

Betty stood, stiffened and silent, still looking at Bill. Suddenly, she became aware of staring and the smile returned, more subtle and polite now. "I'm so sorry," she said. "Donnie will be so excited to see you, uh, to see you both."

Andy smiled and nodded but shifted uneasily from one leg to the other. They were still standing at the door. Betty had not yet invited them into her home. Bill took a step back.

"This is a bit awkward, though," Betty continued, closing the door slightly. "I hope you understand. Donnie's at work, you know? I mean, he's not here and, well, I just think you probably should come back when he is, you know?"

Andy said nothing, nodding sadly.

"We need to go, Andy," Bill said, slightly above a whisper. "Ask her when her husband will be home, but we probably need to be looking for somewhere else to stay."

"Donnie should be home in a couple hours," Betty said. "I'm sorry, but I just really need you to come back then." Andy nodded again, and Betty added, "You might just want to call first. You know?" She smiled nervously and then quickly closed the door. Andy heard the dead bolt slide.

Andy and Bill walked silently back to the Chevy. Andy sat for a few moments behind the wheel then started the car. "I have no idea where to go," he said, mostly to himself.

Bill slid down in the seat. "Well, don't sit here any longer. You saw Betty's reaction, and she at least knew something about you. The neighbors see me sitting here in this lily-white neighborhood, they'll be calling the cops."

Andy drove off, shaking his head. He felt completely deflated. This was nothing like what he had hoped for. Maybe, it was all a giant mistake.

"Get out your Green Book," he told Bill. "Let's see where we'll be welcome in Phoenix. Apparently, it's not at the Winston home."

Bill found four hotels and one tourist home. "I think that's someone's house where they live," he said. "They let people stay there who are traveling through."

"That sounds welcoming," Andy replied, still unsmiling. "Let's look into it. There's an Arizona map in the glove box with inserts of Phoenix."

"Sounds good to me, Andy. But you really need to call Donnie tonight. Whether we stay there or not, he's our connection to work here."

"Agreed. But I won't be where we're not welcome, and I mean welcomed together."

They drove around Phoenix for almost two hours before they found the tourist home, owned by a black couple named Mr. and Mrs. Gardner. It was time for Andy to be peered at suspiciously. Bill thanked them for their time. He considered asking if they could step in to make a quick phone call but thought better of it.

Andy drove until he found another payphone and called the Winston home as promised. Donnie answered. Andy told him that it might be better if they stayed somewhere else and meet him at his workplace sometime the next day. Donnie objected strongly.

"I won't hear of it!" he said. "We've got our guest room all ready and, besides, you and I have three years to catch up on. You're gonna stay here!"

"Have you checked that out with your wife?"

There was a moment's silence on the other end, and then Donnie spoke. "Listen, Andy, Betty feels really bad about that. She really does. Yes, she told me all about it, but I hope you understand. You're both strangers to her, and she wasn't expecting, well, you know."

"Yes, I know," Andy said, trying to stay calm.

"She was scared, didn't know what to do. But we talked and she's okay as long as I'm home. In fact, she wants you to come. Said so herself. I can vouch one-hundred percent for you, and I'm sure you'll do the same for your friend. He was in the war, right?"

"U.S. Army, European Theater."

"Put that with your support and all doubts are gone. Come over now, Andy, please. Let's get started catching up."

THIRTY-THREE

Donnie Winston met them at the front door, stepped outside, and greeted his old army buddy with a giant bear hug.

"My God, you look great," Donnie shouted, now holding Andy at arm's length, a hand on each shoulder. "Please! Come on in."

Donnie led the way, followed by Andy and then, at a distance, Bill. Donnie turned and gestured for both of them to sit down. "We've got a lot of catching up to do, my friend!"

"Yes," Andy agreed, "a lot."

Andy was looking up to his old friend as they talked. He had forgotten how intimidating Donnie could be. Andy was a slender 5 foot 7. Donnie was a hulking six feet, weighing in at about 220 pounds. Tall and fit, he wore his weight well but made Andy look and feel uncomfortably tiny.

Andy introduced Bill. Donnie walked over and took Bill's hand, extracting him from the chair for a handshake and then continued pulling him into an enthusiastic, one-armed man-hug. Andy could see that Bill was painfully uncomfortable. Acutely reserved by nature, such a show of affection by any stranger under any circumstance would have been extremely awkward for Bill. This went over the top. Actually, Andy felt a little sorry for both of them: Donnie because he felt the need to try so hard and Bill because he fell victim to Donnie's efforts.

Donnie released Bill and turned his attention to Andy.

"Betty has made one of her amazing, secret recipe dinners just for you two. How about something to drink right now. You must be exhausted."

Before Andy could respond, Betty, who had been watching silently at the kitchen door, said to her husband, "Actually, dinner will be ready soon, sweetheart. Why don't Andy and Bill get their luggage and things? You can show them the guest room and where to freshen up."

"Hey, I'm sorry about that," Andy told Bill when they made it out to the car. "I guess this could be a pretty difficult stay."

Bill shrugged. "It's okay. We got things to find out and decisions to make. They're all right, and they want to help us, but just don't leave me alone with them, okay?" He smiled. "Betty's still scared of me, and I'm a little bit afraid of Donnie."

Andy laughed. It felt good to laugh. Then, he saw something that brought a smile to his face. "Hey, Bill," he said. "Look at this!"

Bill followed Andy's gaze to the front of the Chevy. What he saw were the flax desert water bags hanging limply on the front bumper – completely empty.

Bill bellowed with laughter. "I guess it's good we made it to Phoenix before our overheating emergency, huh?"

"We'll fill them on the way back," Andy said. "I paid good money for those things; we're sure as heck gonna use 'em."

"Maybe, you can soar up those mountains at about 100 miles an hour. If we don't plunge over a cliff, you might get the car hot enough to need them."

"I'll think about it."

Donnie showed them to their room. "This is the guest room, and you're our very first guests. This has been a year of firsts. In January, Betty and I began the first month of this year with a wedding. Then, we bought our first home with two bedrooms. For now, this is our guest room and one day, well some other year, it will be a nursery for our first baby."

"Sounds like you two are very happy," Andy said. "I'm so glad to hear it. Congratulations."

"Yes, sir. Betty is the best, and I've got a top company to work for. Can't wait to have you meet my boss. He's excited to meet you both, too. I have an appointment set up to meet him at his office tomorrow morning at ten. You two are welcome to sleep in. Know you need the rest."

"You going to work in the morning?" Bill asked.

"Well, it's a work day, but –"

Bill interrupted. "So you're off to work, and we're here till nine-thirty or ten? I think we should leave when you leave."

"Well, normally, I'd be gone by about six-thirty. But I called my boss tonight while you two were getting your things. I asked to come in late and explained why. He said that's fine."

"Yes," agreed Bill, "that's most certainly best. Thank you."

There was a moment of silence and Donnie said, "It'll be good. That way you can follow me to his office, and I can introduce you."

Bill smiled. "Yes, sir. That'll be good."

Betty called that dinner was ready, and they all walked out of the room and into the kitchen-dining area in silence.

THIRTY-FOUR

It was a wonderful meal, what Andy would have called "down home cooking" – complete with fried chicken, mashed potatoes with gravy, and corn on the cob. Andy smiled when Betty brought out the homemade apple pie.

"This is southern hospitality at its best," he said, "and in Arizona!"

Betty laughed. "I guess that's my mother's influence showing. My family moved to Phoenix from Arkansas when I was eight. Arizona's home, but those are my roots."

"And I was around thirteen," Donnie interjected. "We moved from Michigan because my father said he was sick of shoveling snow."

"Seems like everyone you meet's a transplant from back east somewhere," Betty continued.

"Right!" Donnie exclaimed. "And that's good news for you and me, guys, because people mean buildings and buildings mean work!"

Andy nodded. It was good news, indeed.

There was silence at the table while everyone finished dessert. Finally, Betty asked about their plans while here.

"Well, I'm looking forward to catching up with Donnie, of course," Andy said. "And we want to see what might be out there as far as work. We want to make a decision about places to live. Maybe, you can give us some ideas."

Betty smiled and spoke, gesturing with her fork. "I think we have some homes for sale here in the Brentwood area. It's nice." She looked at Bill and paused.

Bill picked up on her hesitation and ventured a comment, a daring action for him in this situation.

"I suppose I would need to look elsewhere," he said, carefully keeping his tone matter of fact, with no hint of malice.

"Well, I'd be worried you might feel uncomfortable here." She looked to her husband for help, but none came, so she struggled on. "It's just that, you know, there aren't a lot of, well, there aren't any of, uh, your people in this area, you know?"

"I see," said Bill. "Yes, I understand completely." He laid down his fork and folded his hands on the table. Every eye was watching him. "And where exactly do my people live?"

"Well," Betty replied, quickly and nervously, "pretty much I think they all like living in the same area. You know? I think they're comfortable like that and the homes are pretty nice, too. I think, anyway. I don't get there much, you know? But I think they like it, you know?"

Andy's mind flashed back to Amarillo and the words of Big Red. "Everybody's got their place here and stays in it." Yes, Andy thought. Just like Donelsburg and Colored Town.

"And where is this place they like?" asked Bill.

"Well, folks say that it's South Phoenix. That's what they say, but I can't tell you much more than that. Yes, it's always called 'down in South Phoenix,' I think."

Donnie finally spoke, much to his wife's relief. "Betty's right, Bill. She doesn't mean anything wrong by it. It's just best to be honest about it. Homes just aren't sold to Coloreds in this neighborhood. And, just to say how it is, I don't think you could buy here or anywhere but in South Phoenix. Unlike my wife, I have been there. There are nice homes and not so nice ones, just like anyplace, I guess."

After dinner, everyone retired to the living room. There was more effort made for conversation, but Andy had to admit that he was exhausted after the long drive. "I'd like to be my best when I meet your boss," he added.

"I know you'll like him," Donnie said. "Walt is not only my boss, he's the owner of the company. Walter Dean Construction is the premier builder for residences and business buildings here in the Valley. He's eager to meet you two."

"And we're eager to meet him," Andy said. With that, Andy and Bill excused themselves and headed for the guest room and blessed rest.

Bill closed the door as Andy sat on the bed, slowly shaking his head with a sigh.

Bill smiled. "What?"

"You know what, Bill. I expected things to be different here. It's not, not really. And I was just thinking about Betty coming here from Arkansas and Donnie from Michigan, and how they said everyone's from someplace else. So I guess it makes sense. I don't like it, but it does make sense."

"What's that?"

"Every person that comes here brings all those attitudes and prejudices right along with them."

Bill nodded. "Yes, I guess they do."

"I'm so sorry, Bill."

"Oh, it's really okay, Andy. Besides," he added, raising his eyebrows, "I'm looking forward to seeing where 'my people' happily live." A few beats, then, "You know?"

Andy winced. "Good night, Bill."

"Good night, Andy."

THIRTY-FIVE

Bill was up and dressed by 6:45, and Andy followed soon after. They walked together into the kitchen, where they found Donnie and Betty at the table with coffee cups before them. Donnie rose from his chair to greet their guests.

Betty also stood as Andy and Bill approached the table. She went to a cabinet, retrieving two more cups. She filled them with coffee and set them on the table, then moved back a couple of feet and looked at Andy then Bill. She seemed to be struggling for something to say. Andy smiled at her, wanting to put her at ease.

"Good morning, Betty," he said. "Thanks again for opening your home to us."

"Why, you're very welcome," Betty said. "I'll put some breakfast on for all of us. Sausage, eggs, and toast work for you boys?"

"That sounds perfect," Andy replied with a smile as he and Bill joined their hosts at the table. "Thank you!"

Betty moved quickly to the refrigerator and got to work.

"We didn't get much of a chance to catch up last night," Donnie said. "Let's just visit a while this morning, and you can follow me to Walter Dean Construction. I'll be heading out from there to the site I'm working right now, actually not far from there. Maybe, we can give you a quick tour around the Valley later."

That set Andy up for a question he'd carried over from last night. "You and Betty called this the Valley several times. What's that mean, exactly?"

"Phoenix and our neighboring towns are completely surrounded by mountains, hence, the Valley. Actually, it's called 'the Valley of the Sun.' Pretty appropriate, I think," Donnie said with a smile.

"We really do appreciate your offer for a tour," said Andy. "We'll definitely take you up on it. Right now, I think I'd like us to just explore a little on our own after our meeting this morning. We have a Phoenix insert on our state map, but I'd like to pick up a city map or maybe a little broader area, you know, the Valley."

Betty joined the conversation from across the kitchen. "We have one you're welcome to borrow," she said. "In fact, just keep it. They're easy to come by, and you'll be moving here soon, right?"

Andy laughed. "We'll see. Thanks." He looked again at Donnie. "I have one more question. You said that there are neighboring towns that are part of the Valley. Do you mean different sections of Phoenix, like the South Phoenix you mentioned? Or are they actually completely different towns really close by?"

"They're towns. Why?"

"Well, I'd just like to explore and keep options open about where we might live if we move to the Valley. I don't know. You've got a lovely home, and this seems like a nice neighborhood, but Phoenix itself feels a little, I don't know, a little 'concrete' for me. We'd be moving from a lot smaller town. How big is Phoenix?"

"It's growing so fast, it's hard to keep up. I think we're just above one-hundred thousand right now."

"See? Donelsburg peaked at 20,000. And we're dropping from that. I know we don't have to live in or close to the city. A neighborhood like this would be great. I just want to keep my options open and look around a bit while we're here."

"Makes sense," Donnie agreed. "Some of those other towns will be on that city map we'll get you."

"Thanks."

"Breakfast is ready," Betty interjected. "Donnie, come help me bring the food to the table."

Donnie got out of his chair, saying, "Let's eat!"

THIRTY-SIX

The offices of Walter Dean Construction brought Bill and Andy once again deep into the heart of downtown Phoenix. It was difficult finding a place to park. There were definitely never this many cars in one place anywhere in Donelsburg, Illinois.

Andy was disappointed that Donnie didn't actually come in to introduce them. He drove ahead of them and pointed out the window to the office building, waved, and drove on. It was understandable since they had already made him several hours late for work, thought Andy. Then, he remembered why Donnie apparently felt he needed to stay with them all morning. Maybe, Andy thought, we should have continued to look for another place to stay. He'd talk more about that with Bill later.

They found a parking place and walked a couple of blocks back to the Dean office. Andy felt apprehensive as they walked through the front door, but that feeling ended quickly. The meeting went splendidly.

Walter Dean was an energetic man in his early fifties with thinning salt and pepper hair, a dark, desert tan, and a friendly smile. Mr. Dean had fought in the European Theater during the First World War. He told Andy and Bill that he knew how hard it is to transition back to civilian life. He was eager to give his fellow veterans a hand.

After a brief visit in Dean's office, he took them for a drive, specifically directing Andy to the front seat and Bill to the back. He took them both to some of his company's current construction sites around the Valley. They were impressed by the number of projects Dean Construction had going at once, as well as its reach into neighboring towns. Mr. Dean drove them to one of those towns northwest of Phoenix called Casa Nueva, to show them a recently completed building.

"The project we just completed is right here on the town square," Mr. Dean said as he parked. "Right there, boys, is the new Casa Nueva public library."

"It's a beautiful building, sir," Bill said quietly from the back seat. But Andy said nothing as he took in the park-like grounds around the building. Grass and trees surrounded the new building with a well-tended flower garden bordering its front door. It reminded him of a much smaller version of Rotary Park back home in Donelsburg.

"Yes, it is indeed beautiful," he finally said. "Can you tell us a bit about Casa Nueva, Mr. Dean?"

"Please call me Walt. We're on a first name basis at Dean Construction. Casa Nueva is Spanish for 'new house.' The town's not really new, but it's taken on new life with the end of the war. Casa Nueva has always been a nice little town with fine local businesses and excellent schools. But over the last few years, it's been in something of a boom, probably more so than Phoenix itself. A lot of our vets have moved here because they like the Valley but think Phoenix is too big and urban."

"I can understand that," Andy replied, looking back to Bill.

Walt began his drive back to the office. "You thinking of settling in Casa Nueva, Andy?'

"Can't say, sir. But I like what I've seen so far."

"What about you, Bill? Have you learned of some places you might live?"

Bill thought a moment about the phrasing of the question. Finally, he said, "I don't know where I'll live yet, sir. But if it's at all possible, I'm pretty sure I would I like to work for you."

"We'll work hard for you, sir," Andy said. "And we're both experienced carpenters. What we don't know, we're ready to learn."

Walt laughed. "I'd like to hire you both. Now, I got a top-notch recommendation for Andy from Donnie, one of my finest workers. Andy, if you're half as skilled, smart, and dependable as Donnie says, you'll be an asset to my company in no time. But as far as I can tell, Donnie's endorsement's all I've got on you, Andy, and I've got nothing on Bill, here. But I like you both so consider yourselves hired with just one condition."

Walt paused to focus on turning another street as he headed back to his office. Andy began to feel uneasy. "What condition?" he asked.

"Oh, it's the same as any new hire. We're a big company with lots of projects going on. I need top skills and employees that are self-starters, if you know what I mean. So you two can consider yourselves hired when we get back to the building and sign the paperwork— you know, contracts and such. The condition is that the contract is what we call probationary. It's a ninety-day probation period for you to train, settle in, and all."

"We're coming all the way from Illinois, sir," Andy said. "That's a big move for something that lasts ninety days."

"That's the way we do it, Andy. From everything I hear, you have nothing to worry about."

Andy was having second thoughts. "What about Bill?" he asked. "He's skilled, and he's smart." Andy paused. Should he go ahead and state the obvious? He decided, yes. "But I've seen every good quality Bill brings ignored because of race. So what effect will that have on his probationary time?"

Bill leaned forward. Part of him wanted to tell Andy to please shut up. But he really wanted to hear what Walt had to say. Like Andy already said, this is a big move.

Walt shook his head. "You've got it all wrong, Andy. I hire people for two things: ability and character. If you're hard working, dependable, and you can do the job, color doesn't mean a thing. You must have seen it when we went by those job sites today. Negroes and whites working together! Bill's got nothing to worry about."

"I saw one," Bill said. "You're saying there's more?"

"Yes," Walt said. "There's more. Now, at this time, all of them are what I would call 'unskilled laborers,' and we pay them accordingly. We have skilled masons and carpenters. Then, we have laborers who help them; mix the mortar and keep it fresh for the masons, drive trucks, unload materials, and set up sites, do whatever needs to be done to keep the job moving. It's important work, Bill. You'll start there until we see what you can do."

Walt drove past his office building and pulled into a drive. Andy smiled as they entered a small parking lot behind the office with spaces for about ten cars. "Could we have parked here this morning?" he asked as Walt switched off his car.

"Absolutely. But, of course, after you're on the job, you'll go directly to our work sites. I've got some work to do in the office. You fellows come on up and visit with Brenda. She'll give you some papers to look over and fill out so we'll be ready for you when you come back." A moment and then he asked, "So when do you plan to make your move?"

"I'm not sure," Andy said. "Maybe, a month or two."

They got out of the car and headed for the office door. Andy paused outside the door. "If it's all right with you, sir, I think we might want to take a drive, you know, look around some for ourselves. Could we come back and look at those papers later? We plan to be here all week. I'd like to see a little more of Casa Nueva."

THIRTY-SEVEN

They walked down the street and climbed into the Chevy. "So, Bill," Andy said as he started the car, "what do you think?"

Bill shook his head. "I think you're going to be fine here," he said. "Me? I don't know. Ninety days probation, and I could be out on the streets."

Andy wanted to argue but discovered he couldn't. "I didn't like the way he talked to you about unskilled labor."

"Not my favorite thing either," Bill agreed. "But he doesn't know me from Adam. He said when I showed what I could do, they'd move me up."

Andy suddenly felt hopeful. "So you want to give it a try?"

"I don't know. He said we'd be guaranteed a start. I guess that's all we could expect."

They drove on in silence. Then, Bill said, "Hey, aren't we in that town?"

"Yep! If I remember right, the square is just ahead."

Andy drove part way around the city square to get a look at some of the stores and businesses that circled it. There was a pharmacy on one corner facing a bank on the next. Next to the bank was a diner and then a florist and a real estate agent. Facing the real estate office on the next corner was a building with "Casa Nueva City Hall" painted on the window. On impulse, Andy turned between the real estate office and city hall. The street sign said, "Casa Nueva Avenue."

This, they decided, was the town's main street, with the business area extending on it to and from the square.

"I just like the feel of this place," Andy said. Bill concurred.

Andy turned off of Casa Nueva Avenue onto Royal Palm Drive. They passed several apartment buildings and then made a left onto Ocotillo Lane.

"Do you have any idea where you're going?"

"Don't know, Bill. Just looking around. I guess I'll know where I'm going when I get there."

As he said this, they arrived in a residential area. Andy liked the look of this neighborhood. Some houses had front yards landscaped with green gravel instead of grass and cactus rather than trees. But most had nicely manicured lawns with what Andy decided was traditional landscaping. In other words, they looked much like what he'd seen in the nicer homes of Donelsburg. Suddenly, he pulled to the curb and stopped the car.

"Look," he said, pointing to a sign in front of one the houses. It read: "For Sale, Wilson Realty, 6018 Casa Nueva Avenue, Casa Nueva, Arizona."

"I saw that office on the square," Andy said. "Just look at that house! That's a nice, little house. Let's see if anyone's home."

"You can go see, Andy. I'm feeling real uncomfortable here. I'll just slouch down in the car seat and wait."

Andy looked at Bill and back to the house. He took a pen and paper, writing down the house address, then pulled out from the curb. "Okay," he said. "Let's go see the realtor."

THIRTY-EIGHT

The first thing Andy noticed on entering Wilson Realty was the smell of stale cigar smoke. He felt his nose wrinkle. Andy had not grown up around tobacco smoke. He'd heard his Grandfather Mayes rolled his own cigarettes, as did both of his uncles, but the smoke badly irritated Jimmy's sensitive lungs. Andy's father was greatly relieved when he moved to the Hartley home where Isaiah did not smoke. But he did chew.

Andy never once tried smoking tobacco out of respect for his father. He did get into Grandfather Hartley's Beech-nut Chewing Tobacco once when he was nine years old. Never again.

His grandfather kept pouches in a drawer in the kitchen. One day, when he saw no one watching, Andy opened the drawer, pinched a wad of out of the bag and stuffed it in his mouth. He quickly placed the pouch back in the drawer and ran out to the front porch for a pleasant chew.

By the time he was out the door, he was already feeling a bit nauseated, but he decided what he needed to do was to start chewing, as he had seen his grandfather do so many times. But hot juices began to pool in the back of his throat, and he panicked.

His grandfather would chew and spit, so Andy hurried to the edge of the porch to do the same. He ended up spitting out the entire wad of tobacco but not before he had swallowed a large amount of the ghastly goo, which he promptly threw up, gagging and gasping. What Andy did not know and only learned months later was that his grandfather had watched the entire episode from a window, enjoying himself to no end.

Andy swore that very day to never touch tobacco again in any form. It was a vow he kept even while in the army when so many nonsmoking enlisted men took up the habit. He did occasionally have a drink, but that was in moderation by necessity. He had a very low tolerance for alcohol and could feel its effects after only a couple of beers.

Andy moved his attention from the acrid odor to the second thing he noticed in the realtor's office: a middle-aged woman with dark brown hair sitting behind a desk, talking on the phone. She smiled and gestured toward a row of metal framed Naugahyde chairs. Just as they sat down, a rotund, balding man stepped from a back office, unlit cigar clenched in his teeth.

"Hello, gentlemen," the man said, cigar still firmly between his teeth. He walked over and extended his hand to Andy. "I'm Larry Wilson. Please come into my office and tell me what I can do for you."

Andy walked through the door with Bill following and saw two brown Naugahyde chairs identical to the ones in the outer office. It must have been quite a sale, Andy mused to himself as he sat down. Mr. Wilson sat behind a large walnut desk and leaned forward.

"Now," he said, unlit cigar finally in an ashtray, "please, tell me. How can I be of service?"

"I'm interested in a house," Andy said, pulling a piece of paper out of his shirt pocket. "It's 1012 Ocotillo Lane, here in Casa Nueva."

"Oh, yes," Wilson said with enthusiasm. "Lovely little home, nice neighborhood, great elementary school just a few blocks away. It'd be a great starter home for a young family. You have a family, Mr. –?"

"Mayes. Andy Mayes. Yes, sir, a wife and little boy. This is my good friend, Bill Davis. We're both from Illinois and thinking about a move here in another month or two."

"Well, pleasure to meet you boys. I'm real sorry, Bill, but I don't really have anything available here in Casa Nueva. No, nothing here right now at all. But I can sure help you find something, son. Yes, sir. Lots of nice homes for the taking in other parts of the Valley."

Bill nodded. "Like South Phoenix."

"Why, yes! Some real nice homes there in South Phoenix. Now, about the house on Ocotillo. Great home, great price. But I want to be completely honest with you because that's what I do. You're from out of town and don't know the neighborhoods here. I can show you some other areas where you might be more, well, let's say, comfortable."

"What's wrong with this one?"

"Oh, not a thing! It's great! But it's on the lower end, economically, you might say. And, really, I think the prices could fall from there. There are only a couple white folks left there for a couple of blocks around. One of 'ems at 1012, white folks moving out, if you see what I mean. Other cultures moving in, takin' over. Now, they're great people, and they keep the property up better'n any white owners I know. Those folks just have a knack for agriculture, you know? It's born in 'em, I think."

Andy was confused. "I don't understand."

"The Mexicans! Now, these are land-owners: good Mexicans, all American citizens as far as I know. But we have lots of illegals here, migrant workers who come through to pick cotton and such."

"You grow cotton here?" Andy had no idea.

"There's lot of cotton fields on the outskirts of town. Brings the wetbacks."

"Wetbacks?"

"You know," said Wilson, "Mexicans! Illegal workers, swimming across the border! Wetbacks!"

Bill could stand it no longer. "Sorry, sir, but there are no rivers on the Arizona-Mexico border."

Andy started to grin, but forced it back. He looked at Larry Wilson to see his response. The realtor scowled at Bill for a fleeting moment and then turned his attention back to Andy.

"So we do have these illegals, some folks do call 'em wetbacks." He looked over to Bill and back to Andy. "Some just move around the U.S. looking for work. Most keep coming back and forth across the border.

"But these folks on Ocotillo live here, send their kids to school here. I'm sure they're good enough people, but I felt like you should know about 'em just in case you're not comfortable. Lots of folks here just don't like 'em. You know, they get together and babble in their Mexican talk, and you don't know if they're talking about you or what. It makes some people uncomfortable."

Wilson leaned back in his chair and interlaced his fingers across his waist. "Just wanted you to know," he added.

Andy sat quietly a moment. Did he really want to do business with this man? He looked over at Bill who smiled and shrugged. Another moment passed. Andy folded his hands on the desk, leaned forward and nodded to Larry Wilson. "I'd like to take a look at the house."

Wilson looked into a file, picked up the phone and dialed. After a moment, he hung it up and said, "Wife's home right now. She said to come on over."

The house was simple and neat, inside and out. Andy decided it was a cottage-style home, small with two bedrooms and a single bath. The kitchen was beside a separate dining room with only a counter between, all of which joined the living room area that made it feel open and spacious. There were beautifully polished hardwood floors throughout. Andy liked what he saw.

As they left and walked to Wilson's car, Andy thanked him. "I'll need to make a phone call and visit with my wife." Then, he added, "If this is already a mixed neighborhood, why couldn't you show something around here to Bill?"

Wilson looked down with an exaggerated sigh. Then, he said, "I'd like that. Sure would, more'n anything I can think of. But it can't happen. No home owner would sell it and no bank would finance it. Not my choice, believe me, son. It's just how it is. But, if you'll get in the car, I can take you where he can buy. I don't deal much in South Phoenix, just don't get the prospects, if you know what I mean. But I know a realtor there. I'll give him a call at the office and give you directions to go talk to him about what's available. His name is Arthur Lewis. He'll take real good care of you, I promise."

They did go to Lewis' office. He was expecting them after Wilson's call and took them for a drive to look at homes for Bill. They kept moving farther south as they looked, and Bill finally said he'd like to rent an apartment they visited on Southern Avenue. He would look for a place to buy later, he said. "I like the smaller apartment just fine, and I like the people we've met."

They again left a realtor with a thank-you, but no commitments. As they got into the Chevy, Andy wondered, *is this really going to happen?* He was actually beginning to think that it might. He started the car and looked over to his friend.

"I'm planning to head back to the Winston's to call Jean," he said. He looked forward, out the windshield, as the Chevy quietly idled. "I can tell her about the job and the house. I have no idea what to say about a move."

"Sure, you do."

Andy looked back at Bill. "What do you mean?"

Bill shifted in his seat to better face Andy and smiled. "You say, 'Jean, my dear, we have a job waiting for us, and I found a house I love. Bill has located a place to stay, and we're both ready to move if you'll just join us."

Andy's jaw dropped and then lifted into a broad grin. "Really?"

"Really," Bill answered with a laugh.

Andy dropped the Chevy into first, still grinning. They were on their way to Donnie and Betty's and a very important phone call. But his smile grew slightly narrower with that thought. How would Jean respond?

THIRTY-NINE

They returned to the Winston's home with plans to call Jean. Andy knocked on the door and waited outside even after Betty opened it.

"I'm sorry," he told her. "I just realized Donnie isn't home. We've been out so long I guess I thought he might be here. We can come back later."

"It's all right, Andy. Donnie and I talked this morning, and I told him everything is fine. Really. Come on in both of you. Please. And besides, you need to make a call right away. You got a phone call from a certain Sergeant Donaldson with the Amarillo State Police. He left you his number. Our phone's there on the end table."

"Thanks."

Andy let out a deep sigh. He looked at Bill as he lifted the phone off its cradle. "Believe it or not," Andy said, "I'd actually forgotten about this."

"Not me," Bill said. "I shudder every time I look at that smashed in grill. What we gonna do?"

Andy looked at the notepad professionally printed with "Walter Dean Construction" across the top. Below that, in blue ink and written with impressively neat cursive, was the name "Sergeant Donaldson" and a phone number.

He looked at Bill. "I think we should do everything we can. This is our chance to make a difference. These creeps terrorize innocent people and could have killed us. I say we make our testimony if it gets them off the streets like the sergeant said."

Andy looked again at the note and then, with obvious resolve, dialed the number.

"Police Department."

Andy asked for Sergeant Donaldson, who picked up the line in just a few moments.

"This is Andrew Mayes, sir. I'm returning your call."

"Andy! It's good to hear from you. I wanted to give you an update on your case. The prosecutor has studied my full report with the evidence we've submitted. He put that with your statement, and he's sure he can make a charge of reckless endangerment stick on all three. We've got the evidence as well as the witness of two police officers. He plans to add a charge of misdemeanor assault, but he'll need you two to testify in court."

Andy was shocked. "Reckless endangerment? I don't understand. You said we'd get them off the street, that we'd put them away."

"Well, Joe was the driver, and it's his truck. With other traffic violations on his record, he'll lose his license for sure. With the other charges, they could get some jail time with probation."

"But you said yourself, sir, they have a history of assault, and then they ambushed us. They swerved that truck around and stopped us and ambushed us. You said you wanted our help to put these guys away."

"Yes, and that's exactly what I believe. But here's how it works. I make the arrest, and I write up the report. I pass on the evidence and my statement of what happened to the prosecutor, and then, it's out of my hands. The prosecutor decides the charges. He knows he can make reckless endangerment stick, and he's ready to charge a misdemeanor assault as well. But we all want you to know the facts about what's likely to happen."

"And he says reckless endangerment."

"That's right. Listen, Andy, there's more you need to know. The three have gotten help from some of their Klan buddies, men of some means. They've hired the area's top law firm who looked at the report and your statement. They contested the reckless driving charge and threatened to bring charges against you, saying their clients never physically attacked you. The lawyers say they were physically assaulted, not the other way around."

Andy began to feel nauseous. He took a deep breath then let it out slowly through his mouth.

"You know that's not true, Sergeant. They chased us and stopped us with their truck. Scarface pulled a knife on Bill. Blondie had a rifle."

"I know, Andy. I saw the skid marks and the rifle. We found the knife at the scene. It's all in my report and your statement. But it's not illegal to have a rifle in the city limits. Joe never fired, and Wyatt never attacked you with the knife. In fact, every actual attack came from you and Bill. You hurt 'em pretty bad, Andy. All three had to be checked out at the hospital. You broke Red's nose. And Bill smashed up Joe's face and knocked out a tooth!"

A few beats of silence passed. Andy had nothing to say.

"I agree these creeps need locking up," Donaldson continued. "We need to be rid of 'em. Say you'll press charges, and we'll hit 'em with misdemeanor assault. I'd like that. But I wanted you to know what you're up against. These lawyers are the best, and our prosecutor says they'll end up taking you for assault and would likely win. I'm just warning you to not run into this without knowing all the facts, Andy. I like you, boy."

"Who are you people?" Andy heard himself ask and then regretted it. "I'm sorry, sir, but this is not what I expected. What would a misdemeanor assault do if they're convicted?"

There was a moment of silence. "Well, they'd be fined, and it would go on their record. They could get a short jail sentence but most likely wouldn't even serve that. Oh, and there was no insurance on the truck so we could force them to pay for the damage to your car themselves."

"I don't care about the car, sir. I can drive it." He paused and said again, more quietly, "You said we could get them off the streets."

"I know, Andy. And we're ready to take them to court. But I want you to know all the facts."

Bill waved his hand to get Andy's attention. He could only hear one side of the conversation, but he had heard enough. When Andy looked, Bill slowly shook his head side to side and mouthed the word, "No."

"Thank you," Andy said quietly and hung up the phone. He looked at Bill in disbelief. "How can that be the same man we talked to in Texas?"

"I'll tell you what I think," Bill said matter-of-factly.

"What?"

"I think someone higher up than Donaldson, a lieutenant or captain or, I don't know, maybe the mayor knows these guys or their families or both. I think Donaldson was ordered to lose it, to get them off. And he just did."

"That stinks to high heaven."

"Yeah, it does. I'll tell you something else."

"What's that?"

"If the tables had been turned and we did the same thing to those local boys as they did to us, we'd be sitting in jail right now."

"You're right, Bill. And, no offense, my friend, but if one of the victims hadn't been Negro, I bet it would have gone different, too."

"Yes, sir," Bill agreed. "I do believe you got that right."

FORTY

Andy asked Betty's permission to make another long-distance call. He then called Jean and was met with his second surprise for the night. He wanted to let her know that he and Bill were considering accepting a job with Dean Construction and that he found what he thought was the perfect house. Then, he explained that he wanted to get her thoughts on these possibilities, fully expecting her to say he was moving too quickly. His big surprise was her response.

"I was anticipating just this call," said Jean. "I've been thinking about it since you left, talking it over with my parents and praying about what to say. I want you to know that I'm ready to move whenever you are, Andy. I love you and trust you. You say the word, and we'll be heading for Arizona."

Andy was completely speechless. First, he was excited that they could soon be moving to the Valley of the Sun. Then, he was worried. What if he betrayed her trust? What if she left her home and family entirely on his word and hated it here? Suddenly, he wasn't sure this was the best idea after all.

"It's really different here, Jean. Don't you think you should visit first just to see what it's like?"

"I'll be with you, Andy. That's all that matters. I'll have Michael and you. We'll make a new home together. I've talked it over with Mama and Papa. They're excited for us and want to visit, to see the Grand Canyon and the Painted Desert. They support us all the way. Let's do this!"

"I'll take some pictures of the house and our new neighborhood. I've been told the town has the best schools in the Valley. It's a nice town, Jean. We need to find a place for Bill before we come back, and then we need to put our house in Donelsburg on the market. Thank you so much, Jean. And thank Mama and Papa Hartley. I love you all."

"That seemed to go well," said Bill. Andy smiled broadly. "I'm happy for you, Andy. I really am. I'll give that realtor, Arthur Lewis, a call and tell him I'll take that apartment."

Andy sighed and looked down to the table. He looked up again at Bill. "It's the same everywhere we go, Bill, telling people where they can live and can't live. It's wrong, just plain wrong. Let's don't assume anything about where you can live until we know for sure and, if we need to, let's be ready to fight."

"I don't want to fight, Andy. I don't want to go to someplace where I know people hate me and don't want me there. I told you, Andy, I don't like to fight. And a fight like this doesn't work anyway. How did we do getting Red and his gang off the streets?"

"I'm so sorry, Bill. I'm putting you through all kinds of hell and just because I want to get away from Donelsburg."

"You remember us talking about looking for something better, Andy? Well, I'm going to find work besides stocking shelves in a store. That's better. I'll live with rugged mountains and starry nights like I saw at Fort Huachuca. That's better, too. I'm going to something better, Andy. It won't be easy, but then, I can't remember when life has been easy. But I do believe it will be better."

Andy smiled and felt his eyes moisten. "I hope you're right. No, I *believe* you're right. So now, we call Walter Dean and Larry Wilson and Arthur Lewis. We've got a lot to do before we head back home."

"And I'll add one more thing," Bill said. "We need to check out junk yards for a used grill. I don't want to wear our busted one like a badge going through Amarillo, saying, 'Hey Big Red, come and get us!'"

FORTY-ONE

Betty looked up salvage yards in the Phoenix phone book. Andy found a 1940 Chevy Sedan on the second call. It had been T-boned, almost cut in half the employee said. The grill was fully intact.

Andy and Bill picked up the grill early the next morning, took it back to the Winston's driveway and easily switched it with their crumpled one by early afternoon. They then made phone calls to Dean Construction and the realtors, Larry Wilson Realty and Arthur Lewis.

Walter Dean gave Donnie Thursday off to spend with his guests. He showed them around the Valley and introduced them to a number of his friends. It was a great day, but that night both Andy and Bill were packed and eager to hit the road early the next morning.

***

Back in Donelsburg, Jean was also eagerly awaiting their homecoming. She was excited to see Andy's photographs, hear news of his trip, and to share a little news of her own.

"Why didn't you tell him?" Papa had asked her after their phone call on Wednesday.

"Lots of reasons," she answered. "I wanted to surprise him, and I didn't want him to get all worried. He's so excited about this move and, if he knew, he'd say we should wait, that I shouldn't travel. Besides," she added, "I'd rather go now than later. Imagine how much harder it would be taking care of a crying, hungry little one in my arms instead of the one that's all happy, content inside me."

Mama, Papa, and Jean all laughed together.

***

On Friday morning, Andy and Bill were on their way with Andy driving the first stretch. They felt confident after the long drive out. They had a book to tell them where they could buy food, gas, and lodging. They had experience to tell them what to do if they couldn't.

The timing was different on the way back, but two familiar places merited their special attention. First was the Fred Harvey Restaurant in Gallup, New Mexico. Bill had made it perfectly clear that he wanted to stop for a visit with a certain waitress named Anna, if that was at all possible. Andy was more than happy to oblige.

The second point of interest was Route 66 through Amarillo. Big Red, Scarface, and Blondie were out on the street again and would likely be watching for the Chevy. Andy suggested calling Sergeant Donaldson for a police escort through town. Bill wouldn't have it.

"That's just what we need, Andy," he said. "Let's make a parade of it so the whole Amarillo KKK knows we're back in town. The police would stop at the city limits and we'd have a band of hooded freaks standing at the edge of town with their crosses ablaze!"

"You've got quite an imagination, my brother," laughed Andy.

"I'm dead serious! And besides, I don't know who we can trust. Donaldson seemed okay, but you saw him flip. Someone in power is all buddy-buddy with Red. No, let's just get through town all quiet-like and not stop till we're in the next county."

But the trip went smoothly and without incident. Bill even got his visit with Anna who seemed genuinely happy to see them both. They promised another stop on the way back to Phoenix.

It was an amazing homecoming. Paul and Margaret Holloway hosted Sunday night dinner for the Mayes and Davis families. All were eager to hear stories of the great Arizona adventure but were saddened by the experiences Bill and Andy shared.

"Are you sure you want to make this move?" Beau Davis asked after they had moved from the dining area to the living room. "Andy, you're pushing something here and pulling our Bill along. It may be great for you and Jean. It sounds like nothin' but trouble for Bill."

"There are problems there," Bill acknowledged. "But those same problems are here and everywhere else we might go. The difference is, I'll have work I'm looking forward to. I think there's a future for me there."

"You go, honey," Lorrie Davis said to her son. "You go and find that future. Just don't forget your mamma and daddy. We'll be coming out to see you to be sure you don't."

"And we'll be there, Lorrie, making sure he's okay," Jean said brightly. "I hope he'll be at our place a lot. We're going to need lots of help with our growing family."

"What?" Andy sat up straight and looked at Jean who couldn't stop smiling. "Our growing family?"

"Yes, it seems our next child will be born in Arizona."

FORTY-TWO

Andy got out of his chair and walked over to Jean, kneeling before her. "How long have you known this?"

"I suspected it before you left, but I didn't want you to cancel your trip. You would've, you know. Anyway, I wasn't completely sure until after you were gone. So I decided to wait till tonight and surprise you."

"That's a success on your part. Wow! Are you sure you don't want to wait to move? I don't want to cause any problems."

"I'm sure."

"I hate to have your parents miss seeing the grandbaby."

"Andy, I'm sure."

"Don't worry about it, son," Paul Holloway said. "We're due a vacation anyway. We'll be there when our grandbaby's born."

"That's right," Mrs. Holloway chimed in. "I wouldn't miss this chance to help out and get my baby cuddling in!"

"It's settled then," Andy said with exaggerated confidence. He was still concerned whether or not what he wanted was really right and fair for all concerned. But all seemed ready to make this move. Andy knew for sure that he was. As conversation settled into quietness, Andy realized something else had been bothering him.

"Did you know they raise cotton around Phoenix?"

"No," said Lorrie. "How can they do that in the desert?"

"Irrigation," Andy answered. "Irrigation and a lot of Mexican migrant workers. It sounds like those people don't have it any better than my grandparents did in Alabama. Why do people take advantage of other human beings like that?"

A long silence settled on the room before Andy spoke again.

"The real estate guy said I might not want to live in the house we're buying because there are Mexicans all around us. I knew when he said it, that's exactly where I want to live. If my experience holds true, they're going to be a lot better neighbors than the likes of Mr. Larry Wilson."

The room was again quiet as Andy's mood turned reflective. He suddenly knew what had been playing in the back of his mind. Remembering the exploitation of his own grandparents in Alabama had triggered another memory. His father had told Andy about a personal vow to visit Alice Mayes, Andy's grandmother, once more. Jimmy never had that opportunity. Andy knew he must follow up on it, at least find out if she was all right, perhaps go see her before they left for Arizona.

He shared his new mission with the others. "I simply have to do this," he told them, "for the sake of my father."

"Why don't you call first?" asked Paul Holloway. "You have a party line, so please feel free to use the store phone. Come by tomorrow, and you can connect to Dearing, operator to operator."

"I'm positive my grandparents don't have a phone," Andy said. "But Uncle Matthew moved from the farm and my Aunt Kate moved in with him after Grandmother and Grandfather Hartley died. They might still live in Dearing. It would be good to talk to them, and they could tell me about Alice and −"

Andy paused in surprise, realizing he didn't even know his grandfather's first name nor those of his two uncles. How sad, he thought. How very sad.

Andy called Dearing, Alabama the next day with the help of his father-in-law. The operator did say there was a listing for a Matthew Hartley and connected them. His Aunt Kate answered the phone. They spoke together for almost a half hour, with Andy intermittently laughing and then becoming solemn in his tone. At one point in the call, a single tear made its way down his cheek.

He was calling from the store office. Jean, along with Paul and Margaret Holloway, were in the store itself to give him privacy. They watched together as he stepped through the office door, walked toward them, and shared all he had learned from his call.

"Kate said that the Kenneth Harris farm was no more. He sold all his land to some big company in Montgomery and told all the sharecroppers they had a month to get out. Nobody had any place to go. They had no money and owned almost nothing. Kate said she didn't know what happened to all those tenants, but everyone was forced to leave." Andy paused and scowled. "And the new owner came in and razed every shack to the ground. It's now one huge cotton field with tractors and mechanical cotton pickers." He looked at his wife. "The people are gone."

Jean gently touched Andy's arm.

"Kate said Alice Mayes had died. She didn't know how it happened or when, except that it was before Harris sold the farm. What Kate had heard was that my grandfather buried her somewhere himself. She's supposedly in an unmarked grave somewhere, maybe on the Harris property, maybe out in the woods above the farm. My grandfather and uncles stayed there on the farm, with the boys working the land until Harris kicked them off. Then, they just left. Kate had no idea where. They just disappeared."

"That's mighty tough news, Andy," Paul said. "Are you going to go to Dearing? Maybe, you can learn more or find your grandmother's grave."

Andy had his answer already. He knew it before he even said goodbye to Kate.

"I've had enough of the past," he said. He took Jean's hand that was still resting on his arm. "Our place is the future, and that future is in Arizona."

FORTY-THREE

Five months passed, along with many hours of planning and preparing for their big move to the Valley of the Sun. A number of those hours were spent in Holloway Hardware's meeting room, debating on timing for the trip, stops along the route, and how to transport the extra people and possessions.

Paul Holloway sat in on one of their early meetings. He listened as they talked about transportation concerns. "It's interesting you bring this up," he interjected. "I've been thinking about how we might help each other."

Jean, Andy, and Bill looked his way, surprised.

"I've been thinking about getting a new delivery truck for the store. The Ford's in good shape, but it's, well, a few years old. I'm fond of that old truck, wouldn't want to trade it in and let any Tom, Dick, or Harry have it. I'd feel a lot better giving it to someone I knew would take good care of it. You know, someone like you, Bill."

Bill looked around in shock. "Oh, you can't do that, Mr. Holloway!"

"Now, Bill, don't you tell me what I can and can't do. I'm getting a new truck, and you're taking the Ford. The decision's already been made. You'll all need something to carry your things for the trip, and it has a nice cover that locks. You'll need a vehicle to get around in Phoenix, and I need the peace of mind my truck's in good hands. It's the perfect solution for us all."

Mr. Holloway stood up and walked over to Bill, extending his hand. "Let's shake on it, son, and consider it a deal." Bill stood, and they remained several moments with right hands clasped. Mr. Holloway waved at the others and returned to his business in the store, his work here accomplished.

Plans for the actual trip were not resolved so easily. Andy wanted very much to retrace their original drive west on Route 66, using the Green Book and stopping at the same motels and restaurants along the way. "We learned what worked," he said. "Why do anything different?"

Bill strongly disagreed. "It's not the same this time," he said. "You've got Michael and Jean. We can follow each other on the drive and stay in the same towns. But you let me use the Green Book. I can take care of myself, you take care of your family."

Andy didn't like it. "You're family, too," he said. "And what if we get separated? How will we find each other?"

Bill laughed. "My brother, we both know where we're going! We'll find our way. And besides, I might want to be separated for just a little bit."

Andy was confused. Then, he suddenly understood. "Are you thinking about a certain waitress in Gallup, New Mexico?" he asked with a grin.

Bill grinned back. "I was thinking we could all eat together at Fred Harvey Restaurant," he said. "And then, I don't know, I just might want to spend an extra hour or two in Gallup."

They adopted Bill's plan for the trip.

***

Jean wondered if it felt like déjà vu for Andy, as he drove his car to Bill's house early that Saturday morning, June

26, 1948. He and Bill were off to Arizona once again, except this time, Bill would be driving his own Ford truck, loaded the night before with possessions the travelers felt they simply must take. And the trunk and back seat of Andy's Chevy were tightly packed with every necessity the two of them could squeeze in.

She and Michael would join Andy in the front seat for the entire journey. Jean decided that their son, almost two-years-old now, could sit up between them, lying down on the car seat when he needed to nap. Andy agreed, saying that they could reach down to hold him and keep him safe in the event of a sudden stop.

Beau and Lorrie bid the travelers a long and sad good-bye. *It must be so hard on them*, Jean thought. Her parents had come by that morning and hugged each of them multiple times in front of Andy and Jean's house. It was hard on them all, but, tears aside, Jean felt like this was the right thing to do. They would start a new life together in Arizona.

Andy shared stories of his first drive out, as he made the pilgrimage again on Route 66 through Missouri, Kansas, Oklahoma, and Texas. They made each stop along the way exactly as planned. And, as predicted, the longest stay was in Gallup, New Mexico.

It was five in the evening when Andy parked his Chevy in front of the Fred Harvey Restaurant. Bill immediately pulled up next to him, and the four walked together to the restaurant door, Michael holding his mother's hand. Andy opened the door, and Jean smiled, as Bill stepped back and directed her and Michael through the doorway.

Ah, our friend is showing amazing self-control, she thought, still smiling. Jean knew how eager Bill was to see Anna once again. And Jean was also eager to meet her. She had heard so much about this beautiful, young woman who had captured Bill's heart. Jean hoped Anna would not also break that heart.

As far as she knew, Bill never had a girlfriend in Donelsburg. Would Anna be his first romance? Jean was suddenly shocked by the awareness that she really didn't know. It was amazing to realize how little she really did know about Bill, even though she considered him her friend. They grew up in different communities and divergent cultures. They went to different schools and, except for Andy, she had met none of his friends. She had known all this before but had never felt the full impact of it until that moment. She suddenly appreciated even more her husband's anger at the racial divide in their little town.

"There she is," Bill said, excitedly. Jean broke from her inner musing and became aware of the smiling, young woman, greeting them with a modest wave of her hand. She was as lovely as Bill had said. Bill took the lead now, with Jean, Michael, and Andy close behind.

The restaurant was packed with people. Should they be moving unescorted, winding their way between the tables? Jean chuckled to herself. No matter! There was no stopping Bill now! He slowed as they neared Anna. She was at work, time to show a little reserve.

"Hello!" Anna said, beaming. "It's so great to see you again. Let me show you to a table."

When they were seated, Andy introduced Jean and Michael. Jean liked her immediately. Everything about Anna radiated warmth and sincerity. Bill was a lucky guy.

The Mayes family walked next door right after dinner, checking into their room at the El Navajo Hotel. Bill said he would check in a little later. He needed to visit a bit with Anna. They were setting plans to get together about ten that night when she got off work. He'd see them for breakfast the next day, he said.

At breakfast, there were still more plans to share. "Anna wants me to come by her house today and meet her family," Bill announced over their eggs, bacon and hash browns. "I hope you don't mind. I'll be just a few hours behind you. I'll bring the truck and unload your things before I head down to my apartment."

Jean raised her eyebrows. "Hmm," she toned. "Home to meet the parents. Sounding pretty serious."

Bill laughed. Then, his expression turned serious. "I like her, Jean. I like her a lot."

FORTY-FOUR

The Mayes family and their friend, Bill, were soon settled into their respective homes. Andy and Bill worked hard through the week, quickly earning their place as respected employees of Walter Dean Construction. Andy spent each weekend with his family, whether relaxing at home or visiting sites around the state.

Most weekends, Bill would be making the five-hour drive to Gallup to spend time with Anna. Andy and Jean could see what was ahead, and it didn't take long to happen. It was only three months after they had settled in Phoenix. Bill and Andy had arrived just minutes apart at the work site in Mesa, a complex of office buildings being erected by Dean Construction on the west side of the city. Bill hurried to catch up to his friend as they walked from a parking lot down the street.

"I have a huge favor to ask you, brother," Bill said, beaming as he slowed to Andy's pace.

"And what might that be?" Andy asked, thinking as he said it, as *if I didn't know.*

"I want you to be best man at my wedding! It's not right away. We're thinking of starting our new life on the New Year. How does that sound?"

Andy laughed and stopped, turning to his friend. "Sounds kind of poetic. I like it. You'll be adding to your family early in January, then Jean and I add to ours at the end of the month."

It was Bill's turn to laugh. "Uh huh. Believe it or not, I thought of that. It's going to be truly a New Year of celebrations." The two friends hugged one another, then turned to the day of work ahead of them.

***

Andy said nothing at the time, but he did wonder about Bill's winter wedding plans. It turned out that his doubts were justified. The year 1949 would go down in history as that of "The Great Blizzard" that swept across much of the United States. Arizona and New Mexico were both affected, bringing rare snow flurries through the Valley and rendering most mountain roads impassable.

Anna and Bill postponed their ceremony until spring. The Mayes' second child, however, was right on schedule.

Friday, January 28, 1949, Andy and Bill again paced side by side in a hospital waiting room, just as they had for Michael. Remembering the aversion to Bill's presence in the waiting room in Donelsburg, Andy made a point to research the medical facilities in the Valley. Then, he made arrangements for this birth to take place at St. Monica's Hospital, the only fully integrated hospital in Phoenix at that time. At 9:00 p.m., the waiting family and friends got the news. Martin Paul Mayes had made his way into the world.

Then, Andy, Jean, Michael, and baby Marty were all there on Saturday, April 2, at the Mount Zion Missionary Baptist Church in Gallup. Anna's older sister, Ruth, was Matron of Honor. Andy stood with Bill as the Best Man. It was a small wedding, perfect for the tiny church sanctuary: simple and profoundly beautiful.

It looked like 1949 would be a blessed year, indeed.

***

Years passed and, in many ways, things continued to get better. In other ways, they were frustratingly unchanged. Andy and Bill progressed in their work and their standing within Dean Construction. Responsibilities increased and, with them, came more pay. Bill had wanted to buy a home from the time of his marriage. He finally had enough income, but he could find no bank that would work with him if he remained within the boundaries of South Phoenix. And he could find no realtor or home owner that would sell to a Negro outside those boundaries. He was trapped. He was frustrated. Andy was furious.

Interestingly, it was some exciting, positive news that elevated Andy's fury to a fiery level. It was Monday, a hot day in June of 1952. The crew was breaking for lunch when Bill called them all around, saying, "I have an announcement. I'm going to be a daddy!"

The announcement was met by enthusiastic applause and cheers. Andy joined in, but then his mood suddenly changed.

"You need a bigger place," he said to Bill. "You need a house!"

"Come on, brother," Bill pleaded. "Don't ruin my mood now. I gotta just let that go."

"I'm sorry, Bill." Andy was sorry he'd said something at that moment. But he wasn't about to let it go. He'd do something. He just didn't know what yet.

Then, their foreman, Jack Barnes, said, "Let's celebrate! Everyone meet after work at La Cholla Bar and Grill. My treat!"

A couple of men shouted, "Yes!" But the rest just stood quietly staring at their boss. Suddenly, he realized what he had said. "I'm sorry, Bill. I just forgot. I-" He paused, measuring his words. "I forget about color." Another pause. "You're just Bill to me."

"It's okay," Bill replied, deflated. "I never heard of that place, but you just told me all I need to know."

Andy fumed. "You mean my friend can't even go have a drink with us? It's his celebration!"

"Not there," said Jerry Corbett, a mason on the project. "They wouldn't even let him in."

"Let's get to work," said Jack. "We'll find someplace else."

"No," Bill said. "I gotta get home to the wife. But thanks. I really appreciate it, guys."

Andy seethed over the injustice throughout the day. One of these days, they'd both go in that La Cholla place together, he thought. Things are going to change. He knew it. They just had to. And that change would begin soon, with Bill and Anna moving into their own house.

After work, Andy went to see the smartest and best connected person he knew. He drove to the office of Walter Dean.

When Andy finished the story of Bill's plight, his boss leaned back in his chair. "It's not right," he said aloud to himself. Then, he spoke to Andy. "We're going to take care of this. I'm good friends with the president of Maricopa Savings and Loan. I'll vouch for Bill, and he'll listen. Bill will get his loan, but he needs to find a seller. From what you said, that could be a problem."

"Not if he stays in South Phoenix," Andy replied.

***

Andy was proud to see so much turn around for his friend. The following September, Bill and Anna moved from their rented apartment on Southern Avenue to their own three-bedroom home on East Broadway. They began immediately furnishing one of the bedrooms to be a nursery.

March 3, 1953, Andy was back in St. Monica's Hospital's waiting room, this time pacing with Bill. Jean and the boys were there too when the doctor brought the exciting news. Bill was the father of a healthy, handsome baby boy, whom he and Anna named William Davis, Jr.

Emotions were high as the Mayes family drove home from the hospital. But then, Andy shifted it with what seemed to Jean a very strange question. "Have you ever thought of moving to a bigger house?"

"What?" she asked.

"You know, a bigger house, maybe in a nicer neighborhood."

Andy felt Jean's intense glare and decided he picked the wrong time to talk again.

"So you think because we have two bedrooms and the Davises have three, we have to keep up with them or something?"

"Oh, no. It's nothing like that. I've been thinking about it for a while now. The boys are getting older, and I think they should have their own rooms sometime soon. And our place is awfully small."

"I love our house," retorted Jean. "And we have the best neighbors possible, you've said so yourself." Andy nodded. Then, always the one to watch their finances, Jean added, "Our house fits great in our budget, we're actually catching up and doing okay. No, I haven't thought about a bigger house, and I don't want to."

That ended the conversation, but the thought stayed alive in the back of Andy's mind. It came forward with full force ten years later when he was told of the promotion of a lifetime and the pay to go with it.

Bill and Andy had been with Walter Dean for fourteen years. Only the owner had a longer tenure with the company. Walt had asked Andy to come by the office after work, and Andy felt like something big was about to happen. The last time his boss called him into his office was the year before to promote Andy to crew foreman. This felt very much like that meeting.

Mr. Dean stood as Andy walked in. He asked Andy to please be seated, then Dean walked around his desk and sat in a chair beside him.

"You've done an excellent job here, Andy," he said. "I couldn't be prouder of your knowledge, skill, or work ethic. And you've been here longer than anyone in the history of this company."

Andy wanted to say, "Bill and I came the same day," but he just said, "Thank you, sir."

"I've never had anyone as qualified as you, and I need to put that knowledge and skill to better use. I want you to consider taking on Construction Manager." Andy was stunned.

"That's a pretty big responsibility, sir. I'm humbled you think I'm up to it."

"I have absolutely no doubt. But you're right, it is a big job. You'll basically oversee all our operations. And it will mean some extra hours with no overtime, because you'll be on salary. But it's a good salary, Andy. You deserve it."

Andy thanked Walter Dean again. "I'd like to give it a try. I promise I'll do my very best for you."

"I know you will. Congratulations, Andy."

Andy's mind was racing as he drove home from work that day. He was mentally rehearsing how he'd break the news to his wife. And he was mentally rehearsing how he would let her know what he truly believed: the time had come to make that move.

To his delight, Jean agreed. They immediately made plans to list their house with a realtor and begin house-hunting. Jean kept their focus practical and frugal and, the first week of June, 1963, the Mayes family moved across town to a three-bedroom, one and one-half bath ranch house at 5038 Sierra Boulevard.

FORTY-FIVE

It was June 11, 1963. *What a night,* Marty thought. It felt like a ghastly dream: Dad's unusually late return home from work, his slurred speech and finally passing out on the bed. It was just awful.

Mom had insisted on cleaning up the mess. Bill and the two boys rolled Andy on the bed to make room for Jean to take off the unbelievably stinking bedspread. Then, she sent the boys off to bed, so she could talk one on one with Bill.

Marty moved closer to the right side of Michael's double bed, being extra careful not to crowd his brother. He couldn't bring himself to return to his new bedroom alone with its creepy shadows. To his surprise, Michael made zero fuss when he asked. It was a hard night for everyone.

Surely, Mom and Bill were in the living room by now. Apparently, Michael was thinking the same thing. Marty felt him shift, then sit up in bed. He looked over, and Michael turned, nodding his way.

The brothers stepped quietly together to the bedroom door, opening it a crack to listen in on the conversation.

"The entire crew was working late on that strip mall down in Scottsdale," Bill began. "One of the guys had a radio on, and we heard the news about integrating the university in Alabama."

"I had hoped Andy heard that," Jean said. "It's great news."

"Well, he did. He got real excited about it and said we needed to celebrate. I told him I thought it was too late to do anything tonight. We're both really tired, I said. But he was so energized and happy about it and, well, you know I can't say no to Andy."

Jean smiled. "So what happened?"

"We both had our cars, so I followed him to La Cholla Bar and Grill. I didn't know that's where he was headed and really felt uncomfortable when we pulled in the parking lot. I got out of the car and told him, 'Let's go someplace else, Andy. I won't be welcome here.' I told him that, Jean, and he knew it was true. But he just grinned and said, 'Come on, brother. It's a new day. The world is changing!' I said that change may be starting, but it's not here yet. But he insisted, Jean, and I was dumb enough to follow."

"You're such a good friend, Bill. It's not your fault Andy is so bull-headed. He gets an idea, and there's no stopping him. No one can."

"We went in the bar and got lots of stares, but no one said anything. I began to think we were going to be fine. We sat at a table, and the waitress came over and asked what we wanted. It was amazing. I ordered a beer, and Andy said, 'Bring me a CC and water.'"

"CC? What's that?"

"Canadian Club! It's whiskey, Jean! I've never known Andy to drink whiskey!"

"Never! Maybe a beer now and then. Andy didn't drink at all till he went in the army, and he's pretty much given all that up since then. Where did he even hear of this CC stuff?"

"I don't know, but, right after the waitress left for our order, this one man walked over to our table and just stood there. Then, another guy stepped up beside him. And that first one said, 'You boys don't belong here. Down those drinks and get the hell out.'

"Andy didn't say anything. The waitress brought our drinks, Andy gave her some bills and said, 'I'm mighty thirsty, miss. Please bring me another.' And then, he started slugging down that drink. I mean, Jean, he just drank it down fast! He was pushing everything, and I knew we were headed for trouble."

Bill's eyes were wide in shock as he relived the whole scene. He took a deep breath and let it out noisily before continuing.

"The waitress looked back at the bartender, and he was already pouring that drink. It should never have happened. He just should have stopped right there. But he poured the drink, and the waitress went to get it. The two men just stood there. They just stood there, Jean, staring at us like they couldn't believe what they saw. Andy got his drink, and I'll be damned if he didn't order another one! I said, 'Andy, no! Let's just go! It's getting late, we need to go home.'

"But they brought him that third drink, and he started drinking it. The men watched him drink, and that first guy yelled, 'Jesus Christ' and slapped the glass out of his hand. Then, the guy on the left grabbed me out of the booth. Andy jumped up and pushed the first guy back and started after the one who had me, but that first guy jumped back in and swung. He hit Andy hard. Andy came back swinging, and the second guy pushed me over and jumped into it. So I jumped in, too. It was fists everywhere, and then the first guy was on top of Andy, punching him like he wanted to kill him. Some people pulled him off and broke it up just before the police came.

"I'm so sorry. I knew I shouldn't go in." Bill lowered his face into his hands.

Jean slowly shook her head. "You've got nothing to be sorry about. This whole thing is so wrong. You had every right to be there, but Andy had no right to put you through this."

Bill looked up and sat quietly a moment. Then, he continued.

"There were two officers. They kept everyone apart and checked on Andy. He was awake, and they asked about a hospital. But he said no. They looked him over because he was pretty beat up. Then, they talked to the bartender and some of the people. Finally, they checked on me. They told me I didn't belong there and, if they ever heard of me in there again, I'd go to jail."

"You'd go to jail because you'd been in that fight?"

Bill looked at her in disbelief. "I'd go to jail because I was in the wrong place in the wrong part of town."

Jean sadly shook her head again. "I'm so sorry. What did you say?"

"I said, 'Yes, sir. I understand, sir, and it won't happen again.' Then, the police checked me over to see if they thought I could drive. I had one sip of one beer. So they told me, 'Take care of your friend and get the hell out of here.' We just left."

"Where's Andy's car?"

"I had to leave it there. I figured we could get it tomorrow. If Andy's able to work, I'll pick him up and drop him off there."

"No, Bill, I'll get Michael to take me tonight, and I'll drive it home. It's too far out of your way, and you've been through enough. Did you let Anna know what's going on?"

"I called her right after I called you."

"I hope this doesn't hurt our friendship," said Jean. "Now, you go on home. Please. Anna and Billy need you. She must be worried sick."

FORTY-SIX

Andy couldn't remember ever feeling quite so horrible with a combination of a headache, body ache, and nausea. But he showered, dressed, forced down breakfast, and let Jean cover his facial bruises as best she could with makeup that was far too light for his sun-bronzed skin. Then, he was off to Scottsdale and work. He said nothing about the night before beyond a sincere apology and an "I love you."

He and Michael were both dressed and gone before Marty made it out of bed. He'd slept very little, waiting for his big brother to return from getting his dad's car. Even then, he lay awake for what seemed like hours. He couldn't get over the shock of seeing his father in such horrible condition. And he wondered if he would ever feel comfortable in this strange, new house.

Marty wanted more than anything to return to 1012 Ocotillo Lane. Everything made sense there. It was home.

Marty had lived in the house on Ocotillo since Mom and Dad brought him home from the hospital. All his friends were there, including his very best friends in the world: Toni and Bobby Garcia, who lived next door. He was at their home almost as much as his own. Marty's plan for this very day was to ride his bike over to the old neighborhood for a visit. He had gotten Mom's okay and couldn't wait to see his friends.

Marty and Toni had grown up together, moving upward grade by grade at Saguaro Elementary. It was one of Casa Nueva's older elementary schools, housing all grades first through eighth. As of last year, with the city's amazing growth, there were now five such schools. All of these funneled into Casa Nueva High School, where Marty would enter as a freshman in the fall. He was glad Toni would be there, too, along with the rest of Saguaro's three eighth grade classes. They would have to wait for Bobby who was two years younger and would only be in seventh grade.

Toni had become very special to Marty the past several years. They both were quiet children, very reserved in crowds. But they talked and laughed easily together, often on the same offbeat wavelength with their humor. Marty was sure he was one of the few people who knew that the name Toni is actually short for "Antonia," which means priceless. Sometimes, when just the two of them were together, Marty liked to call his friend by her full name. She seemed to like it, too.

Bobby was actually Roberto Garcia, Jr. Marty's dad often said that Roberto and Anita Garcia were the best neighbors anyone could ever hope for. Andy seemed to love the old neighborhood as much as Marty. It just made no sense why they would move. Sure, his dad was about to get another substantial raise, and his mother was going back to work. But that was no reason to move when you already live in the perfect home.

Marty hurried through his usual breakfast, a large bowl of Cheerios topped with sliced banana. His mom offered to fry up some bacon and eggs like she had for Michael and Andy. Marty really appreciated that and said so. But today he was eager to see his friends.

He thought about the old neighborhood again as he rode his Schwinn Mark IV Jaguar across town. The bike was his pride and joy, given to him by his mom and dad just last year for his birthday. It had a horn, front and rear carriers, stainless steel fenders and a chrome headlight. With a bright red frame, it was a real beauty.

The Schwinn was his second favorite gift ever. The first was given by his parents for Christmas his seventh-grade year. It was still his most prized possession.

Marty turned onto Ocotillo, passed his old house, and rode into the driveway of 1014, home of Toni and Bobby. Toni must have been watching from the window. She walked out the front door as Marty pulled to a stop.

"Buenos dias, Antonia," Marty shouted, setting the Schwinn's kickstand with his right foot.

Toni laughed. "Buenos dias, mi amigo. Era un hermosa dia."

"Si. Si," Marty replied. "Yes, it is a beautiful day."

"I've got to say, Marty, you sound authentically Mexicano with your Spanish."

"Gracias, chica amable. But, remember, I grew up with your family. Who knows, it may come in handy someday when we want to talk around those Anglos and don't want them to know what we're saying."

"Keeping secrets? I like it!" Toni cocked her head to the side and winked.

Marty grinned. And blushed. Toni was flirting again. It used to make him uncomfortable, but now he really liked it. For a long time, they both had an unspoken understanding that they were more than just good friends. Someday soon, Marty hoped to make it official and ask Toni to be his girlfriend. There were a number of his friends at school who would not approve, but that was their problem.

Although Marty was the only non-Mexican in his immediate neighborhood, Saguaro Elementary School was about seventy percent white. Mexicans were the only minorities in the school, and they pretty much hung together. No one crossed those barriers even at the school lunch room, much less dating.

More often than Marty could say, there were after school fights, Anglo vs. Mexican. He hated it, because he had good friends on both sides. So he let that be known early on and, for the most part, both sides came to accept it. But dating? He'd cross that bridge when he came to it. But when would that be? Why not now?

"Toni?"

"Si."

"Quiero che sepas –" He paused.

"Okay, you want me to know... You want me to know what?"

"Quiero che sepas – me gusta."

Toni laughed. She had such a beautiful laugh. "I know, silly. I like you, too."

"No." Marty was struggling now. "I mean I – you know - like you."

Toni smiled and extended her left hand, palm up. Andy covered her hand with his right palm. Toni stepped closer. "I know," she said. "And I – you know – like you, too."

Suddenly, a loud voice shouted from the house through the screen door, making both of them jump.

"TONI AND MARTY SITTING IN A TREE!!"

They dropped their hands and turned toward the door.

"K-I-S-S-I-N-G!"

"Bobby Garcia!" Toni shouted.

Bobby walked out the door, laughing hysterically.

Toni waved an index finger at her brother and said, sternly, "El braguillas!"

Bobby put his hands on his hips and announced, "I am not a brat!"

"Well," Toni replied in mock annoyance, "you scared me to death!"

Bobby roared with laughter, clapping his hands. Then, Marty started to laugh and Toni finally dropped her angry façade and joined in the laughter. The three linked arms together in one big, three-person hug, laughing, and pushing each other around the front yard.

It's good to be home" Marty thought. *It's so good to be home.*

FORTY-SEVEN

It was a great day together. Toni, Bobby, and Marty walked over to Ricky Sapien's house several doors down. Ricky was the proud owner of a brand-new skateboard, the latest rage among young teens in the Phoenix area. He showed them how to push off and ride the board.

Ricky made it look easy, so Bobby was eager to try it. He put his left foot at the front of the board as he had seen his friend, Ricky, do. Bobby gave two good pushes with his right foot and mounted the board.

"Look at me! Look at me!" Bobby shouted, holding his arms to the side to balance and then fell, landing hard on his back onto the cement sidewalk. The others ran over to him.

Marty got there first. "Bobby! Are you okay?"

Bobby looked up, startled, and then started his usual loud, infectious laugh. "That was fun! I want to go again!"

And he did. And so did they all, perfecting the new pastime after multiple falls with few injuries except to their dignity.

Thus, Marty spent most of his day with Toni, Bobby, Ricky and several others of his friends from the old neighborhood. He walked back to the Garcia's with Toni and Bobby. Bobby went on into the house and Toni asked Marty if he'd like to come in, too, maybe watch some TV. Marty thought a second and said he'd better get home.

"Stay just a little longer," she said. "I want to show you something."

She took Marty's hand and walked ahead of him. Marty followed her lead, which took them to the side of the house and their very first kiss.

When he said goodbye, Marty got back on the Schwinn and pedaled away. But he stopped at the end of the block and gazed back at his old home and the house next door. His mind was spinning with all that had happened that day. So much had happened in this wonderful neighborhood, things that had shaped his very life.

Marty smiled as his mind turned to the amazing nighttime barbecues the Garcias loved to host, sometimes a couple a month through the summer. He had been to some of those, the guest of Toni and Bobby. But the ones that changed his life were before that, as he lay in bed listening through his bedroom window.

Andy and Michael's bedroom was adjacent to the Garcia's front yard, where the parties were held. Roberto, Anita, and guests would grill and eat there on the lawn. Then, they would play guitars and sing Spanish songs long into the night. Marty would lie on his top bunk, awake and enthralled by the sounds. He understood none of the words at that time, of course, but he was moved by often exquisite harmony and an occasional male voice lifting high into a soaring falsetto.

Marty couldn't remember the first time he listened to the Garcia family and their friends making music into the night. He truly grew up with it. But he could remember the feeling it gave him and the desire to have a guitar of his own. He once told Toni how much he loved to listen to the music. She told her father, who brought out his guitar one day when Marty was visiting. It was a Gibson acoustic, clearly old, and somewhat scratched but with a deep, rich sunburst finish. To Marty, it was the most beautiful thing he had ever seen.

Roberto told him to sit down and placed the guitar on Marty's lap. He showed Marty how to hold the guitar, helped him to form a C chord, and instructed him on a simple strum, straight down the top five strings with his thumb. That was the beginning of informal, periodic lessons with Roberto that soon had Marty playing and singing a number of songs, each using only C and G7. He progressed from there and, the more he learned, the more Marty wanted to play.

Marty asked his parents if he could have a guitar someday, and thus he received his most cherished possession on Christmas day, 1961. It was a brand-new Airline, sold by Montgomery Ward. Like Roberto's, the finish was sunburst. Unlike Roberto's, it had F shaped sound holes instead of a large round one in the center. The strings were a little harder to press down than Roberto's, but Marty mastered it and decided it sounded great. He took his guitar to the Garcia's moonlight barbecues twice after that and never felt so much a part of anything else before or since.

Making music with his neighbors was the first time Marty really felt connected or capable. It all seemed so easy for Michael. His brother was an athlete, excelling at every sport. He was popular and president of the junior class at CNHS. Michael had a great personality, at ease around anyone of any age. He was a top student in school and a respected employee where he worked in Phoenix at the International House of Pancakes.

Marty loved his brother dearly, and Michael had never been anything but good to him. But Marty dreaded following Michael as a new high school student. He knew the teachers would say, "Oh, your Michael Mayes' brother!

He was my best pupil!" And Marty would have to reply, "Don't get your hopes up. I'm no Michael Mayes."

Marty was an average student and a below average athlete. He had the personality of a tree stump, or so he believed, and he truly did get nauseated whenever he had to talk in front of his class at school. But something happened when he got behind his guitar. He suddenly felt confident and capable. And when he made music with his neighbors on Ocotillo Lane, he knew he belonged.

All this flashed through Marty's mind as he sat on his Schwinn, gazing at the neighborhood he loved. Then, he sighed, turned his bike, and headed to what now was home.

FORTY-EIGHT

Two more weeks passed in their new home. It was Monday, June 24, and Marty still had not met any neighborhood kids his age. Michael assured him that would change when school started. And it wouldn't hurt, Michael added, "to move on. You know, get out around this neighborhood and just let go of that old one."

Marty had already moved on in some ways. He actually liked their more spacious home now and the privacy of having his own room. He arranged it the way he wanted and even added a straight back chair and music stand to better practice his guitar.

There were other advantages to their new house. For instance, the house on Ocotillo was cooled by an evaporative or "swamp" cooler. It sat on the roof with a fan that blew air through vents in the house. The lower part of the cooler was a reservoir that held water. When the fan was turned on, water was pumped from the reservoir through straw pads. Air was drawn through the wet pads, cooling the house.

The swamp cooler actually worked really well except around mid-August. That's monsoon season in Arizona, when the Valley gets most of the year's rain. Pumping moist air into an already humid house could make what was often 110 degrees feel perfectly sweltering. Marty heard his mother complain about it, but he really didn't mind. At least, he didn't think he cared until they spent that first summer in the new house. It had air conditioning.

Air conditioning was quite a luxury in 1963 Arizona. Marty knew very few people who had it, although more and more of his friends' families were taking the leap. When Marty was younger, it seemed everyone cooled with evaporative. The one place he would go that did have air conditioning was the CN Cinema, downtown Casa Nueva. Marty thought sometimes his friends wanted to go to the summer matinee no matter what was showing, just to be together out of the heat.

He smiled to himself at that thought. It made him miss his friends all the more. But he was in a new neighborhood and new house on Sierra Boulevard. Michael was right. He should take it on himself to get out and about, to meet some new people. He decided to explore his street and beyond, to tour the surrounding blocks on his Schwinn. It felt good to get acclimated, and he actually did see some young teens in the area. He waved and they waved back, and he even stopped once to say hello. This might not be an entirely bad move after all.

There was one boy he did not wave at or speak to, even though he had seen him more than any others. The boy lived in the house behind theirs. The two houses faced in opposite directions with back yards sharing an alley. Each yard had a fence, Andy's a four-foot wooden basket weave, theirs a taller chain link. But Marty could stand at his own kitchen window and see this boy almost every day, staring sadly out the sliding glass back door.

Marty was intrigued by the boy. He looked high school age, perhaps fifteen or sixteen. He was always neatly dressed in a buttoned shirt tucked into what looked like dress slacks. That was standard fare for school, but it was summer in Arizona. It was time for T-shirts and cut-off jeans.

Marty guessed he was about five-foot-ten with light, sandy hair. He was a nice looking young man, but there was something strange about him. Marty had never seen him in his yard or anywhere outside his house. He would always be just standing there, looking out his back door.

At least once, Marty became aware that the boy was staring back at him. Marty started to look away but found he couldn't. Besides, why pretend? So they stood for several minutes, each watching the other without emotion or gesture. There seemed to be a profound sadness in the boy that moved Marty deeply in a peculiar, irrational way. He wanted to go to the boy, to somehow encourage him, tell him that everything would be just fine.

Marty thought about that odd sensation often after that. It made no sense to him, but he wanted very much to meet the boy. He asked Michael if he had seen him and, if so, did he know him.

"Yeah, I know him or at least I know about him. I didn't know where he lived until we moved here."

"What's his name?"

"Charles. Charles Dixon. He'll be a junior this year. But stay away from him, Marty."

"What do you mean?"

"He's weird. No, he's worse than weird. You don't want to know him, and you sure don't want people to think he's your friend."

"Why? What's wrong with him?"

Michael looked as if he was debating whether or not to continue. "Listen, Marty, you just have to trust me on this one. This guy shouldn't even be allowed at our school with all the normal people. But he comes. No one stops him. I've had him in classes, and he just gives me the willies."

"I still don't get it. What does he do?"

Michael seemed to be getting frustrated. He sighed and continued quietly. "He does nothing, at least not at school that I know of, anyway. I mean, he turns in his work. I guess he's smart enough. I've seen his name on the honor roll. But he's weird, Marty. He's a freak! No one likes him. A few times, guys have waited for him after school to just, you know, rough him up."

Marty was shocked. "Why? What's he done to deserve that?"

"It's not what he's done, Marty. It's what he is. Just stay away from him. You don't want to have people thinking that you're, well, you know."

Marty didn't know, and he didn't like the way his brother was talking. There was something terribly wrong in what he had just heard. Why was Michael okay with someone getting beat up for no reason? And Marty couldn't shake the feeling of profound sadness he sensed from the person he now wanted to meet more than ever.

"I trust you, Michael. You're a great guy, and I believe you want what's best for me. But you're not talking straight with me right now. You're not leveling with me about something. So tell me straight up. What's the problem with this Charles Dixon? Why have people been so mean to him, and why are you okay with that?"

"The guy isn't normal. He's a queer, Marty. The pervert is a queer."

FORTY-NINE

Marty had heard the word before. He never liked it. It always seemed hateful and cruel, a slur against a boy who was different, a smear that often triggered smirks or giggles all around. He knew what it was supposed to mean, but it more often referred to the way a boy talked or walked or his preferences of, say, art over sports. Marty's realization of what prompted the word hit home because many of the traits he saw attacked by that word could easily have been turned against him.

The word sounded completely out of place coming from his brother. How could he speak so easily of guys attacking someone, beating him up just because he was different? Michael made a point of saying Charles did nothing to provoke or deserve such a thing. Did Michael see the attack? Did he participate? Marty put that out of his mind. His brother would do no such thing.

Still, Michael talked like he had no problem with it. It made no sense. All the conversations they shared as a family screamed against it. Like that thing Mom kept quoting from the president's talk. How did it go? President Kennedy said all Americans should have "the kind of equality of treatment that we would want for ourselves." Those words sure impressed Mom. They seemed to impress Michael, too.

Michael said nothing about Charles Dixon that made him sound like a bad person. Marty wanted to see for himself. He decided to pay Charles a visit. Michael had told him to get acquainted with the new neighborhood, right?

He told his mom that he was going for a ride. She asked if he was going any place in particular, and he told her. "I'm going to meet the neighbors who live behind us." And he took the Schwinn around the block.

Marty felt nervous as he walked up to the front door. It was a nice home, very similar to their own, what Mom called a "ranch-style" house. He took a deep breath and rang the doorbell. To his surprise, Charles answered the door. He was dressed as Marty had always seen him, with a neatly ironed button shirt tucked into tan dress slacks. A second surprise: Charles broadly smiled and said, "Hi. Come on in."

"Uh, hi! Thanks. My name's Marty Mayes. We just moved into the house behind yours and, well, I just wanted to, uh, get acquainted."

"I'm glad you did. My name's Charles. My family and friends call me Charlie. I've seen you there sometimes. And heard you, too. You play pretty good."

"You heard me play guitar? How?"

"Sometimes, when I'm in the backyard, I can hear you. It's not loud or anything, but sometimes you really get into it! I like it. It sounds like Spanish music, Flamenco or something like that."

Marty laughed. "Yeah. Well, there's a reason for that."

Marty followed Charlie through the living room. There was a Wurlitzer upright piano along one wall, and Marty stopped a moment to admire it. "That's really nice," he said. "Do you play?"

"As a matter of fact, I used to play all the time for our church. I've kind of switched over now. That's what I want to show you."

"Hello, young man."

Marty jumped a bit, as he was still admiring the piano and didn't see the woman walking into the living room from the hallway. He turned and smiled at the attractive woman in her late thirties. Like Charlie, she seemed to be, what Marty considered anyway, dressed for church. She wore a dark navy-blue skirt and plain, white blouse. Her hair was pulled tightly into a bun which seemed somehow out of place with her youthful complexion. Marty suddenly felt underdressed in his typical summer attire of sandals, shorts, and a T-shirt.

"I'm Charlie's mother, Pam," the woman said, standing stiffly with hands folded in front of her. She seemed nervous for some reason. Marty noticed that, when she spoke, her voice was soft, almost a whisper. Her smile looked forced. Marty felt she was a very nice person, but he somehow felt sorry for her. She seemed distressed and unhappy.

"Nice to meet you, Mrs. Dixon. I'm Marty Mayes. We moved into the house across the alley from you a few weeks ago. You have a lovely home." Marty's parents had taught him well.

"Marty's the one I told you about, Mom. The one who plays the guitar. I was going to show him my Guild."

"That's great, Charlie, but you know the rules. Get your guitar and bring it out in the living room. I'll get you boys some drinks. Do you like your ice tea sweetened or unsweetened, Marty?"

"Oh, thanks, ma'am. Sweet, please. My father's family's all from Alabama and he always says, 'Southerners drink their ice tea sweet and the sweeter the better.'"

"Sweet it is." With that, Pam headed for the kitchen, and Charlie led the way down the hall into his bedroom.

Marty saw it as soon as he walked through the door. It was in an open hard-shell case and looked like no other guitar he had ever seen. The body was small, and the three top strings looked like plastic. Charlie read his look and smiled.

"It's a classical, Marty, a Guild Mark 1. I had another used classical that Dad got me to learn on several years ago, saying when I could really play he'd upgrade to something nicer. He kept his promise last year with this beauty."

Marty smiled. "Looks nice." But he still wasn't sure what to make of it.

"Let's take it to the living room. I have an understanding with my parents."

"Sure." Marty flashed back to what Michael had said. But he put the thought quickly out of his mind and led the way out of the bedroom, followed by Charlie, Guild Mark 1 in hand.

Two glasses of ice tea were waiting for them, but Pam Dixon was not in sight. Charlie sat in a chair, and Marty sat expectantly across from him. Charlie strummed an open G chord. Marty liked the sound. It was quieter than his metal string Airline, with a mellow tone. He waited to hear more.

Charlie plucked the bass string with the thumb on his right hand, still holding an open G chord on the neck with his left. Then, the fingers of his right hand played an arpeggio up and down the strings: first, the thumb on the bass and a different finger for each of the highest four strings. He followed that same pattern as he moved through a chord progression. Marty recognized the chords: G, D, E minor, C. Then, Charlie continued higher on the guitar neck with several chords Marty had never learned.

Charlie finished playing through the progression several times, humming a tune Marty had never heard. It was haunting, beautiful.

"What is that song, Charlie? It's amazing."

"It's one I'm working on right now."

"You write your own songs?"

"That's what they call it, but I really don't know. It seems like songs are out there waiting to find someone listening for them. Sometimes, I look at a song that's found me and gets sung through me, and I'm just amazed by it. I don't know where it comes from, but I want to keep open and give it some kind of voice."

"I'd like to bring my guitar and play some with you, Charlie, if that's okay."

"I was hoping we'd meet, and you'd say that, Marty. I was a little worried though."

"Why?"

"Because the first person I saw at your house was Michael Mayes, and I got scared. I know he's your brother, Marty, but—" He paused. "I've said enough."

"No, tell me. It's okay. What?"

"Well, it's like this Marty; I'm sorry to say it, but your brother just isn't a very nice person."

FIFTY

Marty rode his Schwinn home with Charlie's words still ringing in his ears. He didn't ask him to explain or give any details about what he said. Marty felt like he already had a pretty good idea. But everything was so confusing. Michael was the perfect son, the perfect student, the perfect everything. But he knew about the attack on Charlie. It sounded like he was there. It almost sounded like he approved.

Could Michael have been part of that gang of thugs? Marty shivered at the thought. Part of him said, no way. No way could he have done such a thing. But then, he wouldn't have believed how Michael talked about Charlie if he hadn't heard it with his own ears. Michael is the popular kid, the big football hero. Would he stand up to his buddies if it put their friendship at risk?

Marty shook his head as he turned the corner onto his street. Charlie didn't say much, but what he did say matched what Marty had heard from Michael himself. That made Marty horribly uneasy. The more he thought about it, the more it seemed possible, even likely.

Marty rode up the drive and parked his bike behind the house. He walked to the door and resolved not to say anything to Michael yet. He'd watch and listen until he felt more sure, one way or another. But one thing he did know: whatever Michael may have done that caused Charlie to say he's "not very nice person," it wouldn't stop him from pursuing some music time with his new friend. They had agreed that Marty should bring his guitar over the next day, and they would experiment with some songs. Marty had promised Toni and Bobby a visit tomorrow, but he'd call tonight and explain. He'd still come over to the old neighborhood later.

There was lively conversation at the dinner table that night. A lot of changes were ahead in the fall. Good changes. Marty knew that his father was due a big promotion. He was already foreman of his crew, overseeing work on a particular site. Walter Dean was promoting Andy again to Construction Manager for his company. Andy would oversee multiple sites, allocating resources, assuring codes were being met, and so on.

The family knew all that. It was one of the main reasons they had made the decision to "move up" to the new neighborhood. No, the good news Andy shared at dinner tonight was that, when he moved out of position as site foreman, Bill would be his replacement. It was news all the family was excited to hear.

"It couldn't have happened to a more capable or deserving person," said Andy.

"It's wonderful, dear," Jean chimed in. "Just please don't celebrate with drinks at La Cholla Bar and Grill."

Andy winced, and Jean was sorry she'd said it. "I'm sorry," she apologized. "It just came out."

That was an experience Andy was doing his best to put behind him and had actually not been brought up since the night it happened. Jean made a quiet promise to herself not to bring it up again.

The big job changes for Andy and Bill were scheduled to happen sometime in late August. Then, Jean had her own big change scheduled for the fall of 1963.

Jean had been happy to stay home fulltime while the boys were in school. But both she and Andy knew that she would need to return to work eventually. She had kept books at her parents' store from the time she was in high school until they moved to Phoenix. She was eager to return to the workplace.

Jean decided what she would like to do was go back to school in preparation to teach math. She enrolled fulltime at Phoenix College in 1957 feeling, at thirty years-old, very much like a mom to other students. But she persevered and entered Arizona State University in Tempe as a junior. It took her six years, but she graduated the previous May, magna cum laude. She was immediately hired by Casa Nueva High School and would be starting there in the fall when her "baby" was enrolled as a freshman. Talk about changes.

So there was a lot of excitement and chatter around the table that night, which culminated in Jean asking Marty how his visit went with their neighbors. All eyes turned to Marty who said, "Oh, fine. They're nice." He felt Michael's eyes staring at him, but his brother said nothing.

"What neighbors did you visit?" his father asked.

"The neighbors behind us. They're the Dixons and, like I said, they're nice. There's a boy a couple years older than me named Charlie. He's a really good musician, Dad. He plays piano and is amazing on the guitar. I learned a lot just being with him for few minutes today."

"What do you know about his family?" asked Jean.

"His mother was nice, and Charlie seemed real respectful of her. I didn't meet his father. Guess he was at work or something. Charlie invited me to bring my guitar tomorrow. I want to do that. I know it will help me in my playing."

"Sounds like good folks," Andy said. Then, he addressed Jean. "I think I need to stop over and meet them myself. Be good to get acquainted with our neighbors and especially since it seems like our son will be spending a good deal of time over there."

"That's a good idea," Michael said.

All eyes turned to Michael, but he just returned to eating dinner. The others did the same and nothing further was said about it.

Actually, nothing further was said until after dinner when Michael followed Marty into his room. Michael closed the door.

Marty turned, ready for a fight. "What?"

"I can't believe you went over there after what I told you."

"Believe it. I wanted to see for myself, and what I saw was, you were wrong, Michael. Charlie's a really good guy. If I see anything different, I just won't go back."

"You're going to my school next year, Marty. I know how they can be if they see you and Charlie together."

Marty sat down on his bed with a sound somewhere between a growl and a scream. All his speculation during his ride home from Charlie's came back with a fury. This was it. It was time to speak.

"So that's what this is about," Marty snarled with an intensity that startled his brother. "Don't worry, Michael. No one will shun you because of me. And I don't want to be friends with the gang of bullies you hang with. Did you beat up on him, too, Michael? That's it, huh? You were the tough guy, so tough with all of you ganging up on one guy who did nothing to you? So tough because you were afraid the creeps wouldn't like you if you didn't go along?'"

Michael clenched his fist and scowled but turned, opened the door, and walked into the hall, closing Marty's door behind him. Marty's words stung. He was authentically concerned about his little brother, but he was also in a bit of shock at how much of what Marty had said hit home.

FIFTY-ONE

Marty went to his neighbor's at the agreed on time, carrying his Airline across the back alley. Charlie was standing at the gate to let him into their back yard.

Charlie's Guild was waiting for them in the living room. As they strummed some chords together, Marty was surprised by the difference in tone. His pick against the Airline's metal strings sounded strident and harsh next to Charlie's fingers on his classical. But Marty decided that the sounds fit their different styles and made for an interesting contrast. He had learned to play listening to Roberto's powerful, Spanish rhythms. He still liked that sound, but Charlie was opening him to new possibilities.

Marty asked Charlie to play one of his original songs. "I'll watch and follow along the best I can."

Charlie thought a moment, then smiled. "I just finished this one last night," he said and softly began a chord progression Marty found strangely familiar. He realized it was the song Charlie had played the day before, finger-picking its arpeggios, humming its tune, saying, "This is one I'm working on now."

After playing through the chord progression, Charlie started to sing gently, softly.

> The back of the class, the second row,
> He seldom speaks, they mustn't know
> How much it hurts, each verbal blow.
> He keeps himself invisible.

She sits in church, alone, apart
To hide her fear, protect her heart;
Don't say too much, just play the part.
You're safe when you're invisible.

Don't let them know, don't let them see
Your fragile soul, humanity.
Hide every vulnerability.
But you'll die in this invisibility.

It just takes one to be a friend;
Just one, real kindness to extend;
Someone you'll trust, reveal your soul
Or it will die, invisible.

The melody was haunting, heartbreaking. When Charlie finished his song, there was a long silence. Charlie looked at Marty and shrugged. Marty shook his head.

"That was incredible, Charlie. I can't believe I know someone who can write like that. The song, the words, and music are beautiful. But it's so sad."

"Yeah, I guess most of the songs I write are. But I think they're real. Life can be pretty sad."

"I guess so," Marty said. A moment of silence passed between them. "The song talks about being alone in church. You told me that you used to play piano at church. What happened?"

"It's simple enough," Charlie said. "They didn't want me anymore. I was contaminating them." Charlie laughed. "Oh, come on, Marty. You're Michael Mayes' brother! Surely, he's told you plenty about me by now."

"Yeah, sure. But then, I met you. I figured it was all lies."

"I have no doubt that, whatever he told you, ninety-nine percent of it was a lie, nasty gossip nastily spouted by nasty people. But there was one percent that was probably true. Let's go outside, Marty. I don't want to talk about this in here. I'll tell you all about it."

Marty wasn't sure that he wanted to know, but he followed Charlie out the door into the backyard. Charlie led him to a couple of lawn chairs and gestured for him to sit. Charlie paced a moment then sat down opposite Marty. He began to talk softly, carefully measuring his words.

"Gossips don't care about truth, Marty. They just like it juicy. You'd expect that. What's sad is when the church doesn't care, either. Oh, they like to quote the Bible saying it's the inerrant word of God and all. But then, they pick and choose what to quote. I grew up with that, and I believed everything they told me. So when they quoted and said, 'Thou shalt not lie with a man as with a woman; it is an abomination,' I was right there with them. It's so serious, the Bible says that a man with another man deserves to die!

"That's scary stuff, Marty. It was always scary, but it was, like, nightmare scary as a teen who's told it's about him! But I grew up in the church, and my gut said that part didn't fit with what I'd learned about God. I mean, these teachers took it literally that a homosexual deserved to die. I'm not saying they would do it, but they said it was God's word. And even if you had feelings like that, you deserved to die. That just didn't make sense. That's when I started seeing all these verses the church leaders ignored.

"Did you know the Bible tells us to kill a kid who talks back to his parents? It's true! Leviticus 20 verse 9. There goes every teenager I know!

"But the Bible says it's an abomination, like over a hundred other things. Marrying a foreigner's an abomination. So's wearing two kinds of fabric or sacrificing to God when you're a hypocrite, now that covers a few folks I know! But my Sunday School teachers never taught about those. And I can't remember them teaching what the Bible says about lying and gossip, how our words hurt, and the Bible talks about those things a lot more than, well, than the other." Charlie laughed, and shook his head.

"You sure know a lot about the Bible, Charlie."

"Well, I guess I should. My father's the preacher."

"The preacher! You mean the preacher at the church that, uh –" Marty couldn't bring himself to finish the sentence.

"Yeah. That kicked me out. Makes you proud, huh? Oh, they didn't say I couldn't come to church. They said a sinner like me shouldn't be up front, leading. So I couldn't be their musician anymore. And, honestly Marty, my dad's a really great guy. He really is. He's a good father and a great pastor. He's so loved by the church. If he wasn't, he would have been fired on the spot when they heard."

"How did they hear?"

"In a way, I told them. I've always known I was different somehow, but I didn't know what it meant. Then, adolescence hit, and all my friends were talking about this girl or that one. I'd jump in with, 'Wow! Look at her!' Like that, you know? But I was just saying words, trying to fit in. But I started noticing that, well, I started noticing that I was attracted to guys."

Charlie was silent a moment, then lifted both hands to the side, palms up, in what Marty perceived as, "I don't get it."

"Attracted to guys," he repeated. He lowered his arms to his sides and sighed. "I didn't want that. I still don't! I went to our public library and then the big, Phoenix library. I searched the card files and periodical guides, pouring over books and magazines. And I learned a lot, Marty.

"I learned that President Eisenhower signed an executive order just five years ago, banning homosexuals from working anywhere in the federal government. I learned that the medical world says it's a mental illness, and the church says it's a sin."

Charlie looked at Marty and shook his head. Marty nodded, understanding, but not knowing what to say. Charlie continued.

"Everyone seemed to say the answer is easy. Just change. But I also learned that people from the homophile community – that's what they called it – those people said it wasn't their choice to change. It was who they were, how they were born to be. I learned that there are groups now, like the Mattachine Society for men and the Daughters of Bilitis for women. They both formed about ten years ago to support, to welcome, and help. They speak up, questioning the meanness and hate. I want to be someplace like that, Marty, and it seems to me that it ought to be the church.

"I grew up in the church. I've always loved the church and the things my father taught about how God loves and accepts us. I believed that, but the more I learned, the more I was afraid. I needed to talk to someone, and I don't trust anyone in the world more than my father.

"So I just asked him one day if I was saved, and he said, absolutely. And I asked him, what if I sinned, and he said, 'Confess it and ask forgiveness. God is faithful.' So the next Sunday, I came forward and said I was asking God's forgiveness, and my dad prayed for me, and everybody cheered. But nothing changed.

"Then, I realized I really hadn't said exactly what I was confessing, so I told my father in private and asked if I should confess to the whole church next Sunday. Dad asked if I'd ever done anything— with a boy, I mean." Charlie laughed, a sound that seemed to Marty empty and sad. "I said, no, I wasn't even sure what that meant. I just wasn't attracted to girls. He said don't say anything to anyone right now. We needed to pray and think about it first.

"I said, 'okay,' and then my father told them." Charlie let out his empty laugh again.

"Your father told the church?"

"My father has two men he tells everything to. He calls them his prayer partners. He met with them and asked for prayer. He asked them not to say anything to anyone yet, he just needed prayer for me and wisdom for him.

"They agreed and kept quiet. But time passed, and they didn't like the secrecy. They asked my father, and he said not yet. But one of them told one person. Just one. You know how that goes. It spread through the whole church. There was a big meeting at the church, and someone got up and said I would have to repent and turn from my sin.

"Repent! If that means asking forgiveness, I did. If that means stop doing something, how do you stop a feeling? I tried, Marty. It doesn't work."

Charlie sat quietly for a moment and then said, with conviction, "I've worked it out for myself. I've studied the Bible and, as far as I can see, these people pick a few verses and use them to hate when the big word is love. Read what Jesus says, Marty. It's love and not judging other people."

Charlie started to tremble ever so slightly. "The big sin is hate. And the worst things are lies and gossip. That's what they do, Marty. That's what they do."

Marty saw a tear form in Charlie's eyes and felt his own begin to well.

"So I just try to do what's right, to cause no trouble, to forgive when I get punched out by someone like –" He paused and looked down.

"Someone like my brother?"

"I'm sorry, Marty. It isn't just him. It's the whole school; it's the whole church. I hear stories about things I've done with guys and not one of them is true. I just tried to be honest about how I feel, to show people who I am inside. But, well, they won't hear it. They can't see it. Like the song says, I'm invisible."

Marty stood up and walked to Charlie's side and laid a hand on his shoulder. Charlie placed his hand over Marty's, lowered his head, and wept. Marty thought how, any other time, this would feel awkward and uncomfortable, but it did not. At least, not to Marty or Charlie.

However, across the alley and watching from the Mayes' kitchen window, Michael felt uncomfortable, indeed.

FIFTY-TWO

It was dinnertime at the Mayes' home, and Jean had prepared a family favorite. It was "Taco Night," with beef tacos, cheese quesadillas, and chips. All were at the table, eager and ready, when Andy asked if Marty had visited the Dixon's as planned.

"It was really good, Dad. Charlie wrote this incredible song. He just finished it last night. And I found out that his father is a minister."

Andy opened his taco to spoon in hot sauce, homemade by Jean from Anita Garcia's own recipe. "A minister, huh? What church?"

"I don't know, but it seems he's been there a pretty long time. I haven't met him yet, but Charlie seems to really respect him. I think he's a good guy."

"Well," Andy said, "I may get a chance to meet him tonight. I plan to make a visit after dinner."

"What will you say?" asked Marty, feeling a bit apprehensive.

Andy smiled. "Not to worry, son. It's just a neighborly visit, parents of two friends getting acquainted."

Andy wondered about their neighbors as he walked around the block to their home. Marty had told him very little, only that his friend, Charlie, played guitar and that Mr. Dixon was a minister.

Reverend Dixon. Hmm. Andy wondered what kind of "reverend" he was, what kind of church he served. Was it the fire and brimstone preaching he faintly remembered (and feared) from early in his childhood in Dearing? Or was it the more cerebral (should he say, "languid"?) services of the Hartley's Methodist church in Donelsburg?

Andy liked the various pastors he had met through the years at Donelsburg First Methodist. They were open and accepting, always welcoming to him though he seldom darkened the doors of their church. But neither the Dearing preacher nor the several Donelsburg pastors who made their way through First Church seemed to connect to the reality where he lived. He left every church experience thinking, "Nice, but nowhere relevant."

He had to admit, things were definitely better since their move to the Valley. Jean grew up in church and, soon after their move, talked about how much she missed it. He grudgingly agreed to go along with her to visit First Methodist in Casa Nueva. It was quite a surprise. The ritual was essentially the same as in Donelsburg, and the hymns were mostly familiar. The difference was the minister. He talked about the Christian call to justice, and he spoke with passion.

The pastor, what was his name? Reverend Davis! Yes, that was it. Andy remembered because he had the same last name as Bill. Rev. Davis was a veteran of the war, a chaplain in the army serving in the European theater. That first Sunday they visited, he spoke eloquently of another great fight going on back then in 1948. It was the fight for civil rights for all people, regardless of race. He talked about the shameful ways Negroes were discriminated against in our own armed services.

"These brave men were fighting and dying for our country," he said, "but I personally saw how they were not allowed to be with their white brothers in the battle, how they were separated and treated poorly. I applauded President Truman in his executive order, calling for 'equality of treatment and opportunity for all persons in the armed forces.' But the fight goes on here, too. It's a fight for dignity and respect, for all the human family."

Andy remembered how those stirring words resonated with what he personally believed. He was moved again to learn that, just that previous April, their current pastor, Rev. Stephen Moore, had taken leave of his local church duties to march with Dr. Martin Luther King, Jr. in Birmingham, Alabama. Rev. Moore returned, on fire with excitement for the movement King was leading.

Andy had caught that fire. He knew the reality of racial discrimination: in Birmingham, in Dearing and, yes, in Phoenix. It was heartbreaking that a couple as decent as Bill and Anna Davis could be told where they could and could not live. Oh, there were no laws on the books in Phoenix, but the unwritten rules were not to be broken. The homes simply were "not available" to Negroes, except in certain neighborhoods in South Phoenix. It was so wrong.

But there was hope in the air. There was hope with a strong president who was not afraid to do the right thing, even when it was not the popular thing. There was hope when courageous people of faith acted in behalf of justice for all. And it took courage. A large part of First Methodist Church was up in arms, screaming that their minister should be about "religious" things instead of joining some troublemaking agitator like King. But what could be more Christian than reaching out to lift up the needy and hurting?

Andy smiled. That's the kind of minister he wanted to hear. As he walked to the Dixon's front door and lifted his index finger to the doorbell, he wondered. What kind of minister am I about to meet now?

FIFTY-THREE

He was six-foot-two at the very least, or so it seemed to Andy as the minister stood in the doorway before him. He was an impressive man: tall with thick brown hair combed back and Hollywood good looks. He wore dark gray trousers and a long sleeve white shirt, a blue and gray striped tie loosened at its open collar. Andy was glad that he had already showered and changed from his work clothes immediately after arriving home that day.

"Hello," the man said. "Can I help you?"

Andy smiled. "Rev. Dixon, I'm your new neighbor, Andy Mayes. I live behind you on Sierra Boulevard."

"Oh, yes! Please do come in, Mr. Mayes."

"I hope it's not a bad time. I just wanted to stop by a few minutes and get acquainted."

"No, it's fine. Really. We've had dinner and were just relaxing a bit. This is my wife, Pamela."

Mrs. Dixon stood up and walked to Andy, extending her right hand. "Please, call me Pam. I'm so glad our sons have become friends. Your Marty seems like a wonderful young man."

"Thank you, Pam. And I've heard very good things about Charlie."

Rev. Dixon gestured to the sofa. "Please have a seat and let's talk. And please call me Ralph. I still haven't gotten used to 'Reverend,' even after over twenty years in the ministry."

"Thank you, Ralph. Marty told me you are a pastor. Where do you serve?"

"It's an independent congregation here in Casa Nueva called Grace Fellowship. I've been there fifteen years, only the second church I've served since seminary. It's been through huge changes over all those years, some good, some maybe not so good. But that's another story. Tell me about yourself, Andy."

And thus began a conversation that lasted well into the evening, so surprisingly engaging and transparent that Ralph actually forgot that he had a regularly scheduled deacons meeting at the church that night, something he heard about at great length the following Sunday. Charlie had been in his room when Andy arrived, listening with great interest by his bedroom door. After about thirty minutes, Ralph called to him to join them.

Andy came home through their backyards, across the alley. His wife greeted him with a hug. "My, that must have been quite a visit."

"These are really decent people, Jean. And, yes, it was quite a visit. I think we were all shocked at how everything opened up so fast between us."

"How much can you tell me about it?"

"They didn't swear me to secrecy or anything. I think they assumed we would talk. Let's go out and enjoy an Arizona 'sort-of-cool' summer night."

Jean laughed and led her husband out the back door. It was just "sort of" cool at seventy-nine degrees with no breeze. But she directed Andy's attention to the breathtaking explosion of stars above them.

"Such a beautiful night," she said as they sat down side by side in lawn chairs. "And it sounds like I'm going to hear about an amazing visit."

"Ralph Dixon is minister at Grace Fellowship. It's that fairly large church over on Holly Street."

"Oh, yes. I've seen it there."

"It was small when he came there fifteen years ago, but it's grown, I imagine through his leadership. The house the Dixons live in was bought as a parsonage specifically for Ralph, an upgrade of the house the church owned before.

"When the Dixons came to Casa Nueva, the congregation was called Grace Baptist Church. Ralph said it was part of the Northern Baptist denomination. But in the 1950s, the deacons convinced the church members that the denomination was getting too 'liberal.' It had changed its name to 'American Baptist' and started talking a lot about race relations and participation in the civil rights movement."

"Wow," Jean said, wide-eyed. "Now that's interesting!"

"You bet. Even more interesting, Ralph was all aboard with the changes, but the majority rallied against him. He almost quit over it but decided to be there as an agent for change. Unfortunately, over time, he just settled in to keeping it peaceful and comfortable."

"He said 'unfortunately'?"

"His exact word, Jean. The church voted to leave the denomination and go independent, no denominational ties. The leadership changed its name to Grace Fellowship. Ralph stayed with them, and the church grew. And I'm not surprised. He's personable and easy talk to. I bet he's a great preacher and pastor. So, like I said, Grace Fellowship grew, added on to their building and bought a nicer parsonage, the house the Dixons live in now. But Ralph kept thinking about his vow to lead them to change. He said he played it safe. He's got a nice home, good salary.

He didn't rock the boat and now he's ashamed of that, I think."

Andy stood up and began to pace. He turned to his wife and said, "I was amazed how much he shared on a first meeting like that. It was pretty intense, Jean."

"It sounds like it!"

Andy sat back down and leaned toward Jean. "I must have just come at the right time. Something seems to be nudging him back to his civil rights message. I think he pushed the envelope a few weeks ago. He told me about a sermon he did on the church's name; you know, the meaning of the words 'grace' and 'fellowship.' He said half the church thanked him because that message really needed to be heard. The other half was ready to fire him because he was getting too 'political.' Can you believe that? He told me, 'I guess when the gospel hits home, it's called meddling.'"

Jean laughed. "I think I like this guy," she said.

"You'll never guess what he said next."

"What's that?"

"He said, 'I keep thinking about what President Kennedy said. And I truly believe that the church above all places ought to give others 'the equality of treatment we would want for ourselves.'"

Jean's jaw dropped. "You're kidding."

"That's what he said."

Jean smiled. "Now, I know I like this guy."

FIFTY-FOUR

It was Sunday, June 30, and Michael Mayes was up, showered, and out the door before anyone else in his family was awake. He was glad to have a summer job and was banking most of his earnings. But just one month into bussing dishes at Phoenix's favorite breakfast restaurant was already starting to grow tiresome.

He looked fondly at two summers before when he was able to help his father as a construction laborer. It was the summer after his freshman year and his first real, paying job working alongside his dad and the rest of the guys. But that opportunity wasn't available last summer with his dad's promotion and shifting responsibilities. So last year it was working with a landscaping and lawn care company, taking care of various commercial properties around the Valley.

This year it was everything from clearing tables and carrying loads of dirty dishes to the kitchen to taking out trash and mopping up sticky, syrupy concoctions off the dining room floor. But, still, he really was happy to have the income, and it was just for the summer. He'd bank every penny he did not need for gas, auto insurance, and weekend dates with Sarah Hensley, the prettiest girl at CNHS and next year's head cheerleader. He was a lucky guy.

So Michael was actually whistling as he parked in the employee area of the House of Pancakes. It was a song he'd heard on the radio on the way to work that morning, a catchy tune by the Four Seasons, "Walk like a Man." Michael liked that song a lot. It's what he wanted to do, and it seemed to be happening. He had respect. That was important. And he hung out with the popular crowd. He worked hard to be there, to be a top student and athlete, to walk like a man.

Some of his friends had stopped in to see him a couple of times at the restaurant. So far, they all knew better than to bother him at work or get in the way. They were good guys, solid students and athletes. Michael hoped that none of them heard about Marty hanging out with the queer. It could hurt Marty's freshman year. Hell, it could reflect on him!

But something about this whole budding relationship between Marty and Charles Dixon was troubling Michael in a very strange way. He loved his brother. More than that, he respected and trusted him.

Michael hated the way things looked, when he saw Charles take Marty's hand in the Dixon's back yard Wednesday afternoon. But he was also sure that it wasn't what it seemed, at least not from his brother's perspective. Marty was just being kind, he thought, reaching out to someone hurting. And Charles did seem to be hurting, accepting Marty's friendship. It's was all innocent enough, Michael thought. Sure it was! No, he was sure it was innocent, but it was all so confusing. Michael shook his head. He didn't know what to think anymore.

Then, Michael remembered the way he had treated Charles. He thought of the cutting words from Marty, words that had more truth in them than he wanted to admit. His mind flashed with the image of Charles, confused and afraid, as he and five other guys circled around him after school that day.

How did he get tangled up with those guys, anyway? But he joined with them as they mocked and harassed Charles day after day. Then, one day, it just got out of hand. They circled Charles like a pack of wolves after its prey. Six of them surrounded him, calling him names, pushing him from one to another around the circle. And Michael did it, too. He may have been the one who threw the first punch, he couldn't remember. But, at some point, the hassling escalated to hitting and then kicking.

School was out, and they were off the grounds. No teachers came to Charles' rescue, nor did any of his fellow students, though a number of the kids did circle their circle, vultures getting their own bizarre voyeuristic kicks. Though he doubted anyone could tell by watching, it disturbed Michael at that time that he was part of such an act. Looking back now, it more than disturbed him. He was appalled and ashamed.

Work went fine. They were insanely busy, but that was typical of any Sunday. They especially geared up for the after-church crowd. Then, when the majority of the lunch crowd had left, Michael's main duties involved extensive cleanup in the slack before dinner. He was anticipating this when he noticed some of his high school gang, the same cocky, conceited, self-privileged five that he joined in harassing Charles. Michael shook his head and wondered. With all the decent, positive students in all his classes and on all his teams, why in the world was he ever with them? What frightened him was the danger that he was becoming one of them.

These guys were louder than his other friends, rowdier, laughing together at a volume that disturbed other customers. Michael did his best to ignore them and focus on his work bussing tables. But they shouted out to him by name, calling him over to their table. He tried to wave them off. He wasn't supposed to visit with the customers. They were going to get him in trouble. Finally, he stepped over just to quiet them, to ask them to please settle down.

"Hey, Michael!" It was Brian Markey, the loudest and proudest of their little group. He waved Michael closer. "Look over there across the room! Jeff Brown sitting there having breakfast with Gary Johnson. Look at 'em! Right there in public before God and everybody!"

Brian and the others began laughing. Michael was doing his best to quiet them down. "As far as I can see," he said, just above a whisper, "they're just talking and eating. That's what you do here. So just hold it down and eat your meal. And stop calling me over here. You're gonna get me fired."

"Well, ain't you high and mighty," Brian said, again too loudly. "You oughta just quit here and come with us. We got our own work to do."

Michael saw his manager watching from across the room. It was time to shut up and leave this huddle. He turned without a word and resumed his work trying to ignore the chatter and laughter in the background.

What did Brian mean, they had work to do? The words haunted him as he carried dirty dishes to the kitchen. Whatever it meant, Michael was sure it wasn't good.

He delivered the dishes and returned to the dining area to take quick inventory of what else needed to be done. As he stepped out of the kitchen, Michael noticed Jeffrey Brown and his friend walking from the cash register together and out the door. He saw them through the restaurant window as they exchanged words in the parking lot and walked to separate cars. Then, Michael watched as all five of his classmates walked together to the register and paid. They exited together and climbed into one convertible and drove away in the same direction as Jeffrey Brown.

No, this was definitely not good.

FIFTY-FIVE

It was a long-standing tradition at Grace Fellowship of Casa Nueva to host a potluck meal after worship every fifth Sunday. They were usually festive occasions, with each family showing off its finest recipes. Three six-foot serving tables were heavy laden with sinful amounts of every imaginable meat, vegetable, and starch, with yet another full table dedicated only to desserts.

So it was that the good people of the church gathered in fellowship hall on June 30, 1963. But as they made their way through the orgy of food, this potluck meal seemed less than festive. And as they gathered around the rectangular six-foot tables decorated this particular Sunday in red, white, and blue, most of the conversations were more whispers than laughter. The topic was that Sunday's sermon.

No, the message was not on gluttony. It was the Sunday before the Fourth of July, and the topic was, traditionally enough, "Freedom." But the message was far from patriotic to the ears of at least half his congregation. In fact, it sounded suspiciously like communism. Pastor Dixon used as his text the Gospel According to Luke, chapter four. He said it was the mission statement of Jesus at the beginning of his ministry and thus, said the reverend, the primary work of the church if we're to follow Christ.

What was this work? First of all, it involves reaching out to the poor. (Dixon even suggested the church should open up their quarterly potlucks to migrant workers and the homeless!)

"Jesus' mission focused on those his society had cast aside, like the lepers and the hated Samaritans," Dixon said. "Jesus told stories about good Samaritans and about street people invited to wedding feasts. And whom did our Lord condemn? Not the sinners, but the religious elite like scribes and Pharisees; maybe a bit like us.

"We're calling ourselves Christians and we've turned what Jesus taught upside down!" he asserted with more volume than usual. "Jesus wants to set us free from religious ritual and rules and from the prejudices of our society. Jesus wants to set us free so we will finally be free to serve those our culture has abandoned."

***

"That was quite a message," Pam told her husband as they drove from the church parking lot after the Fifth Sunday Fellowship. "Suppose the deacons are meeting now to plan your exit?"

Ralph laughed. "I wouldn't be surprised. But, Pam, I truly believe that for every upset church member there was at least one other who felt the gospel was authentically preached today."

"I thought so, Dad," Charlie said from the back. "It was the right message at the right time."

They drove on in silence for a few minutes. Ralph chose to take a different way home, along quiet neighborhood side streets. There was little traffic in Casa Nueva on a Sunday afternoon and, on this route, there was absolutely none. But, as they turned a corner, all three saw two cars parked to the right side of the road, one in front of the other. Ralph stiffened in shock when he made sense of the scene. One teenage boy was backed against the driver's side front door with four others hovering in a semicircle around him. A fifth boy had climbed on the hood of the same car, apparently scratching something deeply into the paint with a key.

"Dad!" Charlie shouted from the back seat. "You've got to stop!"

Ralph was already slowing in preparation to pull behind the victim's car, a light-blue Ford Falcon.

"I know them," Charlie said, still in shock at what he was seeing. "I know them all!"

Ralph pulled his car to a stop. He and Charlie climbed out as Pam was busily writing down the license plates and descriptions of both vehicles. The five assailants were already running to their car, a 1950 Oldsmobile convertible. The top was down, and they jumped into the car without opening the doors. Two were in the front while two planted themselves into the back seat. The fifth boy was in the back with his feet in the back seat and his rear on the trunk. He was in the middle, and the other two had to grab his hands so he didn't fall out backward as the car sped away with all five yelling and laughing.

The Dixons were focused on getting to the victim with Charlie leading the way, followed by Ralph, with Pam close behind. To the relief of all, the boy was apparently unharmed. They had arrived just in time, Charlie thought. He cringed at what he knew could have happened if they had been even minutes later.

He was a nice looking young man, about five-foot-ten with red hair cut short in a flat top. Charlie didn't know him well but had seen him going quietly from class to class, keeping mostly to himself. They had their sophomore social studies class together last year but had never really spoken. Charlie only knew that his name was Jeffrey Brown, and he seemed very quiet and reserved. Charlie smiled. It was no doubt exactly how his own classmates viewed him.

"You okay?" Charlie asked.

"Sure. I'm fine. Just a little shaken. Thanks so much, Charles. And thanks to your family."

"We're just glad you're not hurt," Pam said. Then, she noticed her husband was not standing with them. He had walked in front of the car to see what the one teen had been so busily scratching on the hood. She followed Ralph's sad gaze and read in horror. There, etched with a key deeply into the paint in six-inch tall capital letters, was one word.

FAGGOT

FIFTY-SIX

Pam began to feel ill. She turned back to the boy and introduced herself. "Charlie says he knows those boys," Pam said. "I got their car make and license plate number. I'll be happy to help you make a report to the police. Those thugs need to be stopped."

"Thank you, ma'am. I appreciate it. I really do. But this isn't the first time. The last time was worse. My parents reported it, but it never went anywhere. I mean, it went to court and all, but we can't afford a fancy lawyer. Their parents got the best. He said how they were good boys, top students and great athletes. Then, they pulled out all sorts of embarrassing stuff about me. Somehow, they turned it on me and put me on trial. So they paid some damages and court costs and got off with a hand slap. It wasn't worth it."

"But look what they did to your beautiful car! They should pay for that. They should at least fix it."

"I'll show my dad and let him decide. He's going to be really mad, ma'am. It's really his car. I think he'll blame me. I'm afraid my father doesn't . . . well, he doesn't really like me very much. I think I'm an embarrassment to him. But thank you so much for your help. I'd better go."

The Dixons drove home in silence. They went to their bedrooms in silence to change from their church clothes. Each felt numb, unsure of what to do or say.

The first sound in the Dixon home that afternoon was the ringing of the phone. Pam answered it and then listened. "That sounds lovely, Andy," she said after a moment. "I'll talk it over with Ralph and get right back to you."

When she told her husband about an invitation to join the Mayes family and some other friends for a cookout at the Mayes' home, Ralph was enthusiastic. "I think it's the very thing we need right now," he said.

Charlie came to his parent's bedroom as Pam was leaving. He asked Ralph if they could talk.

"I've been thinking a lot about your sermon today," he said. "I think it might have been the best sermon I've ever heard. And I think that today, on the way home, we had the opportunity to live it. I believe Jesus reached out to a leper today through us."

"That's a very nice thing to say, son," Ralph replied. "But, to be honest, I don't feel like we did much good."

"Oh, but I think we did. But we've got to keep doing it, we've got to keep caring. That's why I want your permission to talk to Jeff. You said in your sermon that people in Jesus' day thought lepers were sinners being punished by God. Well, I think people believe that about people like Jeff. And they think it about me, too, Dad. You know they do."

Ralph said nothing. He waited for his son to continue.

"It's lonely, Dad. I know. I think it's how the leper felt until Jesus was willing to touch him. It's how the Samaritan felt until Jesus saw his goodness. But most people were afraid to see them or touch them, and they still are. I mean, think about it, Dad. Jeffrey's own father is ashamed of him. His own father blames him when some idiot thug beats him up or tears up his car! I don't know how Jeff can live like that."

Ralph was silent for a long moment. He was somehow unable to say what had occurred to him as he listened to the pain in his son's voice. Finally, the courage came, and he spoke.

"Charlie, I love you. You're my son! You don't think that I'm ashamed of you, do you?"

More silence followed, which spoke volumes to Ralph. The two looked at each other in the silence. Ralph finally looked down. "Oh, Charlie, I'm not ashamed of you. You're an amazing young man. But I just don't understand." He paused and looked into his son's eyes. "It's just so hard to understand."

"I know, Dad. I don't understand, either. I just know I didn't choose this, and Jeffrey didn't either. Who would choose to be hated and called names and worse? But people judge us like we could just change if we wanted to. You said Jesus didn't judge. He cared and touched the untouchable. You said that's what we're supposed to do as Christians."

"Yes, I did."

"I want your permission to go to Jeff, to be his friend. I didn't even know him, and I saw him almost every day. Someone needs to let him know they care."

Ralph reached out and pulled his son close into a gentle embrace.

"I'm so sorry, son. I don't understand, but I love you, your mother loves you, and Jesus loves you unconditionally, no matter what. I want you to know that, and I'm proud you want Jeff to know it, too." Ralph was still holding Charlie when he added, "You go be friends with Jeffrey, and you go with my love and blessing."

"Thank you, Dad"

"I do have one favor, though," Ralph continued, leaning back to look into his son's eyes.

"What's that?"

"Andy and Jean Mayes have invited us over this Thursday for an Independence Day barbecue in their back yard. They've invited another family Andy wants us to meet, their very best friends, Bill and Anna Davis. I'd like you to bring your guitar and, sometime over the next few days, plan some songs you and Marty can share with us."

"That's your favor?"

"Yep."

"Consider it done."

"Love you, son, and oh so very proud."

FIFTY-SEVEN

The Mayes family minus Michael also attended worship on the Sunday before Independence Day. Interestingly, Rev. Stephen Moore's message had many similarities to that of Rev. Dixon. He, too, spoke of being set free to serve, giving several specific ways the members of First Methodist Church could get involved in bringing "deliverance to the captives and setting at liberty the bruised." One of them especially intrigued Andy Mayes.

Andy remembered the difficulty he and Bill faced in just finding a place to eat or a place to stay on their first visit to Arizona. That was so long ago and yet, apparently, little had changed. But Rev. Moore announced that there was a dramatic movement for change growing right there in the Valley. There had been discussion in the Arizona State Senate of a Civil Rights Bill, which would require open access to all public accommodations, including hotels, motels, and restaurants, to all people regardless of nationality or race.

"It's going to be a hot summer in the Valley," the preacher announced. "Yet, local theaters turn away paying customers ready to get out of the heat and enjoy a good movie, simply by the color of their skin. This bill would make such discrimination illegal. People traveling through our state have difficulty finding a place to rest overnight or eat a decent meal, simply because of the color of their skin. Again, the senate bill would make such discrimination illegal in the state of Arizona.

"We have the opportunity like never before to truly make a difference. The week after Independence Day, when we have just celebrated the truth that all men are created equal, when we have remembered again that we are a country founded on inalienable rights endowed by the Creator of us all, that very next week we can join in a march at our state capitol, led by Lincoln and Eleanor Ragsdale to be a voice for those rights. I'll be there! I pray that many of you will join me."

Andy had heard of the Ragsdales, friends of Dr. Martin Luther King, Jr. They were nationally known for their accomplishments for civil rights in Arizona. He wanted to be part of this.

Andy spoke with Jean and Marty about it on the way home from worship. Jean remembered that President Kennedy talked about just this kind of civil rights bill on a national level in his television address.

"Maybe it's time for us to get to work here in Arizona," she said. "I would love to take a stand for this."

Marty and Andy agreed. They decided to share the information with Bill and Anna. Hopefully, they all could march together.

It was then that Jean suggested having Bill and Anna over for the Fourth of July, along with their new neighbors, the Dixons. "We could have an old-fashioned barbecue in the back yard, get acquainted with the Dixons, and let them meet the Davises," she said. "It could be a great experience for all of us. And we share so many of the same concerns, Andy. We just might join forces for more impact."

"I like it," he said.

"And, of course, Casa Nueva Parks and Recreation will have their annual fireworks display at Veteran's Park. We'll all be able to watch it right there in our back yard."

"I'll call Ralph and Pam a little later, along with Bill and Anna. It'll be a great time."

And it was a great time. Just as Jean predicted, the Dixon and Davis families immediately connected like longtime friends. Charlie and Marty had practiced several songs together and amazed everyone with their vocal harmonies and the intricate counterpoint accompaniment of their two guitars. Billy Davis had learned about the plans for music and brought his harmonica which, it turned out, he could play quite well. He joined Charlie and Marty whenever it felt appropriate.

Billy was ten now and seemed mature beyond his years. He even listened attentively as Andy spoke of the march on the capitol the next week in support of the civil rights bill. The adults talked together about racial discrimination in accessing public accommodations. They were surprised when Billy said, "Our teacher had to change plans for a field trip. She found out we couldn't go inside one of the businesses we were supposed to visit." Then, after a pause, Billy matter-of-factly added, "We're colored."

Andy was indignant. "That's exactly what I'm talking about! And a young child just accepts it as if that's how it's supposed to be. That not how it's supposed to be!" All agreed and planned as one to participate in Ragsdale's march.

The mood throughout the night was exuberant. Andy said it was one of the most positive evenings he had shared in a long time. After a great meal, they all settled in to enjoy the fireworks, clearly visible from the Mayes' back yard. Anna Davis commented that she felt they were "right there," as they watched the display.

Marty and Charlie sat side by side on lawn chairs, talking quietly, as the rest joined in "oohs" and "ahs" throughout the show. Marty was shocked to hear about the thwarted attack on Jeffrey Brown and the vulgar vandalism on his father's car. Charley recited the names of the five attackers. Marty knew none of them but said his brother, Michael, might.

"Oh, yes," Charlie said. "Michael knows every one of them all too well."

Michael was several feet away from the other two, teasing and laughing with Billy. But he heard most of Charlie's rendering of Sunday's aggression. He also heard Charlie's last remark loud and clear. Yes, he knew every one of them. All too well.

Michael felt an impulse to excuse himself from Billy and walk over to Charlie and Marty. He imagined himself kneeling on the ground, facing them, saying he was sorry for all he had said and done. But he couldn't do it. *Why not?* Michael wondered. *Why am I just sitting here?*

Yes, he was embarrassed. And ashamed. But he was also confused. What he and his friends . . . No, wait. They were not his friends. They never were. What he and those *five jerks* did was wrong. But he'd always known what Charles did was wrong, too. Where had he learned that? Who knows? Who cares? It's wrong! Wasn't it? But was it so wrong that he deserved to be attacked?

Michael's head was spinning. *Who made us judge and jury?* he thought. Just hearing what happened to Jeff sickened him but so did what happened to Charles. He never deserved that.

I should get up right now and tell Charles. I should just come clean and apologize.

But Michael sat there, snuggled next to his buddy, Billy. *Charles didn't deserve what we did*, he thought again. But Michael didn't make any move to tell him. Maybe, he would. Maybe, someday, he would.

FIFTY-EIGHT

The next morning, Charlie opened the Casa Nueva phone book to look up Jeffrey Brown's phone number and address. He stared at the columns of names. It looked like several hundred households were listed as "Brown."

Discouraged, he put away the directory and poured himself a glass of milk. Charlie then carried his milk into the living room and turned on the television. It was a morning news show on NBC. He sat on the sofa, not terribly interested in the TV but letting it play, while he wondered how to locate Jeff.

Hugh Downs, anchor for "Today," had just finished a segment and announced that local news was next. This caught Charlie's attention. Perhaps, they would say something about the upcoming civil rights march in Phoenix. They did not. What the Phoenix news anchor said caused Charlie to pull back in shock, spilling some of his milk on his shirt. But he didn't even notice. His body went numb.

The anchor said that the body of a sixteen-year-old high school student was found late last night in a 1960 Ford Falcon, parked in the desert north of Casa Nueva. The vehicle was parked well off the road with the windows rolled up, the engine still running, and the car's tail pipe connected to the vehicle's interior by a garden hose. The boy was pronounced dead at Good Samaritan Hospital, the cause of death being carbon monoxide poisoning. There will be further news at six.

Charlie didn't need further news. He knew the boy's name, and he knew the cause of death. The medium may have been carbon monoxide. The action may have been suicide, but the cause of death was something much more subtle and deadly. The person was Jeffrey Brown. The cause of death was a cruel mixture of isolation and hopelessness.

Charlie heard the guttural sound of a deep gasp and realized it was his. This was exactly what he feared. Charlie knew Sunday that he needed to reach out to Jeff. He had even talked to his father and gotten his blessing. Why did he wait the entire week? Why?

Charlie looked down and saw the spill on his shirt. He carefully held the glass level and carried it to the kitchen, dumping the milk into the sink. He walked half-dazed into the bedroom, tossing his shirt into the hamper, and taking a clean one out of his closet. He sat on the bed, shirt still in his hand, burying his face into the soft cotton material, and cried.

Pam Dixon walked by the open door to Charlie's room. "Charlie?" she said softly. "May I come in?" Hearing nothing, she entered his room and sat next to her son on the bed. The two sat there together a moment, Charlie's face still covered by his shirt. He lowered his shirt and turned, wrapping his arms around his mother's shoulders, resting his head on her neck. She held him there, mother and son, not knowing what was wrong but not needing to. This was her boy, and he needed her. She was there.

After what seemed like several minutes, Charlie composed himself. They continued to sit together as he told his mother about the news report.

"But you don't know that it was Jeffrey," she said.

"Oh, but I do, Mom. He didn't have to say it. I know. And I might have been able to do something if I only hadn't waited."

Mrs. Dixon started to argue with him but decided to not talk at all. She hoped her presence would make a difference. She would let him talk if he wanted, or she would just be there with her son in his pain. Time would tell soon enough if he was right about the boy.

And time did tell. Charlie was right. Jeffrey Brown had driven his father's car home after the attack that past Sunday. He told his father all that had happened and showed him the word scratched into the car, his father's car.

Mr. Brown flew into a rage. He never directly blamed his son, but, then, he didn't have to. He never spoke of finding the boys who did the vandalism, even though Jeffrey told him he knew their names and that he had access to their vehicle and license plate numbers. He never spoke of the terrorizing of his son by these same vandals. He only raged at the damage to his car, his beautiful, baby blue Ford Falcon.

Jeffrey was hurt. His hurt erupted into anger. His anger dissolved into shame. His shame imploded into hopelessness. His parents watched a bit of television that Fourth of July evening and then, tired and bored, decided to go to bed early. Jeff was already in bed, awake, wondering what to do, where he could go. Everywhere he went, he was a screw-up: ridiculed at school, rejected at home.

He had one friend, someone he was sure was more than a friend. But Gary Johnson realized their being together was causing rumors and he was getting scared. They had already planned to have lunch at the Pancake House last

Sunday, so Gary used that opportunity to say they needed to lay low, break it off for a while.

If he couldn't go to Gary, then who? There was no one. There was no place. There was only hate and rejection. So Jeffrey developed a plan, as he lay there alone that Fourth of July. It was poetic, really. He was going to finally be free, and he would find his freedom in his father's beloved, baby blue Falcon. He knew what he needed. He knew where he'd go. When he was pretty sure his parents were asleep, Jeff found his father's keys, put a garden hose along with a roll of duct tape in the back seat of the car, and drove away into the night.

Charlie, of course, knew only the barest of details about Jeff's actions. It was enough to confirm his worst fears. What would he do now? He decided he should go to whatever memorial service might be held. And what else? He must do something else. Charlie sat in his room with his Guild Mark 1, and he wrote a song.

FIFTY-NINE

The Mayes, Davis, and Dixon families met in downtown Phoenix, a few blocks from where the march was to start. As they walked to the site, Andy laughed, reached his arm around his wife's shoulders, and pulled her close.

"Look at this," he said. "Just look!" They all looked: Jean, Marty and Michael; Bill, Anna and Billy; Paul, Pam and Charlie. They all looked and smiled, as they saw the hundreds of people joining them, young and old, black and white.

They had heard that music would be a big part of the demonstration, so Marty and Charlie brought their guitars. They were glad they did.

The city had closed off the roads for the event, so there was no traffic. When the march was to begin, the participants were called together, and someone started singing "We Shall Overcome." And they all walked toward the capitol, many hand in hand, singing together.

The three families remained close together at the center of the stream of marchers. They were excited to be a part of this amazing throng, all united in one cause. But each family member was also aware of the sizable number of uniformed police, deployed by the city to keep peace along the route. They also couldn't help but notice the small clusters of people, spread out along both sides of the street. Andy, his family and friends, couldn't make out much of what these people were shouting. But they could hear the angry voices and see the loathing on their faces.

Some carried signs saying, "Black and White Don't Mix" and "Coloreds Go Home."

Pam and Ralph Dixon were dismayed to spot Elton and Harriet Phillips, active members of their congregation, screaming at the sidelines. Pam was horrified by the hostility and hate. She took her husband's hand and leaned into him. "What are we going to do?" she asked, loudly enough that he could hear over the singing.

Ralph gently squeezed her hand and smiled. "We're going to march and sing," he said. "And in the weeks ahead, we'll teach and serve however God leads, and trust the Lord for the rest."

Charlie also saw the church members. He had been walking beside Marty, but stepped over to his mother's side after overhearing his parents' conversation. "Don't worry, Mom," he said. "They're the past. Just look at them all. They're standing still. We're moving!"

Pam laughed out loud, taking her son's hand as he walked beside her. And Ralph, Pam, and Charlie marched hand in hand, singing together.

There was already a small, temporary stage erected at the capitol plaza. As the great throng arrived, a man took his place behind one of the three microphones there, introducing himself as Pastor Frederick Williamson from Bethel African Methodist Episcopal Church. Andy was pleased to see his pastor, Rev. Moore, also on the platform with several other men he presumed were local ministers.

It's good to be here, he thought. It felt good. It felt right. It felt– Andy was surprised; no, more than surprised. He was in awe. A powerful but familiar feeling swept over him as he gazed around the great crowd, united in the cause of justice. And he knew: it was the Presence. He closed his eyes and breathed deeply as he remembered his last moments with his mother and the Presence they shared.

The Presence is here. This is a holy time. This is a holy place.

Pastor Williamson greeted all and thanked them for sharing as important witnesses for justice. He invited his colleague, Rev. Stephen Moore of First Methodist Church, to open with prayer. After the prayer, Pastor Williamson again stood at the microphone. He said he was going to introduce Lincoln and Eleanor Ragsdale, but, first, he asked someone named Andrea Jones to lead them together in song.

Andrea came to the microphone, guitar in hand, and looked over the crowd. "I saw a couple young men here today with guitars." She pointed directly at Charlie and Marty. "Why don't you two come forward right now and help me lead this music?"

As they joined her on stage, Andrea stepped away from the microphone and shook their hands. She asked their names and asked if they knew how to play "Keep Your Eyes on the Prize – Hold On."

"No, ma'am," Charlie said, "but I'm sure we can follow you. Not a problem!" And they joined her, excited to hear so many of the crowd singing along, clapping hands to the bluesy beat. Marty loved the song and decided he had to add it to his repertoire.

Charlie was surprised that it was the only song they led at that point. When it was finished, he again spoke quietly with Andrea Jones, away from the microphone and from Marty. She nodded and stepped over to Pastor Williamson. She returned to Charlie and Marty. "The pastor will call you up later in the program."

Marty wanted to ask what that was all about as they stepped down from the stage. But another man who introduced himself as Pastor Jonathon Monroe was already at the microphone, inviting another singer to the stage. She walked past Marty and Charlie, stepping confidently behind a microphone and began to sing, unaccompanied, the most beautiful song Marty had ever heard. It was completely unfamiliar to him, but most of the marchers seemed to know it well. They sang it with such deep conviction and passion that Marty was deeply moved. He noticed that Bill and Anna were singing it also, and he asked them later what it was.

"It's called 'Lift Every Voice and Sing,'" Bill said. "It's also known as The Negro National Anthem. 'Lift every voice and sing till earth and heaven ring, ring with the harmonies of Liberty. Let our rejoicing rise high as the listening skies, let it resound loud as the rolling sea.'"

"It's an exciting song," Marty said.

"Yes, it is," Bill agreed. "Exciting and true."

Lincoln and Eleanor Ragsdale were the final speakers. All were moved by their words, especially Bill who said to the others, "I need to stay after this is over. I need to talk to these people."

Lincoln Ragsdale closed his presentation by calling Pastor Williamson to offer a benediction. The pastor walked to the microphone. "Before I pray," he said, "I want to invite back one of the young men who played guitar earlier. He says he has a story to tell and a song to sing."

Charlie stepped nervously onto the stage, put his guitar strap over his shoulder and, with instrument ready to play, walked slowly to the microphone.

"Thank you, pastor. And thank you all for allowing me this time," he said quietly but directly into the mic so all could hear. "We are here today for an important cause. It's the cause of justice that recognizes the worth of every human life as a precious creation by God. We recognize as self-evident the truth that God created each human life as equal, with rights that are divinely given to us by that creator."

Charlie paused a moment, took a deep breath, and continued with increased conviction and volume.

"But we see people denying those rights just because someone is different than the majority. So we're here today to unite around that cause which says, 'No!' No rule or law of a human majority can deny any minority the dignity God has already given!"

Marty smiled as the crowd erupted in applause, with shouts of "Amen!" and "That's right!" Would his friend, Charlie, ever cease to amaze him?

"I've asked to come forward in honor of one of those precious lives," Charlie continued. "The life of Jeffrey Brown was taken from this earth on the night of July fourth. He was only sixteen years old. But he's gone now because he saw a world that refused to accept him, simply because he was different. It was a prejudice that was everywhere he turned, that said, 'You're not worthy to be welcomed, to be loved, to even be here at all.'

"I want to honor Jeffrey Brown by reminding us all that we have a responsibility as citizens of this planet to not make anyone feel like less than the creation of God that they are. So, in honor of every child who is snubbed because she's poor – and every boy who's beat up because he's 'too feminine' – and every immigrant who's cast aside because she speaks with an accent – and every person held back or kept out because of color of his skin, I would like to sing a song that I've written especially for today."

The people applauded, with several shouts of "Yes!" and "Sing it!" Pastor Moore brought another microphone and lowered it on the stand so that it was in front of Charlie's guitar.

Charlie strummed his first chord. "President Kennedy called us all to work together so that all Americans can have, and I quote, 'the kind of equality of treatment that we would want for ourselves.' Think of that! It sounds so simple, doesn't it? Do you know why? Because it is! It's been around thousands of years. It's called 'The Golden Rule.' And we can do it! And it could change the world."

Charlie strummed a chord again and began to sing,

> Her dress is old, a hand me down,
> but it's clean, it's neatly pressed.
> Yet, other girls won't talk to her
> because of how she's dressed.
> But her father takes two shifts at work,
> and her mother takes in ironing.
> And they teach their girl to stand up tall,
> to always do her best.
>
> She's learned to be a friend to all,
> whatever others do;
> She's learned 'do unto others as you
> would have them do to you.'
>
> His spirit's gentle, his words are kind,
> but his classmates never hear.
> They're busy pointing out he's odd,
> spitting names like weird and queer.
> They should be ashamed,
> but he's the one who feels the guilt
> And he wonders if life's worth the pain,
> if he'll always live in fear.
>
> Give him half a chance and he'll be your
> friend, it's not so hard to do
>
> If you'll just do for this one good soul
> as you'd have him do for you.

The people block kids from their school
　　with shouts, 'You can't get in!'
　　'And you can't live here or worship
　　there: it's the color of your skin!'
But cut them, see? They, too, bleed red!
　　Inside, we're all the same!
　　We love our children, want them to
　　learn, to rise and live and win.

So let's teach all children right from
　　wrong, to know the good and true
　　Till all the people do to others
　　as you'd have them do to you.

EPILOGUE

He was driving to the Scottsdale site the day after the march, forming in his mind what he wanted to say to Bill. Andy had been away all morning, driving to multiple locations, getting familiar with the duties he would soon assume with his new position at Walter Dean Construction. He timed his visit to Scottsdale for lunch with Bill. One of the goals of his visit was to see if his friend had any concerns or needed any help as he assumed team leadership. The other was to check out a gut feeling that Bill might be thinking of leaving Dean Construction altogether.

Bill and Andy sat in the shade of a tree apart from the other workers and, with lunch boxes open, started chatting about what each had packed for that day. Bill lifted a sandwich neatly wrapped in wax paper. "You know, my lunches aren't nearly as good since Anna went back to work," he said. "My sandwiches just can't compare."

"When did Anna go to back to work?" Bill asked.

"Oh, it's been some time now. She started waitressing again. I told her there was no need, that I made enough money to support us. Boy, she got all hot and bothered about that one! She said, 'You don't understand, Bill Davis. I've always worked. I want to work. The extra money would be good, but it's not about money. It's about me being me.'"

"Jean's going to be teaching next year. I told her about the raises ahead and how we were doing fine on my pay, and she said about the same thing." They sat quietly a moment.

"Where's Anna working?" Andy asked. "I might want to stop in some time."

"You'd be welcome there, but you might feel a little uncomfortable. It's a place on the Southside she found in the Green Book."

"You're still using the Green Book? Here in Phoenix?"

Bill gave his friend a look that said, "Did you really ask that?"

Andy shrugged and shook his head. "Yeah, I know. I'm sorry, Bill. But some things are better. Aren't they? I mean, you did get promoted to site foreman."

"Yes, and I'm getting big push-back from some of the crew. One walked off the job when he learned that he'd be taking orders from me. And I still can't live anywhere I want in this fine city." Another moment of silence followed. Andy wasn't sure what to say. Bill finally spoke again.

"Don't get me wrong, Andy. I'm glad we moved here. I love the Valley. And I do own my home now, and I like it, too. But realtors won't even show me a house anywhere outside the area I live now, in spite of the fact I could well afford it. And it took me forever to find a banker to finance the home where I do live. I was caught having to rent for years in between that rock and hard place. You know that."

"I know, Bill. That's why I wanted to talk to you today. Jean told me you were really affected by yesterday's march on the capitol. I guess she talked to Anna last night, and you were all on fire about joining Ragsdale's movement in a big way. I was excited, too. I want to be a part of it. But I'm just concerned about you taking a big step before you think it through."

"You're worried about losing me as an employee?" Bill asked with a wry smile.

"No! Well, yes. But it's more than that. I want what's best for you whatever happens to this job. I just want to be sure you're okay, that's all."

"Sure. I know." Bill sat quietly, apparently deep in thought. When he spoke again, Andy heard unmistakable conviction in his voice.

"Andy, you are my true brother. I'll never have a better friend, and I don't want our friendship to ever change. But there's a hole in my life, and I'm the only one who can fill it. I finally figured that out. I've figured out a lot of things lately."

Andy had no idea what to say. He sat and waited for Bill to continue.

"I figured out that, when we were just kids, I was always afraid, and the thing that drew me to you was your fearlessness. You stood up for things, and you did it no matter what. I wanted to be like that. I guess I thought it might rub off, I don't know.

"So when you went to the army, I enlisted. When you said, 'Arizona,' I was there. I even followed you into an exclusively 'white' bar when we both knew we might not even come out alive. I knew you did it for me, and I loved you for it. But it was me following you to things that didn't fit me."

Andy was feeling ill. How could he have not known all this? Was he losing his best friend? Did he ever really have him?

"I'm so sorry, Bill. I had no idea. So tell me, you said you've figured out a lot of things. Have you figured out what's been missing?"

"I think so, at least, I've got a start. It's something I've been thinking about for a long time now, but it all seemed to come together yesterday at the march on the capitol.

"We stayed after you all left. I wanted to talk to the Ragsdales. To my surprise, they invited us all, Anna, Billy, and me, to stay and visit with them, then and there. They wanted to hear our stories, about our lives. They asked about our talents and skills and then told us how those very things might help the cause."

"So that's what you're going to do? You're going to work with the Ragsdale's in their movement?"

Bill smiled. He could see the worried look on Andy's face.

"Don't worry, Andy," Bill assured his friend. "Nothing's going to interfere with our friendship or take away from our time together. And I don't plan to leave my job. It's been a good job, and I'm thankful for it. But, while none of that will change, I am going to move on to something more. I'm going back to school. I'm going to use my GI Bill and go to college."

Andy never expected that. But he liked it. "I think that's great," he said.

"I've always known you're a fighter, Andy. But I don't think you ever knew that I'm a reader. You taught me to be a builder, and you taught me well. But, my nature isn't to build, it's to study. I'm not about tools, Andy. I'm about books.

"I told that to Lincoln Ragsdale, and he grinned this big grin and said, 'Wonderful!' He said that this movement for equal rights has to happen in the realm of ideas. We have to show people how we're missing the mark on our nation's very creed, and he said it will happen in the area of ideas and communication. That's who I am, Andy. And when I'm there, I'm courageous, too."

Bill took a deep breath and smiled. "I'm not afraid anymore," he added. "I know who I am."

Andy nodded. "That's amazing. All you've told me, it's just amazing. But, I'll be honest. I was worried. I knew things were about to change, and I was worried what it would mean for our friendship. Anyway, whatever does happen, just know I'm glad for all we've done together."

"Look at me, Andy. Listen! You're my brother, and I'll love you forever. You've helped me more than you'll ever know. But you're right. There are some changes ahead, and here's how I'd like them to start. You always give. I always receive. It's my turn now.

"Anna and I would like to invite you, Jean, and the boys to our house for dinner. Please come this weekend and bring nothing but yourselves. It's time that you're our guests. I've talked about it with Anna, and she agreed, which is really important. You wouldn't want me to serve you one of my miserable sandwiches!"

"Very true, my brother, very true," said Andy, in his most serious tone. "That fearless, I am not."

A NOTE FROM THE AUTHOR

"We're here today to unite around that cause which says, 'No!' No rule or law of a human majority can deny any minority the dignity God has already given!" Charlie Dixon

Of course, the Charles Dixon in this novel is not an historical person. Nor are any of his family, their friends, and acquaintances. Nor are the cities of Dearing, Donelsburg, or Casa Nueva actual places. The characters and their stories in this novel are entirely fictitious. Some are creations from whole cloth, but, for the most part, these people with the joys they experienced and struggles they encountered are each an amalgamation of many people and their stories that have personally crossed my life.

There are, however, some people and events in this novel that were lifted directly from the pages of history, though fictionalized in as much as they interact with the characters herein. Here are just a few key examples.

- President Kennedy's action to integrate Alabama State University and his subsequent speech on civil rights did take place on June 11, 1963.
- The practice and conditions of sharecroppers as represented herein are, to the best of my research, historically accurate.
- The horrific mine disaster in the fictional town of Donelsburg was loosely based on an actual

explosion in the Orient 2 Coal Mine at West Franklin, Illinois, in 1951.

- *The Negro Motorist Green Book* was an actual book, annually published from 1936 to 1966.
- Lincoln and Eleanor Ragsdale were truly a remarkable force for civil rights in Phoenix and beyond. They led two marches to the Arizona state capitol building to encourage passage of a bill that would make illegal the denial by race to places of public access. One of these rallies was held in 1962, the other in 1964. I combined the two into one event, held in the summer of 1963. I could not find details of either march, the numbers attending or anything about the programs. Thus, every detail of the march in this novel is entirely fiction. However, the events are historical and apparently met their goal. The State of Arizona Public Accommodations Bill was passed into law on July 16, 1964, just fourteen days after the enactment of the national Civil Rights Act that President Kennedy envisioned.

This is my first attempt at writing a novel. I decided it would be helpful to begin and end it in a location and situation with which I felt familiar. My family also had moved from the South to the Midwest, then the Southwest. Like Marty Mayes, I was fourteen the summer of 1963, preparing to enter my freshman year in high school. My family also lived in the Phoenix area at that time, and I, too, was powerfully affected by the national events of that year, beginning with President Kennedy's daring stand against segregation at Alabama State and the presidential television address that evening.

Beyond that personal location and situation that gave me bearings to write this story, this is truly a book of fiction. The fictional characters and their stories do provide a vehicle, however, to examine the all too factual realities of prejudice and injustice. And they, hopefully, have represented the also inherent pursuit for something better, a quest when, at its best, is grounded in the eternal foundation of faith, hope and love.

My hours with this novel have returned to me a beautiful gift of personal growth. Writing it, many times well into the early hours of morning, has proven an often surprising adventure of discovery. I cannot say what discoveries the reader will or will not make, but I would be so bold as to send this book forward with a prayer: May the reader discover somewhere within these pages a character, situation, phrase, or idea that will spark personal reflection and shared dialog.

I am honored that you have given of your valuable time to read *In Pursuit of Something Better*. I do ask one very important favor. Please take a few more moments to return to amazon.com and review this book. Your honest opinion is not only valuable to me but also important for any who may be considering reading it. Thank you.

Ed Varnum
Columbia, Missouri
October 2017

ACKNOWLEDGEMENTS

There are so many people who made this effort possible, beginning with my family, friends, and the many teachers who encouraged and inspired me from childhood to adult.

I need to especially acknowledge Miss Carolyn Jeter, my eighth grade English teacher, who was the very first person to draw me aside and say, "You truly have a gift for writing!" One wonderful consequence of writing this book was a renewed incentive to reconnect with Miss Jeter after fifty-five years. I'm pleased to report that I found her well and active at age seventy-nine. We had a delightful visit.

My wife, Jan, has been a source of continuous encouragement. She was the book's first reader, giving invaluable suggestions to make it a better work. I was blessed by a number of friends and colleagues who generously served as beta readers, offering important advice that helped shape and greatly improve this book. Thank you David Avery, Vanessa Barnes, Judy Boss, Timothy Carson, Don Carter, Robert Eichenberger, Jane Elledge, Pam Gordy, Paul Koch, Walter Lee, Bill Rose-Heim, Danny Stewart, and Chris Varnum.

Chris Varnum, a graphic artist in Austin, Texas, designed the book's excellent cover. Check out his work online at http://www.asleepstanding.com.

Cara Lockwood edited this book with expert skill, a keen eye for detail, and invaluable advice. Want to greatly improve your writing? Go to Cara's web page, http://www.edit-my-novel.com.

My thanks to Genevieve Howard who also encouraged me and directed me toward publishing through amazon.com. Learn more about Genevieve at http://genevievehoward.com.

And thank you for taking the time to read my first effort on a novel. Please share your feedback! Drop me a note on Facebook: https://www.facebook.com/edvarnumauthor.

Made in the USA
Columbia, SC
23 December 2017